To Sue
Kate

Gifts In The Night

GIFTS IN THE NIGHT
BOOK 1

KATE HAWKINS

XULON PRESS

Xulon Press
2301 Lucien Way #415
Maitland, FL 32751
407.339.4217
www.xulonpress.com

Unless otherwise indicated, Scripture quotations taken from the New
English Translation (NET Bible). Copyright ©1996-2006 by Biblical
Studies Press, L.L.C. Used by permission. All rights reserved.

"Collected Poems - Edna St. Vincent Millay"
Harper & Brothers Publishers New York - New York 16, NY
Library of Congress catalog card #56-8756

Printed in the United States of America.

ISBN-13: 978-1-54564-996-1

I DEDICATE THIS BOOK TO MARK WILLIAMS
FOR HIS TECHNICAL EXPERTISE AND
FOR BEING SUCH A GOOD FRIEND.

Door To The Future

Chapter 1

He stood on the tarmac, watching the small Starbird C52 quiver as its propeller developed the smooth rhythm that would lift it from the ground. When he returned his mother and sister's eager waves, he could see that Beth had her face turned away from the window. His dad would be too busy checking all the instruments and, being the almost compulsively careful pilot that he was, to be looking for his son. Nash was so grateful to them for bringing him to his senior year at Colorado College because that had allowed him to work until the day before they left. His things had been stored from the previous year, and they had even helped him move into his new room at the fraternity house. He knew he could not have a better family than he did.

Then there was Beth. His heart was swept with alternating waves of relief and guilt. He had purposely driven her to the airport alone, so he could tell her. The whole three days had been so hard since he knew their relationship was over, but he didn't want to ruin her time in Colorado and make everyone uncomfortable. Their engagement had been a mistake from the beginning, but because the Wentworths and the Williams had been good friends for years, everyone seemed convinced it was a good match—except Nash. He felt her clinging and her childishness even though she tried so hard to be what he wanted. He wanted to convince himself he had done her a favor by putting an end to it on the way to the airport, but he had seen how devastated she'd been. Apparently, she had fantasized that all was well. She had seemed shocked, but how could she be? Beth didn't even know what he was talking about when he tried to

2

explain his plans and dreams to her, and she hadn't really been very interested. She'd find someone much better for her than he would be; he was sure.

The plane was roaring down the runway, and he was about to turn away when it seemed to waver and then went completely out of control. He watched with horror and disbelief as it went nose down and catapulted into flames. He heard himself screaming as he ran across the tarmac. Others were running and shouting, too, but he reached the plane just before the fire crew. He tried to rush into the flames to pull his family out, but as he touched the hot metal, someone grabbed him forcefully and threw him to the ground. Burning gasoline made a red-yellow curtain around the plane, so it seemed to glow. He tried to see his family, but everything was blurry and strange. Then it was dark.

He woke in darkness and fear flooded him. Where was he? Why was it so black? Something terrible had happened but he couldn't remember what it was. He really didn't want to remember. Maybe he had been buried alive. Terrified, he called out. "Where am I?"

"Mr. Williams, you are in the hospital, and your eyes are bandaged. You were badly burned."

Burned? How did he get burned? And then it came back to him, and he gratefully returned to unconsciousness.

The next week was a repetition of waking and slipping back into oblivion. But each waking period was a little longer until the day they removed the bandages from his eyes. The doctor was elated at their condition.

"I really didn't expect you to recover much sight, and now I believe you will be able to see just fine. You're a lucky young man!" Nash looked at him in disbelief. Finally he mustered up his courage and asked the question he had been avoiding. "Did my family make it? Did they get out of the plane?" He was holding his breath as he stared at the doctor's face. The expression on it told him everything. With a grief too great for words, he turned his face to the wall.

Physically he did well and was released from the hospital after two weeks. The burns on his face were healing, and they assured him the scars would be minimal. He didn't care. He didn't care about the pain from his arms and shoulders where his shirt had burned right into the flesh. He didn't care where he was or where he was going. A college friend drove him home to Cedar Rapids, Iowa, and got him into his house. "His house"—he supposed it was now. There'd only been Nash and his sister, Kitty, and their parents, not even any uncles or aunts or living grandparents. He was alone!

The next three weeks were a blur to him ever after. Apparently, he just sat and looked at the wall, turning off any life that went on around him. He didn't answer the phone or the doorbell and ate only when it crossed his mind. He may have slept but wasn't aware of it. He didn't shave, didn't wash, and didn't move except for the necessities. It was as though he were frozen in a block of ice. On Tuesday of the third week, someone kept pounding on the door, banging on the windows, and shouting his name. The sound reached through his lethargy, and in irritation, he rose to see who was making such a commotion. When he opened the door, Ed Hanson, the family lawyer, stepped in before he could tell him to go away.

"My God, you look terrible, Nash. And you don't smell too good, either. What have you been doing to yourself? There are lots of things that need to be done, and it's time we got to them. But I think a shower is the first priority. I'll wait here for you."

Nash didn't really care, but he went to his bedroom, washed, grabbed some mismatched clothes, and returned to the living room, hoping Ed had given up and gone away. He hadn't.

"I brought several papers that need to be signed. There are all sorts of legalities, but your dad had his estate in pretty good shape, and his will is up to date. As you might imagine, everything will be yours with small bequests to the church and the YMCA. It leaves you relatively wealthy, able to go to school and get started in whatever direction you want to go. There is one problem, and I'm sorry to have to tell you this, but Sam Wentworth is suing your dad's estate for four million dollars for negligence in Beth's death. Since the crash hasn't been fully investigated, we won't know how that will work out. If it goes to court, and he should win, I'm afraid everything would be taken. I'm sorry to tell you this, but I think you have to know about it sooner or later."

Nash said not a word. It was hard to keep track of what Ed was saying, but he got the part about Sam suing. How could he want money from Beth's death? What kind of man was he? You think you know someone and then when they're under pressure, you find what they're really made of. What if he'd married Beth and then found out what her father was like? Well, he hadn't been going to marry Beth anyway. But her father didn't know that so that wasn't the reason for his legal action. Then he remembered that Beth was dead, and even if he wanted to he couldn't marry her.

All this time Ed was talking, so Nash finally took the pen he held out to him and signed where he pointed. That was probably the quickest way to get him to go away.

Ed did go away because it's hard to keep talking *at* someone. At least he'd gotten the legal work started. "I'll have Nancy bring over some food for you tonight. You must eat. You're just skin and bones. And tomorrow night I want you to come to dinner, so I can watch you eat. I know your folks wouldn't want you to carry on like this. I'm here for you, Nash, and so are your friends. They're worried about you. Start getting out and let us support you through this sad time." He gave the boy an awkward hug as he turned to leave.

When Nash saw Ed's car pull away, his weary mind capitulated. His life was over. With his parents dead, his engagement broken, and his former fiancée dead, his sister dead, and his home and everything that might have been his lost in a lawsuit brought by a family friend, there seemed no reason to go on.

Suddenly he had an urge for one last look at the place he'd been happiest in his whole life. It was the place where his family really spent time together with no interruptions, where he and his dad had their heart-to-heart talks, where his mom could be young and silly, and where even his little sister was a good companion. He tried to remember when they'd first rented a cabin at Island Idyll in Door County, Wisconsin. It must have been the summer he was five because that was the year he broke his arm falling from a tree, and he'd had to go in the water holding the cast high in the air. He smiled as the memories started to come into focus. They'd gone each year until he got a full-time summer job three years ago, and now he realized the money wasn't worth anything in comparison to the joy of those family vacations. Then he remembered that he would never be able to go there again with his loving, laughing family. But he decided he'd go there one last time, and then he would end things up there, which would be the best place he could think of. Weary as he was, he still felt some strange enthusiasm to have a direction, a place to aim for.

Since he wouldn't be there long, he just stuck ten dollars in his pocket, walked out the door, locked the house, and drove away in the ten-year-old compact car that he'd bought used three years ago. He was relieved to see that the tank was full, as he pulled out of town on highway 151 on his way north.

His nervous energy lasted for the first four hours, and then he began to get very tired. His lack of food and sleep started to catch up with him. Walking around at rest stops helped a little, particularly as he got further north and the weather became colder. He hadn't bothered to bring a coat, and he shivered as he put five dollars of gas in the car outside of Madison. By the time he reached Sturgeon Bay at twilight, he could hardly stay awake.

What made him come wide-awake was the engine stopping. He managed to guide the little car into a bay overlook area before forward momentum completely ceased. He was so weary that it took him a minute to focus on the dials and see that the gas gauge showed empty. What to do? He decided to take a little rest before he made any decisions.

He woke up cold and stiff five hours later, wondering where he was. Then a passing car's headlights illuminated the stone wall in front of his car, and he remembered his predicament. He was too tired to do anything, and besides, it was dark. He drifted back to a restless sleep punctuated by crashing planes and being on his way somewhere, but he didn't know how to get there. He saw Beth's tear-stained face coming toward him. Finally he just sat in the driver's seat in a stupor and waited, shivering, for the dawn.

It came finally, bringing with it a beat-up old VW van with peace signs painted over the rusty body and a driver to match. The man climbed stiffly from the sagging front seat and stretched his scrawny arms above his head as he took in lungfuls of the fresh, cold morning air. His stringy hair and scruffy beard looked compatible with his Limp, old, stained tee shirt and faded, kneeless, oversized blue jeans. Nash realized he was looking at a senior hippy. Apparently some of the flower children never really grew up.

The young man felt concealed in the car but knew he'd have to get help somewhere, and he might as well start now while he could still move. He opened the door and eased himself out. Mr. Hippy must have heard the door because he quickly turned to face Nash.

"Hey, Man, you don't look so good. Are you sick?"

"No, I'm just tired after a long drive and no food. I ran out of gas, so I couldn't get to a restaurant and I wonder if you could give me a ride to a gas station. I'm on my way to Door County."

"No kidding? So am I!" This didn't seem like such a big coincidence to Nash since they were on the only road that led to the peninsula, but it gave him a new idea since he only had five dollars left. "It would help me even more if I could hitch a ride with you because I have friends up there who'll put me up and come back with me to get the car. I'm almost too tired to drive it right now, and they're waiting for me." He was a lousy liar due to lack of practice, but he must have looked pretty pathetic.

"I could use some company cuz I've had a long-ass drive myself. Are you sure you want to leave your car here? How far up are you going? I'm on my way to Ephraim."

"Sister Bay is where I'm headed. Ephraim is close, so that would be great if you'd give me a lift. I'd really appreciate it."

"What's your name, Kid? If we're going to travel together I'd like to call you something. I'm Billy." And he held out a large, soft hand.

Nash took it as he said, "Nash. And it's sure nice of you to help me, Billy."

"You look a little down on your luck, Nash. Maybe this'll get you to better company and a better place. You gotta watch drugs cuz they can get you in a lot of trouble. I learned that a while back."

His rescuer had to move pop cans, tape cassettes and portable tape player, maps, half-empty food cartons, a wadded-up tee shirt, and a partially consumed half gallon of milk from the passenger seat so Nash could sit down. It took a while for him to transfer it to the back which was piled with musical equipment, some old chairs, piles of what looked like clean clothes, a cooler, and things unseen that were buried beneath the rest.

The young man hoped they didn't have an accident because he might never be found under the contents of the van. Fortunately, Billy talked a lot as he drove so Nash didn't have to answer any questions or make up any stories. The older man was going to Ephraim for a reunion with a man he'd known years ago in San Francisco.

"Those were the days! Fred and I played our gigs on street corners, so we could get some bread to buy what we needed. There were so many great people out there then. Everybody was so free and shared what they had. After a while, the drug scene gave it all a bad name, and there were some mean guys who'd do anything for a fix. Some of the idealism went, and some of the kids began to grow into the establishment. I tell you, it was a golden age until then."

"So I go up to see Fred about every five years, and we play together like old times. I doubt if anyone would pay to hear us now, but it brings back some happy times. He went home to Door County when things went bad in Frisco and started doing some carpentry and then got into cabinet making. I guess he got pretty good. He's retired now and lives back in the woods outside of town."

Nash had a fleeting picture of two skinny old men, sitting out on the porch of a shack in the woods, playing their guitars and dreaming of "the good old days."

Billy reached into the back with his right hand and dragged out the tape player, and Nash listened to Joan Baez, Judy Collins, "Blowin' in the Wind," Pete Sager, and others that he didn't recognize. Billy sang along with gusto.

When the music stopped, Nash thought he could see some questions coming, so he asked, "Where did you come from and how did you end up out in California? I don't think I ever knew anybody personally who'd been part of the flower child world. Did you live in Haight Asbury?"

His host was off and running. He rambled on about college protests and marches and what had happened to various friends at the time. If Nash had not been beyond sociability, he would have been fascinated to hear the memoirs of a hippy. It was during this soliloquy that he noticed snow was starting to fall in big wet flakes.

"Damn! This snow is going to be slippery. I hope I don't get snowed in up here. I don't want to spend my winter in Door County. It's a good thing we're almost there. With this weather, I wonder if you'll be able to hitch a ride." He paused and thought a minute. "I think I'll just drive you up to Sister Bay. I don't think your family would want you out in this weather since you don't even have a coat. That's the trouble with this place. You never know what the weather is going to do, especially in late October. I should have started this trip earlier."

The mention of his family almost made Nash sick to his stomach. He'd shut off the news from his mind for a few hours and it came back in sickening reality.

"Are you okay, Nash? You look kind of white. Maybe you should go see a doctor or something. I don't know if there's one up here, but maybe your friends could take you to Sturgeon. You take care of yourself. If you don't have your health, you don't have nothing."

"I'll be okay once I get there, Billy. I'm just tired. Just let me out in Sister Bay, and I'll call my friend."

After that there was little conversation because Billy was giving his full attention to the road which was beginning to accumulate a thick layer of snow. True to his word, he took Nash all the way to Sister Bay. As Nash got out on the main street, he had to steady himself against the van. Billy looked at him anxiously. "I've got an old army blanket in the back somewhere. I'll get it and you put it around you so you don't freeze before you get to your friend's house." He looked at his companion with a worried frown. "You sure you're alright, Dude? I don't feel good about leaving you."

Nash was touched and could feel tears stinging his eyes, but he lowered his head and growled, "I'll be fine once I get there. You've been a Good Samaritan today, and you've done your work. Get off to Fred and play a tune for me." He took the outstretched blanket and walked off into the snow.

Chapter 2

R alph "Hairy" Peterson was getting impatient. He'd let Ringo out five minutes ago, and the darn dog was still barking instead of doing what he was sent out for. There weren't any neighbors to worry about disturbing, but he was afraid the dog had found a skunk or a raccoon, and he didn't want Ringo to tangle with either one of them. And the stupid animal wouldn't come even though he'd called him several times. If it got any darker, he might have a hard time figuring out what was the trouble.

"Now I'll have to put on my coat and boots and go get that damn dog in," he snarled. He really loved that dog, but he liked to pretend he only put up with him. In reality, the hound was the only family and good companion he had since Mary died. He frowned as he felt that loss sweep over him again as it did so often. He just couldn't seem to get over it, and she'd been gone three years now. After she died, he had stopped renting the cabins that were in the surrounding woods and had left them empty, as was his heart. It had been fun to get to know the families who had rented them when Mary was alive. He remembered the little kids who would come to their door to ask his wife for some of her homemade cookies. She always welcomed them into her big, warm heart and her cookie jar. She'd have been a wonderful mother if they'd ever been lucky enough to have children of their own.

He shook his head to clear it, and, grumbling, he made his way across the snowy yard. He didn't bother to keep the yard up so there was just a path through the weeds during the summer and in the winter it was outlined by the frozen growth along the edges. He walked carefully as an old man does who has no one to take care of him should he fall.

Ringo was barking by one of the closed-up cabins where the name, Island Idyll #4, was still faintly visible above the door. He made a grab at the dog's collar, and still the animal resisted leaving his find. Hairy took a closer look and saw there was a long mound on the path, almost the length of a man. He started to brush the snow away with his foot but drew back when a dirty white sneaker was exposed. Hairy's first thought was that he didn't want to get stuck with a corpse and have all sorts of gawkers poking around his place. His second thought was that he'd better check and see if it really was a dead person. He went to the other end of the mound and with his shaky hand brushed the snow from a face the same color. My God! He must be dead, he thought. But he'd been a medic in the Second World War, and he remembered to feel for a pulse in the neck.

"There is one! He's alive. Now if I can keep him that way until I can get him to a hospital, then it won't be my problem."

In his relief, he boldly reached through the snow to get his hands under the person's armpits. Forgetting he was seventy-one and prone to a bad back, Hairy dragged the body back up the path. And for once the path looked cleared as the dead weight pushed the snow aside. He dragged the limp form up the steps, across the porch, and stopped at the door. Taking the broom standing next to it, he swept off his burden, and then hauled it into the house.

He got the unconscious figure on the couch by pulling and pushing, having decided he'd better see if there was anything he could do. Then he'd have to figure out how to get it in the car—and then how he'd get the car out through the snow.

Wiping off the face, he saw, much to his amazement, that it was somewhat familiar. Yes, it was that boy, Nash, looking older and thinner, but he was sure that's who it was. He hadn't seen him in four years, but he recognized him. Why was he here this time of year? He became more interested.

His next move was to strip off the boy's frozen, wet clothes and rub his arms and legs and cover him with a warm blanket. Maybe the young man would come around, and Hairy wouldn't have to take that miserable drive.

But he didn't come around, and the night grew long. There was a change though because instead of being cold, the boy became very hot and started thrashing around and calling out names and isolated words. Hairy was scared and realized things were out of his control. What could he do? He couldn't get him to the car by himself, and he doubted if he could get the car more than four feet from the garage. The snow had drifted right in front of it as always.

He'd ignored all his old friends for so long that there was no one he felt he could call on for help. But then he thought of Jack DeLong.

Jack was the skipper of the ferry that ran between the mainland and Washington Island. He was big, strong, and seemingly invincible. Also, he wasn't a man who carried grudges. He lived on the mainland side and had a big four-wheel drive truck that could go almost any place. If anybody could get this sick kid to the hospital, it was Big Jack DeLong.

Feeling better, he went to the phone and called him. He was startled to hear the gruff, "What do you want?" but he heard the clock strike two and knew he'd awakened the poor man. Jack was silent as Hairy explained his predicament and then said quickly, "I'll be right over," and hung up. Five minutes later, Hairy saw lights coming down his drive, and the big Ford truck pulled up to his door.

Hairy wanted to let Jack take over the problem, but Jack insisted he needed someone to hold the patient as he tried to see through drifting snow. Grudgingly Hairy put on his old gray coat and climbed into the big green truck and let the boy's head rest on his shoulder while he kept him on the seat. Later, he was surprised to find himself at the hospital in Sturgeon Bay still holding the boy he hardly knew. When they stopped in front of the emergency room, it was Hairy who went with the gurney and gave the name and signed as the person responsible for the bill. Hairy knew he was a fool, but in some way he felt closer to Mary than he had in a long time. It was the kind of thing she'd have wanted him to do.

So here he was, trying to talk to the unconscious boy in the ICU for the five minutes that he could be with him every half hour, and feeling foolish—but worthwhile at last. The nurse suggested that Hairy call Nash by name and try to talk about familiar things even though there was no sign that the boy heard anything. So he dredged his memory and quietly spoke to Nash about those early summers and the broken arm, about his visits to Mary's kitchen, and his endless consumption of cookies, and all the things he knew about the Williams family. It seemed to calm the sick young man.

The doctor had talked to him very seriously in the waiting room, explaining that the patient appeared to be severely malnourished and his physical condition was badly weakened by his exposure to the cold. He looked questioningly at Hairy, but the old man could only tell him that he hadn't seen the boy in at least three years. Dr. Heller looked at him quizzically but added a warning as he went back to the emergency room that he shouldn't hope for much because pneumonia was a real killer of the weak.

As Hairy waited for the five minute monologues, he talked to Mary about the situation in the deserted waiting room, and through the night, he felt her presence more and more and a growing sense of determination that the boy must not die. The conversations with Nash grew more animated and forceful. He was not to give up and take the easy way out! He didn't know what had happened, and he hadn't been able to reach the boy's parents because no one answered the phone when he called the number that information had given him in Cedar Rapids. Hairy was amazed he'd remembered where they were from, but in a way Hairy was beyond amazement. What *was* he doing talking to a dying boy he barely knew in the strange hospital in the middle of the night? Yet in his heart, he knew he was doing just what Mary wanted, and that thought brought a warmth to his heart that he hadn't felt in three years.

It was two days later that the boy's head rolled over, and his eyes were opened as he looked at the older man with puzzlement. "Where am I? What are you doing here, Mr. Peterson?"

"You're in the hospital in Sturgeon Bay, Nash. You have pneumonia, and you've been very sick. I found you lying in the snow by my house, and I don't know how you got there. Jack DeLong and I brought you in here three days ago."

"I think I remember you talking to me. Were you here the whole time?" he asked in amazement.

"Yes," the older man answered simply.

"Why?"

"Mary wanted me to."

"How is Mrs. Peterson?"

"She died three years ago."

Nash looked confused and then the word *died* brought other things to his mind, and rather than face them he closed his eyes and willed himself back to unconsciousness.

A week later Hairy and Jack eased a white, emaciated Nash into the cab of Jack's red truck, and they started back up to the County. The young man had said very little beyond finally forcing out the words that reported his family's demise. It was such a fresh wound that Hairy (still feeling Mary's influence) decided to take him home to heal rather than try to sort out the boy's options.

Jack made small talk about the latest news on the peninsula most of the way home, and the middle passenger seemed to sleep. It was with relief that they got Nash settled in the guest room bed with its pristine sheets from three years ago and closed the door.

"Will you be alright, Hairy?" Jack asked with concern. "Oh, I think so. The nurse told me what negative signs to look for, but she thinks with food and rest, he should be okay. It's his mental health that really worries me. I don't think he wants to live, and I don't know what to do about that. I can feed him and house him, but I can't make him chose life. If you don't mind, I'll call you if I find I can't handle things."

"Feel free. From what you've told me of the boy and his family, he has a lot to offer, and it would be a shame to lose him." With awkward gentleness he said quietly, "Mary would be really proud of you." And he was out the door, blowing his nose as he got into his truck that was parked out in the yard.

Thus began the challenge.

Hairy carried carefully prepared meals to his guest three times a day. He became quite a cook, trying new recipes and spicing up old ones. His thin, Scandinavian frame began to round out a bit as Nash's appetite improved. The boy's mind might not be interested in the things around him but his young body responded to the food that kept appearing so regularly. He rarely talked or showed interest in anything. He did sometimes say, "Thank you."

This went on for two weeks before Hairy lost patience. On Tuesday morning, he announced with the breakfast tray that lunch and dinner would be eaten in the kitchen. Nash just looked at him and said, "Thank you."

When the smell of the beef-noodle casserole wafted through the house, the boy didn't appear. Noon came, and Hairy sat down to eat. One o'clock still brought no sign of his guest, so he covered the dish and put it in the refrigerator.

He peeked into the guest room to see if Nash was all right, but the boy was just lying there looking up at the ceiling. He decided to bide his time.

Dinner was underway when he heard a noise behind him and turned to see his pale visitor swaying in the doorway. He still had on his hospital gown, his hair was every which way, and his beard was scruffy and unkempt.

"I think tonight is bath night. You are beginning to smell a little ripe. I'll lend you my razor, too, and we'll see what we can do about your hair. I'll throw your sheets in the wash while we have dinner."

"Thank you."

Though the meal was eaten in silence, the boy had two helpings and cleaned his plate. When he rose, Hairy went to the bathroom and started running the bath water. As he handed Nash a towel, he received the usual, "Thank you." The sheets were back on when the naked patient returned to his burrow. Hairy laid an old pair of his pajamas on the bed and left the room.

The next morning he had to smile as Nash entered the kitchen. The young man's shoulders were so much broader than Hairy's that he could only button the bottom button of the top half and the lower half ended about the middle of his calves. It gave him the appearance of a child who had grown up overnight in his pajamas.

The next few weeks weren't as quiet, but Hairy's houseguest was now sullen and morose with no apologies. After two weeks more Hairy grew impatient, and three weeks was the breaking point. When Nash walked into the kitchen, looking strong though pale, and sat down to receive his prepared meal in silence, Hairy let him have it.

"You eat the food I get for you, sit and look grim, never lift a hand to help, and I'm sick of it! You are not only going to help with the food preparation, but you are going to get a job and learn to smile again."

For just a moment, Hairy regretted his outburst because the boy looked stricken. Then he said, barely above a whisper, "I'm sorry. I never thought of the trouble I was causing *you* because I was so busy feeling sorry for myself. Can you forgive me?" and he put his head down on the table and wept.

Hairy didn't have a clue about what he was supposed to do. He watched the boy's shoulders shake with grief and heard the groans of emotional pain and wished Mary was in the room. And maybe she was because he seemed to move without being aware of it, and as he put his arms around the anguished boy, he somehow felt comforted himself.

Chapter 3

Jack DeLong didn't seem surprised when Hairy called. "I've been wondering what happened to the boy, but I didn't want to seem nosey. How's he feeling?"

"I think he's feeling all right physically, but he doesn't talk and seems to brood all day. It's time to get him outside and working. Do you know where he could find a job this time of year? Without the tourists, there isn't a whole lot of work to be had."

"Hairy, I think you called the right man. Young Ben McGrath told me yesterday that he'd decided to go back to school and wants to quit next week. It's hard work, especially in the winter, but at least we don't run as often, and I'd have a little more time to teach him the ropes," and Hairy heard the man's booming laugh, "if you'll pardon the expression. Seriously though, do you think he's strong enough?"

"He's strong, but he hasn't used his muscles in a long time. It'll take him a while, but if you're patient, I believe you'll have a good worker. When could he start?"

"Let's see . . . today is Tuesday. Why don't you bring him over on Thursday, and Ben can show him what he does, and then if he'd come on Friday, too, he'd be pretty well set to begin working the next week. This should be good for the ferry, but do you think the boy wants to do it?"

"I don't know if he wants to do anything, but he can't go on like he is. I told him he's got to pay room and board, which may get him moving. If he can get outside and feel useful, it may help him come back to life."

"Well, at least we can give it a try. And if it doesn't work out, you'll have to be my deck hand, Hairy."

"I don't think you'll ever get that desperate, Jack," Hairy chuckled.

When Nash was informed of his new employment, he made no comment. Hairy drove him to work on Thursday through Ellison Bay and Gills Rock to North Port and the Ferry Landing. He barely spoke to Jack and stood around looking grim. The captain just raised his eyebrows and shepherded the boy onto the Merry Jane. Hairy left before they set out for Washington Island and talked to Mary all the way home, hoping for some comfort from her memory.

Captain DeLong dropped the young man off on his way home. The eyebrows rose again, but Hairy knew Jack was not a man to give up easily. When the older man asked Nash how the day had been, "Okay," was the only answer he received.

The next week was Thanksgiving, so the ferry was busier, and the new worker was putting in more hours before falling into bed after eating everything in sight—quietly. Hairy was beginning to despair, but he was trying to put the situation in God's hands since Jack had started taking him to the men's morning Bible Study lately. The older man hadn't really wanted to go, but it was as though his heart had opened up when he found the sad young man, and he knew he had to fill his emptiness with something. At first he felt awkward and isolated in the group of warm friends, but after about three meetings, he found they were his friends, too, and he looked forward to those Tuesday mornings all week. Then Tom Alder and Russ Swenson said they'd pick him up for church the following Sunday, and Hairy really enjoyed that. People he'd known when Mary was alive apparently remembered him, and he began to feel connected to the world again. He tried to talk to Nash about it but met the usual silence and disinterest.

Hairy knew something was amiss the Wednesday before Thanksgiving. Nash stormed into the house and started pacing around the living room. "Why don't you go for a walk instead of wearing out my carpet?" he suggested. At that the young man slammed out the door without even stopping for his coat. Hairy worried that he might go lie in the snow again but the agitation seemed to suggest action, not capitulation. He waited.

18

Slam! Bang! Nash came striding up to him and exclaimed, "I am such a jerk. I have been so busy feeling sorry for myself that I wasn't aware of anyone else. You've been wonderful to me, Hairy! I don't know how you put up with me! Somehow I'll make it up to you."

"Slow down, Nash. What happened to open your eyes?"

"I was obnoxious to someone who was trying to help me, and it was so uncalled for and so dumb," he started pacing the floor again. "that even *I* couldn't miss it. Dumb, dumb, *dumb*!

"Think of my carpet," Hairy pleaded. "Sit down and tell me what happened."

As the younger man began, his host really saw him for the first time, not as a little boy or a wounded adult but as a living person. His eyes were snapping, his voice was strong, and he certainly didn't seem at a loss for words. Hairy listened.

"It was on our third run that a cute little white car pulled on. A cute young girl got out and stood on the deck as we cast off. It was so obvious that she was home from college, and she looked so happy and intelligent and as though she had everything and was enjoying it. I looked at her and thought of all the things I didn't have and knew I didn't like her. My self-pity turned me quite green with envy. I was so busy disliking her that when Jack said to pull in the starboard hawser, I went to the port side and started to pull on that one. Very quietly, so no one would hear and I wouldn't be embarrassed, she said, 'The other side.' And do you know what I said? Dumb, dumb, *dumb*! I hissed at her, 'It must be nice to know everything, Miss College Girl,' and went to the starboard side. I looked for her later, knowing I had to apologize but didn't see her until she was pulling off, and she certainly never looked in my direction. I don't think I've ever been remotely close to being that rude. I was so busy being angry at my losses and thinking I was the only person in the world who suffered that I didn't notice how much you missed Mary or how ungrateful I'd been. How Jack has put up with my sullenness is beyond me. Boy, do I have a big apology for him!" He stopped for a breath.

"Welcome back to the world, Nash. It sounds like you've been raking yourself over a lot of coals. How will you make things right, so you can relax? You may have some fence mending to do, but I have to tell you how absolutely delighted I am that this has happened.

I was beginning to despair that you'd ever start to heal from your grief. I had the men at the Bible Study praying for you, and I believe I've done my share, too. Apparently, God can even use college girls for answering prayer."

Nash smiled painfully.

Everything was different after that. Nash made an appointment to talk to Jack the next night and was whistling when he came home. Hairy couldn't even pick up a dish because his houseguest had it in his hand before the older man reached for it. Nash even asked to help with the cooking, and he had a very satisfied grin on his face the night he produced the whole meal. Harry ate it down and silently asked Mary to forgive him for his extravagant compliments, which pleased the cook enormously. He went to work with a spring in his step and a smile on his face. Hairy saw what a wonderful son he must have been.

December was cold and snowy, and in spite of the reduced ferry schedule, Nash worked about eight hours a day. Jack did much of his maintenance during the winter, and he made use of Nash's new eagerness to help. The younger man was learning many new things about machinery and boats. He came home at night, tired and hungry. Hairy had convinced him it was all right to let the older man do the cooking (much to his relief), but Nash did the dishes and other clean up chores enthusiastically.

It was as though, when his spirit returned, it brought a special joy and awareness of living. Every small thing was a cause for gratitude, and it rubbed off on everyone around him. Hairy found himself looking at life through Nash's eyes, and even he began to whistle when no one was around.

A few days after his reentry, Nash asked Hairy if he could go with him to Bible study. His friend almost cried. It became a regular pattern and even included church. Door County residents, usually very slow to accept newcomers and then only partially, took the wounded young man to heart and included him in some of the outings and events that were open to the residents. He and Hairy were invited into homes that the older man had never seen. And he brought joy along with him wherever he went.

Chapter 4

One day when Nash looked up from fastening the hawser, he saw a familiar van, rustier than before but with the peace signs still evident. It was empty, so he went in search of the driver. He found Billy up in the top deck, face to the wind, long stringy hair blowing free behind him. It looked like he had the same tee shirt on and a newer pair of holey jeans.

"Billy!"

The man looked around, startled to hear his name and unable to identify the source.

"Billy, it's me, Nash."

"My gosh, it is. You sure look better than when I saw you last fall. I wouldn't have recognized you. You've filled out some, and you're not a bad looking fellow now."

"Why are you going to Washington Island?"

"I'm just going to drive around a bit and look it over. I know it's cold, but I thought I'd find me a sheltered beach to sit on and play a couple of quiet tunes." Nash then saw how sad he looked.

"What's the matter?

"I just came from Fred's funeral, and it's hard to lose an old friend and so many memories."

Billy looked old and alone, and Nash said quickly, "Can you come for dinner with me tonight? I'm living with a friend, and he will be out for dinner, so I'll be eating all alone. Come and break bread with me, and if your ears don't get too tired, I'll tell you the story of my life and how I came to be as I am today. I really came up here to die the day you picked me up. Will you come?"

The older man perked up a bit. "Sure, Man. You tell me where, and I'll be there. Maybe my van can jazz up your neighborhood a little." He grinned and to Nash's surprise, his teeth were white and even.

The man who showed up at the door of Hairy's house looked like Billy but was different in an indescribable way. Nash grabbed the hand that was proffered with both of his. "It's good to see you again! You were so nice to a desperate kid. You know, I almost cried when you left me because you really seemed to care."

"I've thought about you a lot and wondered what happened to you. You can't imagine my relief at seeing you today. I somehow knew you were really down, and I've always regretted that I left you. Now I don't have to worry about that anymore." He smiled into Nash's eyes with real affection. "I want to hear your story." They had a beer in front of the fireplace, and by the time Nash got up to put the dinner on, he'd covered his survival under Hairy's caring outreach. Over the ham, potatoes, and green beans, he progressed to his nautical career, and during dessert, he introduced his growing religious convictions.

"That's some story, Nash. It sounds like one that's moving toward a happy ending. I'm really glad for you."

"Thanks, Billy. I've talked your leg off, and you've been a really good listener. Now it's your turn. I know it's been a tough day for you with Fred's funeral and all. It's your turn to talk now. I'll be quiet. But before you start, I have something for you." He went to his bedroom and returned with an army blanket, clean and folded, and put it in Billy's arms. "I'd hoped I could return it to you or pass it on to another needy soul. I'm so glad to see you again and tell you how much I owe you."

Billy looked embarrassed but pleased and accepted the blanket with grace. "I'm glad you told me where you were coming from. On the way over here, I thought I'd *like* to tell you about myself—the one you haven't met yet. When you reached out to me this afternoon, I decided you had a right to hear it. If I could have a glass of water, I'd be ready to help you with the dishes and tell my tale."

And so he did.

"I told you about going to San Francisco and all that. I finally moved into a commune south of there, on the ocean. It was about this time that things started to unravel for the flower children, and gradually, one by one, the brothers and sisters in the commune started to drift off. The fellow who had originally bought the property we lived on had gone off the deep end into drugs, and one day he realized what he was doing to himself and came to me in despair. He said he had no family to go to and no one else to turn to. I tried to help him and did for a while, but the drugs had a terrible hold on him. The last day I ever saw him he came to thank me for being his friend and standing by him. 'I want to give you a little gift to thank you,' he said, and handed me an envelope. I protested that I didn't need anything and I was glad to be his friend, but he brushed it off, gave me a hug, and drove off. I didn't think much about it until I heard he'd driven his van off a cliff into the ocean. The envelope was lying around and I opened it, just to be in touch with him one more time, I think. You can hardly imagine my shock when I saw it was the deed to the property, signed over to me. So all of a sudden I was the owner of fifty acres of ocean front property south of Frisco. I wasn't interested in money, or so I told myself, but when a developer came to me with an offer to buy it, I decided maybe I could develop it myself. I wanted it to be a pristine, ecologically sensitive, esthetically pleasing community and one which common people could afford. It might just be a fitting memorial to the former owner. I set to work and made mistakes and learned more than I ever did in college. But I built a fine community, one that was written up in magazines as a model of what could be done with good planning.

A few landowners called to see if I could do something with their land and thus began an exciting career. I loved the creativity of it and the feeling of doing something for people that increased their pleasure in life.

Along the way I met a fine woman whose most controversial act was marrying me. She softened my rough edges and led me to see that I could only change the establishment by being part of it. We had two sons and a daughter. One son became a lawyer and is working as a public defender, though he has just been offered a judgeship, which I don't know if he'll accept because he believes in what he's doing. Our daughter is married with three children who I adore, and she teaches in an inner-city school and lectures about how to encourage the underprivileged. My younger son works with me, and his main interest is in providing affordable housing for worthy applicants and in helping them maintain those houses. So you can see my ideals haven't disappeared.

Things were fine and life was worthwhile and exciting, and then Helen developed cancer. We tried everything, but it was no use, and bit by bit she died. It broke my heart. She was my partner, my support—my other, better half. I lost interest in everything, even my children. Life was gray. I went through the motions, but there was no heart in it. Finally my son said, 'Go away, Dad. Find yourself. You are a person in your own right, and you have to get to know who you are.' So at fifty-six I was sent off to do what most kids do at twenty, and I was scared I wouldn't find anything at all when I looked inside.

I was still thinking about it a few days later when I drove by a used car lot in my Mercedes and saw the VW bus, peace signs and all. It brought a whole era back to life, and without any doubts I walked in and bought it, had them drive my car to my son's house, and I started my travels.

I began by looking up a few friends from those days, and those connections led to others. I wanted to see who those young people had become. I visited with them and heard their stories and found that some of them were my stories, too. And I found Fred again.

All that took about a year. I kept in touch with my kids and swung by to see them occasionally, so I stayed connected, and then one day I went home. I hadn't really found myself but I saw who I'd been, what I'd become, and I was looking forward to seeing what I would be in the future.

I went back to work, energized, and I believe I do a better job than I did before. But once a year I arrange for a month for myself, get in the overhauled van, and drive. I visit old friends, make new ones, and recharge my batteries. It's sort of a treasure hunt. I try to find people like you who look beyond appearances to see who I really am. Lots of folks write me off as an old over-the-hill hippy who never grew up, but the ones who look closer are the treasures I seek. I don't hold it against the others, but I feel sorry that they live in such tight boxes that they can't see possibilities."

"Billy, I have a confession to make to you. I thought those hippy thoughts when I first knew you. I pictured you and Fred sitting by an old shack playing '60s songs and never growing up. How hard it is to get past the stereotypes to the real person! I was always grateful to you, but now I thank God I had a second chance to know you, to really know you."

"Don't worry, Nash. I could see what you thought, but I could also see the pain and confusion in your face, and I knew you needed help." He laughed now. "Your mental picture of Fred and me is kind of funny though. Fred actually was nationally famous for his furniture creations. There are a couple of them in the White House, I believe. He sold his stuff for big bucks and built a fabulous house way back in the woods where very few people see it. When we were playing, it was in his sound studio above his indoor pool"

"What a jerk I've been! I think you've a lot to teach me, and I *know* I have a lot to learn."

A new voice was heard saying, "Why don't you stay here a few days? We have plenty of room if you don't mind sharing a bath. I think you have a lot to teach me, too, and I don't want to miss it."

Nash turned to see his host sitting back in the flickering shadows and said, "Billy, I'd like you to meet Hairy Peterson, the man who saved my life and is my best friend. How long have you been home, Hairy?"

"Long enough to hear some interesting things. I didn't want to interrupt you, so I just sat here quietly. I hope you don't mind."

"Not a bit. A good friend of Nash's is a good friend of mine."

The young man was aware of a connection in the room between the two older men. He didn't understand it, but it was almost as if they'd known each other before. Was it shared experiences? But how would they know that without talking to each other? Was it that they were both people who'd had to find themselves after loss of their beloved wives? Was it a basic goodness? Was it a gift from God? Whatever it was, he had the feeling he wouldn't be missed when he went to work the next day.

Chapter 5

D ecember 15 turned out to be an important day. Nash was helping get the cars on the ferry and encouraging the novices to park as close as possible to each other when he saw the cute white car. The young lady within met his eyes coolly, then looked puzzled at the delight that showed on his countenance, and finally settled for wary.

As soon as the ferry was underway and his most pressing duties done, Nash hurried to search for the girl. He found her looking out of the forward window, watching for her first glimpse of Washington Island. She stepped back when he approached, but he quickly spoke.

"I have desperately wanted to apologize to you for my inexcusable rudeness in November. I was a jerk, and I can only hope that you might find it in your heart to forgive me."

He was so earnest that she took another step backward, and he was afraid his apology would go unaccepted. To his surprise and relief, she laughed. "Well, you certainly go to extremes. First you insult me, and then you practically beg for forgiveness. Do you ever travel the middle of the road?"

Her eyes danced, and he wanted to join them. Up close, she was really lovely. Her brown hair was shiny and clean and curled around her bright face. She had green eyes that sparkled, a sweet short nose ("*sweet*?" he thought), lips that looked like they were made for smiling, and an overall appearance of health, intelligence, and happiness. He dared not look any further as he felt the silence lengthen.

"Do you ever travel the middle of the road?" she repeated.

"I do when I'm not busy being rude or apologetic. Which me do you think you'll like best?"

"I don't believe I've seen the whole array yet, so I can't tell. A rough guess would be the middle of the roader."

Nash caught a glimpse of the ferry landing approaching rapidly and with a startled, "Oops!" he raced down to the deck to get ready for docking. Captain DeLong frowned out the pilot house window at him, but Nash just bowed his head apologetically and hurried to get the ship ready.

The rest of the afternoon saw a grinning young man leap to do his work, to help the passengers, to open doors for old ladies, and to entertain small children. While they were waiting to load at North Port, Jack DeLong caught up with him.

"What's happening to you, young man? You look like the cat that swallowed the canary. Do you want to spread the good news to your captain?"

"Jack, have you ever done something really dumb and felt just awful about it and then finally had a chance to apologize and maybe make it right? I just got that chance, and I feel like a weight is off my shoulders. And besides that, she's really pretty!"

"I won't ask more. Just don't dance off the boat when we're in the channel."

And then the day got even better. On their last run from Washington Island to the mainland, the little white car pulled on. This time the young lady waited until Nash had a moment and approached *him*. "There's a dance tonight at the high school in Fish Creek, and a lot of kids from around here are coming and lots of students who are home for Christmas. You probably already know about it."

"No, I didn't. If I came would you dance with me?" he asked boldly—and then turned a rosy red.

She gave him a bright smile as she turned to head up the stairs and said an emphatic, "Yes!" over her shoulder. She missed seeing him turn a somersault on the deck, which was lucky because the ship moved toward him just as he was landing, and he fell flat—and didn't even feel it.

Anyone watching the preparations that night would have thought there was a teen-age girl getting ready for a dance. Nash showered and shaved and used Hairy's after-shave lotion. He studied his face in the mirror carefully for any blemishes that might detract from his appearance. That was when his host walked in after knocking, unheard, on the door.

"Hairy, do you think I look all right? If you were a girl, would you think I was okay looking?" He turned his face anxiously this way and that, trying to see it from every angle. His blond hair seemed a little too curly, and he wondered if his straight nose was too short. The sun and wind had toughened his skin, and his lips were chapped. He wondered if she liked blue eyes. Maybe he shouldn't go to the dance after all.

Hardly able to hide his smile, the older man answered in a high voice, "I think you're a doll, Honey."

Nash jerked around with a sheepish smile on his face.

"I guess I am being kind of silly. I don't even know this girl's name, and I already want to impress her. And I have impressed her but not very favorably. It's been a long time since I had a date, and maybe I'm just rusty. I went with the same girl for a long time, and I don't know what to do anymore."

He looked so young that Hairy took pity on him. "Nash, I've watched the girls turn and look after you as you pass. You are a handsome young man, and anyone would be proud to be seen with you. Once you get started, it will be all right. I don't know that it's ever easy to know what to say to a girl. Try to think of them and not yourself, and that will help, I think."

"Thanks, Dad." And he meant it. Then worry set in again. "I wish I'd bought a new shirt. I just have the clothes I came in and they don't even fit very well anymore."

"I have a good wool shirt that might do the trick. Mary gave it to me shortly before she died, and I've never worn it. I was bigger then. Come and try it on. It may be a little tight in the shoulders but we can see."

It turned out to be fine. The predominantly blue plaid picked up the blue of Nash's eyes and made his wind-burned face look healthy and tan. His blond hair shone in the light, and as he looked in the mirror, he imagined for a moment that he *was* handsome.

"Thanks for letting me use your car, Hairy. I probably will be home early—especially if I chicken out." Then he shrugged on his coat and was gone into the snowy night. Hairy said a quiet prayer for his young friend, grown so dear to him.

The dance was in full swing when Nash arrived. He felt horribly shy and stood in a corner behind several people, so he could look over the situation unseen. It was so strange to be in a room full of people close to his age and not know any of them. He was comforted by the knowledge that they were all children of God, but he wondered how many of them were aware of that. He knew he'd just found out about it.

He saw her in the midst of a group of laughing young people. They looked so happy to be together, and it made him feel lonely in spite of his resolution not to feel sorry for himself. He resolved to be happy for *them*. There was one tall, good-looking guy that seemed to hover over her, and Nash imagined that he was a former (he hoped not a present) boyfriend, who would like to be reinstated. He waited for the Ferry Princess (he didn't know what else to call her) to be alone for a moment, and then he would boldly walk over and ask her to dance. He waited. And he waited. And he waited. Everyone seemed to want to talk to her—and did. Occasionally she would look around the room, but he was careful to stay out of sight. What was she looking for? Could it be for him? He was being egotistical! Probably she was just seeking more old friends.

After an hour and a half he gave up and walked dejectedly back to Hairy's car. It was a quiet young man who walked into the house at ten thirty.

When the white car pulled onto the ferry at noon the next day, Nash managed to be very busy. He carefully didn't look around and felt relief and regret when the little car pulled off the ship. He found himself preoccupied the rest of the afternoon, kicking himself for not having walked right up to her and asking her to dance and for convincing himself that she was already involved and not the least interested in him. While he having this discussion with himself, he felt a tap on his right shoulder. Turning in surprise, he looked into the face of the Ferry Princess. He couldn't imagine what expression came over his face, but he saw a surprised look in her eyes.

"I don't want you to think I'm chasing you but," she blushed quite pink, "I want to know why you didn't come to the dance last night." The last part of the sentence was said in a rush as though she had to get it out quickly or not at all.

"I did. But every time I looked you were in the midst of all sorts of people. I was waiting until you were alone, but you never were. So I went home."

Some of his disappointment must have shown through because she said apologetically, "Most of the kids from my high school class were there, and we hadn't seen each other in quite a while. There was lots of catching up to do. But I kept looking for you and didn't see you." She looked puzzled.

"You were looking for *me?* I saw you looking around, but didn't think it could possibly be for . . ." He left the sentence unfinished. Before he lost his courage, he quickly asked, "Will you go out to dinner with me tomorrow night? It might not work because I don't know how you would get back home when the ferry doesn't run at night now."

"I'll ask the girlfriend I stayed with last night if I can stay tomorrow, too. I don't think she'll mind. And I can take the first ferry in the morning, so I won't miss much vacation time with my parents. Yes, I'd love to go out to dinner with you. I want to hear what happens between rude and apologetic." Her warm smile took any sting out of the words.

"Will you catch the last ferry, and we'll go from there? I'll need to go home to change clothes, but the friend I live with will be there, and he's in his seventies, so he'll be an experienced chaperone." And so it was arranged.

Hairy silently thanked God that he wasn't young anymore when Nash came whistling into the house that night. It was the same boy who'd looked so glum when he left in the morning. He didn't think he could handle the ups and downs at his age. But when he thought back on some of the ups, he wasn't sure he should be quite so thankful.

"And she was looking for *me!*" the young man concluded.

Hairy hoped the unknown girl would not hurt his young friend. It was part of growing up, but Nash was still grieving the deaths that claimed his family. The girl might help him heal, though, and Hairy wished for that with all his heart.

Nash had borrowed Hairy's car with the understanding that the older man would get to see *the* girl. In the car on the way to Hairy's home they discussed Door County and found that they had both come up as children with their families and had fallen in love with the water and trees and sunshine. She explained that finally her parents had moved to Washington Island permanently, and she had gone through high school in Fish Creek.

They arrived at Hairy's home and Nash hoped very hard that the owner would not be looking out the window. He was not. When the young man held the door open for his date, no one was in the living room, and then Nash began to worry that Hairy wouldn't come out at all.

It was a well-dressed Hairy that appeared around the corner, his best manners in place. "I'm Ralph Peterson, but most people call me Hairy because of my curly locks." He patted his very bald head. "I've heard nice things about you from my friend here."

"I'm Neenah Kingman. It's nice to meet you and awfully nice of you to let Nash use your car."

"Won't you have a chair while he gets ready? Would you like a cup of coffee or a soft drink in the meantime?"

Nash could hardly believe his ears. He'd never seen a soft drink in the house the whole time he'd been there. Had Hairy been shopping? What would they talk about? Well, he couldn't worry about that, but he still hurried as fast as he could.

When he walked back into the living room, all showered and shaved and in Hairy's wool shirt, the two were talking like old friends. In fact, Neenah (so that was her name) didn't make a move to leave. Nash had to mention that they were expected at the restaurant in fifteen minutes before she rose. And when they left, she hugged her host.

"You come back anytime, Neenah. You don't have to bring Nash, either. I'm glad your folks decided to move here. You were a cute little girl, but I had no idea you'd grow into such a beauty." She blushed a gentle pink.

"Nash, I knew her family years ago when they rented the old Larson place down by Ephraim, and a big windstorm blew part of the roof off. I spent a bit of time getting things back together, and her mom fed me some great meals." There was a twinkle in his eye as he added, "I was tempted to reroof the whole house just to get more of that good food."

After they ordered from the menu, Neenah asked him how he'd met Hairy. The story was a long one, and they were eating dessert when Nash finished talking.

"I'm so sorry about your family, Nash! What a terrible time you must have had!" Then she added quietly, "And must still be having."

"I think I'm healing," he said thoughtfully. "I noticed the other day that I could laugh with pleasure at a memory and not just feel pain. They were such wonderful people, and without them my life is forever changed. But I see growth in me, spiritually and emotion-ally. They say you meet God on your knees most often, and that's certainly where I've met Him. And now I know about good people like Hairy and Jack and the men in the Bible study. And I know more about hard physical work and independence. I've had time and motivation to look at my life and try to figure what I want to do with it—or to try to find what God wants me to do. I'm just sorry that my mom and dad aren't here to be part of it."

"I believe that they know and love you from wherever they are. And I think they'd be proud of you."

He gave her a grateful look and reached for her hand. "Thank you, Neenah."

The silence that followed was a comfortable one. "Now it's your turn to tell about yourself," Nash declared.

"My story is really very simple, I'm especially grateful after hearing yours. I hardly know what to say about myself. You've been through so much, and I've had a wonderful, happy, carefree life. I'm an only child, and my parents love me. I grew up in Milwaukee before we moved here, went to high school at Gibraltar High School, worked at . . ." He interrupted her. "Let me guess. I'll bet that you were homecoming queen and that you were first in your class, academically. Am I right?" She looked startled. "How did you know? I was the homecoming queen my junior year, and I graduated second in my class."

"I was guessing, but you just seem like that kind of girl. Please go on. You started to say you worked somewhere."

"Yes, I worked summers at the Summer Kitchen restaurant and went off to Cornell College in Mt. Vernon, Iowa, where I'm now a junior, majoring in education." It was his turn to look surprised. "You go to Cornell?"

"Yes, have you heard of it?"

"I'm from Cedar Rapids and often went to visit friends at Cornell when I was home on vacation. I went to Colorado College with the same one-course-at-a-time schedule. I would have been a senior this year if I'd stayed in school."

"We went into Cedar Rapids often for entertainment, and I got to know it fairly well. On what side of the city did you live?"

"On the southeast. I went to Washington High School and worked at Fin'n'Feather weekends and summers. Some of my classmates went to Cornell. Did you know Amy Fraser, Jenny Jones, Bill McCoy, or Fred Green? Those are the only ones I can think of right now."

"Would you believe that Amy and I have been roommates since our freshman year?"

"Amazing! I actually dated her a couple of times. She lived right down the street from me."

"Which way? I spent quite a bit of time at her house over breaks and a few holidays."

"If you face her house, my house was two over, to the right. It's surprising we never saw each other." He paused. "Maybe we did." "So you lived in the beautiful gray house with the curving drive and all the flowers around it? I always thought that was a wonderful house."

"My mom was a super gardener." And for a moment he thought grief would engulf him again, but the bright face of the girl beside him seemed to dissolve it.

"I guess this fits into the Small World category. It makes me wonder if our paths have crossed at some time. It's really possible."

"Well, the important thing to me is that they crossed now. I'm not sure what there is about you, Neenah, but I feel it's really special and almost as though I already know you somehow. You don't remember me from anything, do you?"

"No. But what if you hadn't been feeling out of sorts that day and hadn't spoken to me as you did? Would you have sought me out if you hadn't needed to apologize?"

He looked thoughtful. "I really don't know." Then his face cleared. "I believe the Lord would have brought us together if that hadn't worked. Who knows in what bizarre way I'd have appeared in your life." They both laughed.

When he took her to her friend's house, he walked her to the door, held her face between his hands, and gently kissed her on the cheek.

"See you in the morning and thanks for a super evening, Neenah!" was what he said as he turned back to the car.

Chapter 6

Five days and four dates later, Nash was invited to dinner at the Kingman's home. Neenah explained that her parents wanted to meet the young man with whom she was spending so much time.

"Actually they've seen you on the ferry when they cross to the mainland, but they've never had the opportunity to talk to you. It's no big deal. They just want to be sure you've a good person because they want to protect me. So if you'd avoid your rude self, you won't have to get into your apologizing mode." She laughed with pleasure at her small jibe. "Seriously though, there is one thing I should mention. My folks did have another child, a boy. He was four years old when he was killed by an out-of-control car while playing in the front yard where they lived. I was born two years later, and I think they feel a little over protective of me. I can't blame them for that considering all they've been through. I thought you should be aware of it."

"Thanks, Neenah. One doesn't know what other people have suffered unless someone tells you. It may save me from hurting them in some way."

"And I hope it won't hurt you to be in a family again. I know Hairy is your family now, but mine is more like the one you had."

A sad look crossed Nash's face, but then he brightened. "I thought of that but I plan to just enjoy your family because they're responsible for your being here. And that is definitely a cause for happiness." He reached out and put his arm around her. "I haven't figured out what I'll do about getting back home, but I'll work on that."

35

"Would it be alright if you spent the night?" He looked startled. She laughed. "Don't get your hopes up. We have a guest cottage behind the house. It's heated and everything. If you can work it out with Captain DeLong, you could just go to work the next morning from Washington." And so it was arranged. Neenah picked him up at the ferry in her little white car and drove him through winding, tree-lined roads to a small lane, which led them to an imposing building, set among the trees and looking out on the bay. He had wondered what kind of home she lived in, and now he realized she probably came from a very wealthy family. What would he have to offer a girl with a background like this? He involuntarily stopped, and Neenah, misunderstanding, said, "Don't worry. They are dears and certainly won't eat you—unless the roast didn't cook or something." When Nash and Neenah walked in, they were greeted by a slender middle-aged woman wearing an apron. She was gracious and warmly welcomed the young man after giving her daughter a quick kiss. "Please excuse the apron, Nash. I found long ago that if I didn't want to change my dress before dinner every night, I'd better wear an apron, and a big one. I seem to splash a great deal."

Neenah hugged her mom. "Maybe that's why you're such a good cook. You'll have to teach me to splash more."

Nash was about to sit down in an indicated chair in the living room when a handsome, strong looking, middle-aged man appeared around the corner. He exuded an air of confidence and success and power. The young man snapped erect and took the proffered hand, careful to return the strong pressure.

"I'm Stan Kingman, and you must be the Nash we've been hearing so much about. It's nice of you to come tonight, so we could meet you. Doris and I like to get to know Neenah's friends, especially because they're such a nice group of young people."

At that point everyone did sit down, and the conversation centered on the day's activities. It gave Nash an opportunity to look around the massive room that was built to resemble a lodge with log construction and large-scale rustic furniture brightened by colorful rugs and cushions. He didn't understand how such a big space could be cozy, but Mrs. Kingman, or someone, had managed to make it so.

The evening went smoothly at first, with delicious food and interesting conversation. He found that his host was the owner of a trucking company and was able to manage much of his business on the phone or by computer and fax machine. He did travel part of the time but arranged it so he could do a series of things and then return home for an extended period. Nash assumed it was a very successful business.

"Neenah told us about your family tragedy, Nash. I'm so sorry. But she said you lived in a town not far from her college. And that you actually have some mutual friends."

"We were both surprised."

"What business was your dad in, Nash?"

"Well, sir, my dad started out as a carpenter and then bought out the small construction company he worked for and ended up buying land here and there and building houses on the properties. He believed in doing the best kind of job he could, and people appreciated that. Mom started teaching school when Dorie, my sister, was in fourth grade. She loved kids, but it was really funny to have your mother be one of the teachers in your school." He smiled for a moment at some of the memories and then felt the weight of their sadness.

Mr. Kingman went on with the examination. "What do you intend to do with your future? Have you made any plans?"

"When I was in college, I was a premed major, but I've changed in many ways in the past four months. I have another year of college, but I think now I'll go to a seminary to become a minister."

He looked around the table as if seeking the reaction to that announcement. He saw the disapproval on Neenah's father's face, the amazement on Mrs. Kingman's countenance, and a lack of surprise on her daughter's face. Silence reigned.

"And how do you plan to finance all those years of study?"

"I haven't figured that out yet. I have no money from my parents, so I imagine I will apply for scholarships and work part time. Actually, I just realized that is what I want to do."

"Will it be something different tomorrow?" Mr. Kingman asked, dryly.

Then Neenah said quickly, "After dinner, would you like to see the house? It has fun nooks and crannies."

"I'd like to do that." Nash knew how expensive nooks and crannies were in new houses but he doubted that Neenah would be aware of the costs. Maybe he could hide in one.

"Let's have our dessert on the porch after you explore the house. Oh, it's glass enclosed, so you don't need to sit and shiver in your coat while you eat," said Neenah's mother, brightly, as she hurried to carry some plates to the kitchen.

As soon as they were alone in an upstairs bedroom, Neenah came over to him and put her arms around his waist. "Sorry about the interrogation, but my dad has become absorbed in business and making money. Mom said he didn't used to be that way, but when Todd was killed, he apparently found it safer to handle figures than get involved with people. My mom and I are the exceptions."

"Neenah, did you hear me say I wanted to go into the ministry? Where did that come from? After the words were out, I couldn't believe they came from my mouth. And why didn't you look shocked?"

"Have you listened to yourself lately, Nash? You talk about your faith so much and the men's Bible study and church. I thought you were headed that direction, but maybe you weren't listening. I guess you heard it tonight, though.

"Is that all right with you?'

"It's your decision, Nash, and only you know what you want to do with your life."

"This is a stupid time to mention this, but I hope you will want to share that life with me. I feel like you are part of me, the best part, I'm sure, and I don't ever want to lose you."

"We haven't time to talk about it now." She saw his face fall. "But when we do, I'll tell you I feel the same way."

He gathered her to him and kissed her tenderly. "We will talk about this later. Now which are you going to show me first, a nook or a cranny? And what is the difference between the two? And what actually is a cranny?"

She just laughed and led him quickly through the rest of the big house.

Neenah had the whole month of January away from school, and Nash was looking forward to spending as much time as possible with her, but after that night it seemed like her parents needed her to run errands, and for Christmas they gave her a trip to London with them for two weeks in January. Nash wondered wryly how they managed to get the tickets on such short notice. He knew Neenah's father was making a big effort to keep his daughter away from a penniless, would-be minister. He didn't know if the object of the plot knew, and he wasn't going to say anything. She really wanted to stay with him, but how can one turn down a Christmas present from one's parents? So she said goodbye, with tears, and left for England.

When she returned she had only a week before she had to start packing to go back to Cornell. She and Nash squeezed in as much time together as they could. Two nights before she was to leave, she managed to spend the night with her girlfriend again, and she and Nash spent the evening in Hairy's living room in front of the fire.

"I'd hoped to have more time with you, Neenah, and now you'll be going off to school. When will I see you again?"

"Spring vacation isn't that far away. I'll be back then."

He couldn't hold it in any longer. "I'm sure your dad will have some trip planned by then," he said bitterly.

She looked uncertain. "I think they just want to spend time with me before I leave to start my own life. At least, I think that's it. I must admit I was surprised that my dad would take so much time off since he seldom did before." She frowned, deep in thought. "Why would they want me to be away?"

"Because a penniless drifter has designs on their daughter and their money!"

"Nash, you can't be serious!"

"Think it over, Neenah. Did you think he was excited about me the night I came for dinner? I haven't seen your parents since then except for a nodding acquaintance on the ferry crossing. I love you and thought we would spend our lives together, but I don't think I can argue with your dad. What *do* I have to offer you? I'm not sure where I'm going, and I surely don't know how I'd get there if I did. I know I'll find what I should do, and I'll find a way to get there, but it's not at all clear now. Would you be willing to wait, I don't know how long, while I figure things out? You could have anyone you wanted, and there are so many easier lives than any I could offer you."

"Do you really believe I could have anyone I wanted?"

"Yes. I watched you at the dance that night, and boys were around you like bees around honey."

"Okay. If I can have anyone I want, I want *you!*" She put her arms around him and kissed him very seriously, as though taking a vow.

He held her tight. "I don't want to ever let you go, but I don't want to mess up your life. I want the best for you, and I'm sure your parents do, too."

"When they get to know you, they'll realize you *are* the best. I'm only a junior and we have time to think things through and find our direction. I'll be able to teach when I graduate, so I can support you while you go to school. There are student loans and scholarships and things. We'll have to do without some things, but that'll be fun. My parents often talk about the happiest time in their lives that was when they didn't have anything except a future and could work together toward it. And now, let's get back to the part where you said you love me and want to spend your life with me. We kind of skipped over that, and I'd like to investigate that further."

"You are wonderful! Here I thought I was down and out, and you make it all seem possible. Bless you, Lovely One! I want to marry you and love you and hold you and protect you and live with you and eat breakfast with you and sit beside you when you're sick and laugh with you and go through life with you. I do believe the Lord blessed us together, and for a little while I lost sight of that and doubted. We do have time to figure things out and win your parents over. I know that my family would love you the minute they saw you. How I wish they'd had that opportunity!"

The rest of the evening was spent in conversation (mostly) about how wonderful it was to love someone so much and how fortunate they were to have dreams of the future.

Chapter 7

Two days later Neenah's was the first car on the ferry from Washington Island to the mainland. It was a gray day, and snow had been coming down gently for about two hours. It matched Nash's mood. He was watching for that little white car with its DOORCT license plate. Captain Jack knew she was going off to school, and he made sure Nash had some time with her before she went on her way. In fact, the ferry was a little early arriving at the dock, and Nash drove off it with Neenah, so they could say goodbye. He had the feeling it was forever. The memory of saying goodbye to his family rose up in his mind with the sure knowledge that sometimes goodbye is forever.

"Neenah, I'm going to miss you so much! Please call me as soon as you get safely there. Maybe I'll even come down and see you or something wild like that."

"I'd love it! Oh, do! I'd be so proud to show you off to my friends. And I can't wait to tell Amy about you and me. In fact, maybe I won't tell her, but we'll surprise her when you come down."

"I've got to go, Honey. You be careful! I don't like all this snow. It's supposed to turn into a blizzard."

"I should beat the heavy part by my early start. They don't think it will be really bad until this afternoon. And besides, I'm accustomed to snow driving. My car has good tires, and I'll take it slow. Once I get up the hill at Ellison Bay, I should have a straight shot out of the County and I hear that there's less wind down south. I promise to be careful."

"I love you, Neenah!"

"And I love you, too, Nash. And I always will."

He watched her drive off, and his heart felt like lead in his chest. He was going to have to relearn that when you say goodbye to someone you love, that doesn't mean the end. But he couldn't seem to rid himself of the fear.

The captain noticed his dejection, and on one of the landings at the mainland, Nash saw Jeff Randall waiting on the dock.

"What are you doing here, Jeff?"

"Captain DeLong asked me to work for a while this morning because he wants you to run an errand or something. Has it been busy?"

"No, not really. I'll run up to the bridge and see what he wants me to do if you'll take over here."

Jack asked Nash to pick up a package for him at the Sister Bay post office by eleven o'clock. He guessed that it was a diversion to take his mind off saying goodbye to Neenah. It was now a full-blown snowstorm and the young man was glad that his girl (*his girl!*) had an early start. He hoped she'd driven out of the heavy snow by Green Bay.

He was almost to the top of the hill south of Ellison Bay when he noticed there was a break in the underbrush to the west of the road. He was past it when he realized it was about the width of a car. He'd never noticed it before. Could a car have spun off the road and gone down the steep hillside? Would anyone have noticed? Surely someone would have seen it and sent for help. But what if there hadn't been any traffic on this snowy day? He was well on his way to Sister Bay, but the worry seemed to get more intense as he went south. Reluctantly, he turned the truck around and headed back to Ellison Bay. Proceeding slowly on the slippery snow-packed road, half covered with drifting snow, he went back to that opening, and parked his vehicle carefully off the road to the right. He walked over to look for tracks and realized the snow had covered any trail. He peered into the ravine below and stiffened. Even through the veil of snow he could see the dark underside of a car facing skyward. Horrified, he slid down the steep slope, falling and slipping, frantic to see the color of the automobile.

It was a white sedan, and fearfully, he read the upside-down license plate. DOORCT stood out in black boldness. He ran round to the driver's side and fell on his stomach to try to see in the darkened window. There was a snowy, deathly silence.

The window was fogged over and desperately he searched for something with which to smash it. Finding a stout tree branch he used adrenalin strength to break the glass, never thinking that the flying glass might cut Neenah.

When he was able to peer in, his worst fears were confirmed. She hung, crumpled, from her seat belt and the gas fumes made him sick to his stomach. He managed to croak, "Neenah?" and heard a tiny groan in response. Even though he had broken away the window as much as possible, he still felt some of the glass cutting his skin as he inched his way into the crumbled, reeking front seat area. He reached for the girl's hand.

His relief was immeasurable as he felt her fingers tighten on his. He tried to see her face, but it was covered by her long, dark hair. "Are you hurt?" he asked anxiously.

"My foot seems to be caught under the engine or something," was her muffled answer. "And the gasoline has drenched my clothes. For goodness sake, don't light a match."

"Are you in much pain?"

"Not really. I can't tell if it's frozen or not, but my foot and lower leg seem quite numb. I think it will hurt a lot when the pressure is off it. I'm so glad you're here, Nash! I was afraid I would just die here, and no one would know. But all the time I kept thinking, 'Nash will find me. God will send Nash to find me.'" And she started to cry great, gulping sobs.

"You'll be out of here in no time. I'll have to leave you for just a bit to get help but I'll be back as soon as I possibly can. I hate to go, but we must have help unless you think we can get you out. I worry you may be more injured if I try to pull you. I'm even afraid to try to cut you out of the seat belt because I don't know where you might be injured and I don't dare move you. Be brave!"

"I can't get out anyway because my leg is caught. I've tried to loosen it but it just doesn't move. I think I'll scream if you leave though. I can't bear to be alone here again!"

43

"Be brave, my love. I'll be back as soon as I possibly can. You know that the Lord is right here with you, and I want you to picture Jesus on your other side with his arm around you. Don't lose that picture—and I'll be right back. I'm going to put my coat around you as best I can because you must be almost frozen." Having done that, he tried for an unseen smile. "Even if I wouldn't come back for you, you know I'd come back for my favorite coat."

He released himself from her clinging hand, scrambled backward across the glass shards, and slid *up* the snowy hillside, powered by desperation and fear. He ran to the hotel at the crest of the road, hoping so hard that someone was there that his teeth were locked tight.

The third frantic ring brought a tired-looking woman to the door. When she saw his face and bloodied shirt she looked ready to close it, but his foot was in the door before she could do that. He hurriedly explained and asked her to call for help. She was moving to the phone as he turned away and called over his shoulder, "I'll be down there with her. Tell them to hurry. It's a matter of life and death!"

He scurried back to the car, and he could almost feel Neenah's relief. Holding her hand again, he assured her that help was on the way. He tried to talk about normal things, but her responses were getting slower and fainter. *She must be in shock*, he thought. It was amazing that she wasn't unconscious after hanging upside down for so long in the cold. The time seemed to creep by, and an eternity later, he felt someone pull on his leg.

"Help is here, my darling. I'm going back out to talk to them. I'll be right outside." But there was no response, and her limp hand dangled in the air when he let go.

Two county patrolmen were beside him when he stood up. He recognized Eric Slater who went with a girl who lived on the island and rode the ferry often. He was also a member of the Bible study class. "Eric, where is the equipment to lift the car and get her out of there?"

"It's coming but we have to bring it by water because there's no way to get it down here. We won't know the best way to handle things until we see what the situation is so we can advise them when they arrive. It shouldn't be long. How many people are in the car and are they alive?"

"It's Neenah, and I think she's in shock. Her leg seems to be pinned under something. She's awfully cold. Can you radio in to bring a medic and some blankets?"

Eric's transmitter went right to work. The scratchy response assured them that help was on the way. "Are they bringing in a crane to lift the car? Why isn't there an ambulance here by now?"

"The ambulance is held up by the snowstorm and the slippery roads. When the wind blows like this during a heavy snowfall, you know how the plows can't keep up with it. They know it's an emergency, and they'll get here as fast as they can. It'll take a while to bring a crane here and by then we should figure out the best way to free Neenah from the car."

The other patrolman who had wormed his way through the broken window looked worried. "Her pulse is steady, but weak. The gasoline worries me. There's no way we can use any cutting torches around here. That fuel would ignite in a minute and," he looked away from Nash as he finished his sentence, "I believe her foot and lower leg have been crushed between the engine and the frame of the car." Eric kicked the snow with his foot, unable to meet Nash's eyes.

The nightmare continued. Time seemed as frozen as the ground under their feet. Nash shook himself and headed back through the window like some animal going into his burrow. He took Neenah's hand and rubbed it, trying so hard to warm it and transfer some of his life into her limp body. Finally, he heard more voices and backed out once more. The fire department had arrived, but their faces were grim after talking to the patrolmen. Then the medic, Stan Jenkins, pushed his way through and headed for the accident victim.

When he backed out, Nash was waiting for him. "What do you think, Stan? How much longer can she stay there? When will they get the car lifted up and free her?" But even as he asked, he feared the answer because Stan's face was so grim.

"Nash, I hate to say this. I dread making a call like this, but I can't see any way we can get her leg freed. The car must have hit hard on its side and the engine was slammed into the frame right where her lower leg was resting. The boys and I have talked about it. That darn gasoline is another problem, and also we have to get her out of there soon, or she'll die of hypothermia."

"What about lifting the car up?" "We'd have no control over what that would do to her leg. It could sever an artery, and if we couldn't reach her she'd bleed to death."

Nash felt like screaming at him. "What *can* you do?"

"I'm sorry, Nash, but I'm afraid that to save her life we'll have to remove her lower leg. There won't be anything easy about it because of her position but we can be fairly in control of the procedure. Then she'll be taken to the hospital in Green Bay immediately. We must try to keep her as warm as possible until the ambulance arrives with supplies and trained help. And pray that they get here soon!"

Nash slid back through the window with two blankets and tried his best to pack them around the unconscious girl, listening all the time. And then he heard the most beautiful sound he could imagine––the wail of a siren blown on a gust of wind.

After that things happened fast. The medics came sliding down the hill, carrying a stretcher, headed for the car, surveyed the situation, and raced back up the incline to their vehicle to get needed equipment. In three minutes they had blazing lights set up, had managed to pry one of the doors open, and were injecting an anesthetic into the limp form.

Eric had stepped out of the way after giving the emergency personnel all the pertinent information that he had. He stood beside Nash and explained some of the procedures, hoping to give him some understanding of the problems.

"They can't give her much anesthetic because she is in shock, but because she's unconscious she wouldn't need much anyway. They will apply a tourniquet below her left knee to control the blood loss and remove as little of her leg as possible. If they find they'll have to go above her knee, they'll move the tourniquet higher. I hope they can take it off lower. It would make a prosthesis so much easier."

Nash must have looked stricken because the patrolman said kindly, "Don't fret too much about her leg, Nash. It's that or her life, and if they don't do it quickly and warm her up slowly, it may not make any difference anyway. I hate to say it, but you must prepare yourself for the real possibility that she won't make it at all." He put his hand on Nash's shoulder.

There was a strange unreality about the whole scene. The blowing snow, caught in the glare of the intense lights, glistened and whirled, partially obscuring the drama that was going on inside the overturned car. It looked like some surreal stage set. The vehicle seemed to have sprouted all sorts of legs and parts of equipment, overflowing the constricted space within. Nash longed to hold Neenah's hand but knew he'd be in the way and that she wouldn't know anyway.

Then he heard a scream that even the wind could not carry away. It would haunt him all his life. And after it, silence. They slid her body out the misshapen doorway and carefully laid it on a stretcher before carrying it up the steep slope to the waiting ambulance. He ran after the last man trailing the silent procession, asking frantically, "Is she alive?"

The man turned. "Do you know her?"

"Yes, I do."

The man stopped and pulled out a pen and clipboard. "Please give me her name and address. And will you spell it please?"

Nash did as requested. "Is she alive?" he pleaded. The answer was, "For now." Nash didn't think he could pray any harder, but it was as though his whole spirit lifted to God in supplication. He pleaded for Neenah's life, he pleaded for his own happiness, and he pleaded for the strength to ask that God's will be done. He reminded God that his past had been taken in a plane crash and prayed that his future would not be destroyed by an automobile accident.

Eric came to walk beside him. "I've been in communication with Captain Jack on the two-way radio. He said the Coast Guard was picking up the Kingmans in one of their big boats that can handle the storm. They'll take them to Gills Rock where Hairy will meet them in Jack's Land Rover, after leaving his car at Jack's house. Then he'll bring them here to Ellison Bay to the General Store where you are to meet them with Jack's truck. If you're up to it, will you drive the Kingmans to the hospital in Green Bay in the Land Rover? It's probably the safest car for this weather. Then Hairy will take the truck back to Jack's, pick up his car, and head home for the rest of the storm. Jack has to stay with the ferry, and Hairy isn't real confident about driving in this weather. What do you think?"

"I have to admit that I'm a wreck, but I think I can handle it, and I surely want to be there even if I have to walk. Can you take me to where I left the captain's truck? I hope I'll get to the General Store before Hairy gets there. The Kingmans must be frantic. How much do they know?"

"As far as I know, they have only been told that Neenah's been in a serious accident. It will probably fall on you to tell them just how serious it is if you're up to doing that. I suppose you could plead ignorance. I remember the Bible story of the messenger who brought bad news and was killed. Get in the squad car, and I'll drive you up the hill. I noticed the truck when I came down here."

And so it was that a white-faced Nash was on the snowy porch of the store when Hairy pulled up in front of it. He got out and exchanged keys with the younger man, put his arms around him for a moment, offered a gruff, "I'll be praying," and headed for the truck.

Chapter 8

Nash greeted the Kingmans as he climbed wearily into the driver's seat of the Land Rover. He'd barely started the car when Stan Kingman snarled beside him in the front seat, "What did you have to do with this 'accident'?' She was supposed to be well out of the county by now. Did you hang around and keep her from leaving? I'm going to damn well hold you responsible if you are involved in any way. Just what the hell happened anyway?"

Doris Kingman spoke in a shaky voice from the back seat. "They haven't told us anything except that Neenah was involved in an accident and was being taken to the hospital in Green Bay. Please tell us what happened. Is she all right?"

Nash hesitated, not knowing what he should tell them or how he should say it.

"Did she wreck the car? I shouldn't have given her that darn car if she wasn't going to take care of it!"

And from the back seat, stronger this time, "Stan, I know you're upset, too, but stop being such a bully, and let the young man tell us what has happened to Neenah."

"I'll tell you as much as I know. Neenah left just a few minutes after the ferry docked. Her car apparently slid on the snow and went over the cliff on her way up the hill at Ellison Bay. I don't know why, but it must have been shortly after she left because she didn't plan to stop anywhere since she knew she was racing the weather. Jack asked me to pick up a package in Sister Bay about 8:30, and as I was driving up the hill I noticed a break in the undergrowth on the right side of the road about the width of a car. It's amazing I would notice it because the snow was already heavy by then, so there were no tracks leading off the road. I thank God that I did! I was almost in Sister Bay when I realized how much that disturbed me, so I turned around and went back to check on it. When I got out and looked over the edge, I was looking down at the bottom of a car. I slid down, and my heart almost stopped when I saw Neenah's license plate!" He paused. "Mr. Kingman, would you mind sitting in the back with your wife? I think she'll need you beside her to hear the rest of this."

For once, Stan Kingman was silent as Nash pulled over and waited for him to get out and join his wife in the back. When they were underway again, Nash continued reluctantly. "I could see her hanging upside down by her seat belt but the doors were jammed so I broke a window and climbed into the car. She was conscious and frightened, but when I suggested I cut the seat belt she told me that her foot was caught and numb, so I went for help right away. The county patrolmen came shortly after I got back to her, but she was going into shock by then, so she was hardly aware I was there. The gasoline smell was so terribly strong that they couldn't use their cutting torches, and they couldn't turn the car upright because they didn't know what that would do to her foot. Finally the ambulance and the medics arrived." He stopped. How could he tell them the fact that was so terrible that he couldn't even say it to himself?

The silence stretched on. Finally the man in the back seat said in a hollow voice, "Please tell us the rest. I have my arms around Doris."

"I don't want to tell you!" For the first time since he'd seen her frightened face earlier that day, he broke down. He pulled off the road and tried to get himself together, so he could say the words he so dreaded. They came out in a strained whisper. "They had to cut off her lower left leg to get her out."

The mother in the back seat started to sob. Nash put the car in gear and pulled back on the road. He wanted to get to the hospital quickly, and he was afraid of what he might find when he got there. He drove in silence until Mr. Kingman asked, "But she'll live, won't she? That's what matters. Once they got her out, they could take care of her, couldn't they?"

The silence of the young man in the front seat gave him his answer.

"People lose limbs and get along fine. And that's all that was holding her in the car, wasn't it?"

"Yes, but she'd been hanging upside down in freezing weather for at least two and a half hours. She probably lost some blood, but I don't know for sure because I couldn't see where her foot was. I've heard that most cars are tested for front-end collisions but if a car is hit from the side, the motor can swing over and crush the driver's foot. So they are fighting shock, trauma, blood loss, and hypothermia. I think we have to prepare ourselves for what we may find when we get to the hospital."

Nash let them out at the door to the emergency room and parked as quickly as possible. He was afraid to go in, and yet he ran to the door. He found the Kingmans huddled in the waiting room, doing what the name implied. The doctor had been paged.

Dr. Newman was an elderly, kindly looking man who seemed to understand their emotional confusion. He took them into a small room with a couch and two chairs before telling them anything. The tension in the room was palpable.

"Your daughter has been through a terrible ordeal. I'm sure you are shocked by the amputation of her leg." Nash saw Mrs. Kingman flinch as though he had struck her in the face. Her husband's visage was stony.

"But that is something that we all will deal with later. At the moment we are working to keep her alive." A gasp was heard. "I don't want to frighten you, but you must be prepared for the seriousness of her condition. She has been through the trauma of the accident, has hung inverted for a length of time in extremely cold conditions, and has a severe injury. Fortunately the ambulance team is very well trained and capable of handling situations like this one. They were careful to bring her body temperature back up to normal gradually, which is a sensitive procedure. She is in intensive care now but is not conscious. It's difficult to tell when she will become aware of her surroundings. You may go up and see her briefly if you wish. In the ICU, you are allowed in every thirty minutes, and that is only one person at a time. For the initial visit, I think both of you can go in." He was looking at the patient's parents as he said this.

Then he turned to Nash. "May I ask your relationship to the young woman?"

Nash paused. It was Mr. Kingman who spoke up. "He is a good friend of our daughter's, and he is the one who found her. She wouldn't be alive now except for him." The young man whirled around and met eyes that were sad and apologetic. "Would it be all right if the three of us went to see her now?"

More shocks lay ahead as they were led into the cubical where the injured girl was placed. Neenah's hair was matted and scraggly around her white face that was just beginning to show the emerging bruises. At first it appeared that she was not breathing, but then she began to moan piteously, and her hands reached out in alarm. Mrs. Kingman tried to hold one of them, but the girl pulled away as though she had been burned. The visitors looked at each other helplessly. Then a nurse came in and told them their time was up.

"Can anything be done to calm her?" her father asked.

"No, we can't give her any painkillers while she's in shock. She's unconscious, so she isn't really aware of the pain." As they walked out all three of them tried not to look at the flat spot on the bed where her foot should have been.

There were couches in the waiting room, and a kindly receptionist informed them that there was a single bed available down the hall. Both men looked at Neenah's mother who tried to refuse but, in the end, agreed to rest on it if they promised to call her when it was her turn to go into the ICU. After that, it was a regular routine. The three of them rotated their visits every half hour and tried to rest between times. It seemed to go on endlessly.

Twenty-four hours later, they were all exhausted, and Neenah's condition hadn't changed at all. It was Nash who said, "Why don't two of us go to a motel, clean up, get a bite to eat, and try to rest for a few hours? Then one can come back here, and the one here can leave. I'm sure none of us want to go, but I wonder how long we'll last if this goes on for a week. Let's ask the nurse if she would advise us to do that."

The nurse told them she couldn't predict what might happen, but she knew of cases where the patient had been in a coma for two or three weeks, and Neenah's vital signs were fairly stable now. "And as long as one of you is here if we should need you, I think it will be better in the long run."

And so it was arranged. Mrs. Kingman insisted she would take the first watch, so Nash and Mr. Kingman emerged into the weak sunshine and piles of clean, white snow a few minutes later. It seemed like a foreign world after the intensity of the previous time period. They blinked foolishly in the light and had to hunt up the car which Nash had parked without noting its location.

They found a motel three blocks from the hospital, and both men showered wearily, managed to eat a sturdy breakfast, and enjoyed the luxury of horizontal sleep. Nash set the alarm on the little clock between the two beds, and when it went off in two hours; they rose groggily and made their way out to the car.

Mrs. Kingman leaned heavily on her husband's arm as he walked with her out to the waiting car. In passing the baton to Nash, she said that her daughter was just the same, though maybe a little less restless than the last time she had been able to see her.

A routine was soon established. One person stayed for four visiting periods while the other two usually rested back at the motel. This gave about a two-and-a-half hour window to be out of the hospital. And sometimes they all sat and talked or just were silently together, each with their own thoughts. They soon were on a first-name basis with the nurses. They knew that Sandy was there on weekends, working ten-hour shifts, and then during the week, there were Alice, Beth, Noreen, Pat, Kay, and Shari. They all seemed genuinely concerned for the unconscious girl, and it became a vigil for them all, not just her parents and Nash.

To a passerby, those three would have appeared like a family of parents and son. And it felt that way to Nash. It didn't seem to matter if he and Stan went to the motel or if he and Doris went there. The emergency had made them into a tight group, holding on to each other for support.

Three days later, the two men were at the motel. Nash had just lain down on the bed and was drifting off to sleep when he heard a sound that jerked him back to consciousness. For a moment he didn't recognize it, but when it came again he flinched. It was a sob so deep that it came out as a groan. Rolling over, he saw Neenah's father doubled up on the edge of the other bed. He silently went to the grieving man and put his arm around him.

"Stan, is there anything I can do to help?" A muffled, "No," came back to him, but the older man didn't pull away.

"Are you afraid Neenah won't make it?"

From the depths came, "I don't know. But I know I've failed her time and again."

"She certainly didn't give me that impression. When she talks about you and her mother, it's always with love and gratitude. How could you have failed her?"

"Could you get me some Kleenex?"

When Nash had accomplished that task, he sat beside the older man on the bed and waited.

"We had a son, and I loved him beyond any idea I had of love. He was so dear, and we were so happy, and everything looked wonderful for the future. Then it all ended in a minute. A man who didn't even live in our neighborhood, after a fight with his wife, was going too fast on our street, lost control of his car, and ran off the street. Tommy was riding his tricycle on the sidewalk, and that's where the car went. I carried his little broken, bloody body into the house and laid him on his bed, and a part of me died. I didn't want to have any more children. I didn't want to ever love anybody that much again. I think I walled off a part of my heart. But Doris wanted another child, and she became pregnant with Neenah. I tried so hard not to become emotionally involved. From the very beginning, I made it known that she was Doris's child.

"I worked hard. That started when Tommy died. I could go to work and forget for a while. My anger at the unfairness of it all became directed toward my competition, and I went for the jugular. I traveled a lot and built up quite a fortune, but I don't know how Doris stood by me through it all. On my fortieth birthday, I realized I'd gained the whole world, but it was sawdust. I went home, talked for hours to my wife, and moved to Door County to start a new life as husband and father.

"I grew to know Neenah and her dear, loving heart. I found out again what it was like to love far more than was safe, and now I feel faced by the same loss I had with Tommy. I don't think I can stand

54

it! And on top of that, I know how much less I gave to Neenah for all those years, and I can't ever change that." He broke into sobs again and Nash just held him in his arms and didn't say anything.

When the worst of the storm had passed, the man in his arms whispered, "And almost the worst thing is that I've been mad at God for so long that I can't go to Him to ask him to heal Neenah. I've cursed Him, ignored Him, and laughed at those who believe. When you said you were going to be a minister, you can't imagine the disgust that filled my heart. I thought you a senseless fool. Now, who is the fool? I have no hope."

"I hesitate to speak for God but the Bible says He will forgive those who seek Him and are sorry for what they've done. Will you pray with me now?"

A nodding head was his answer.

"Gracious Father, Stan and I come to You today, seeking forgiveness for our unbelief. Please heal us. We come to You not only for Neenah who we love so much and wish to see well but for the health of our very souls. Stan, do you believe in God and His son, Jesus Christ?"

"I want to!"

"Are you sorry for the way you have been, and do you wish to change your life?"

"Yes!"

"May the Lord bless you and give you His peace and guidance and healing and strength to accept whatever comes and grace you with faith. Amen."

Nash lifted Stan's feet up on the bed and gently covered him with a blanket. When he came back with a Kleenex to give to the older man, he found him fast asleep, his face peaceful in rest.

As he and Doris were changing places, Nash suggested she be quiet when she got to the motel room because her husband was sleeping soundly.

"Oh, I'm *so* glad! He has slept very little since we've been here. He just lies next to me staring at the ceiling. I guess when you're tired enough, you finally sleep."

"I guess so."

Two days later, they were all sitting in the waiting room. They'd taken to playing a card game called Spite and Malice that Doris's grandmother had taught her as a child. Even in the midst of an exciting play, they watched the clock carefully. Pat, one of the afternoon nurses, had told them to talk to Neenah because she might be able to hear them even if she didn't respond, and they didn't want to miss any opportunity.

There were nine minutes to go when Shari came rushing out of the ICU.

"Nash, can you come in right away? She's thrashing and flailing and calling for you, and we're having difficulty restraining her. Perhaps if you could assure her that you are there, she will probably quiet down. She's already pulled out some of the feeding tubes."

The Kingmans had risen, too.

Glancing at them, she said over her shoulder, "I don't think you should come in because there isn't much room, and I think it might upset you." She hurried Nash through the door.

He was horrified at what he saw. Neenah was fighting two orderlies frantically and screaming, "Nash! Come back! Don't leave me! Nash!" Blood was dripping from her arm where the IV had ripped loose, her hair was in her face and mouth, and her eyes were open with a look of such terror that it made him shudder. He didn't know what vision she was seeing, but it made his blood run cold to see the horror written there.

Trying to appear calm, he started talking in a quiet voice. "Neenah, I'm here, Honey. I won't go away. I just went to get help. Now I'm back, and I won't leave you again. It's going to be all right." He kept on repeating the last part and gathered her in his arms, holding her firmly against his chest. She struggled, but he kept reassuring her, and gradually she quieted. It was almost like letting air out of tire. She became more and more limp until he couldn't hold her anymore and lowered her back on the bed. She was ashen.

Frantically Nash looked at Shari. "She isn't . . . ?" He couldn't bring himself to say it.

The woman took one of the girl's hands in hers and after feeling her wrist said, "No, she seems to be resting normally."

The experience was more than the young man could bear. He knelt beside the bed and wept. All his anxiety and despair broke loose in great sobs. Everyone left the room to give him privacy and the space to pull himself back together. Or at least he thought they'd left until he felt a hand on his head. He looked up to see who was in the room, but no one was there. It was then he realized it was Neenah's hand, and he stood up shakily to see her looking at him with real awareness.

"Neenah, dearest!" And he put his arms around her and held her close, rocking gently back and forth, babbling incoherently.

"Nash," her quiet voice said, "You are squeezing me very tightly."

He carefully released her. Shari had reentered and stood nearby, in tears. Some of the orderlies had come back in, and they watched with happy smiles on their faces.

"Her parents!" Nash said belatedly. "Shari, will you go get them?"

Mr. And Mrs. Kingman looked ill as they walked through the door, but when they saw their daughter smiling at them and Nash standing by the bed holding her hand, they just went into each other's arms and hung on. Neenah's dad turned his ravaged face to them. "When Shari called us in, she didn't say why, but we saw the tears running down her cheeks and feared the worst. It will take us a minute to take it all in, and then we'll celebrate the safe return of our dearest child."

Neenah was quite confused by the personnel who trouped in to see her. She didn't know any of them, but her return had made them all very happy. She just smiled politely but she held tight to Nash's hand the whole time.

Chapter 9

For the first time, all three of the waiters were in the motel room. The supervisor had told them that Neenah would be given something for sleep, so they could all have the night off. Around noon, they would be moving her to a room on the surgical floor, so they could come back in the morning when they wished.

Mr. Kingman was the first to bring it up. "Do you think she knows about her leg yet? I don't know how she'd react. She's never had to face anything like this before. Life has been very good to her, and I doubt if she's prepared to handle anything this serious. I don't think *I* am either. I wonder if she knows yet."

"I don't know," her mother replied. "She certainly didn't mention it to me, but everything was so new and confusing to her after being unconscious for almost a week. And she seemed a little groggy. I wonder if she knows."

Nash spoke next. "If she doesn't, who will tell her? What a dreadful thing to tell a person!"

Both parents said, almost in unison, "I don't want to tell her!"

"Neither do I. Maybe a nurse will break the news. But if it falls on any one of us, we must be able to do it. And if it doesn't, we'd better think what we're going to say next."

When they entered the familiar cubicle for the last time, they were very nervous but one look at Neenah's bright eyes and their relief at her recovery was so great that the anxiety was forgotten momentarily.

"Why am I here? What happened? I was on my way to school and woke up in the hospital."

"You had an accident, and your car went over the hill on the way out of Ellison Bay. Nash found you trapped in your car and went for help. Do you remember going off the road?"

Her brow furrowed, and there was silence.

"I remember saying goodbye to Nash when I drove off the ferry. And I remember going through Ellison Bay." More silence. "And I started up the hill and . . . there was a deer in the road. I tried to avoid it and heard some branches scrape against the car and . . . that's all I can remember. Did I scratch the car?"

"Don't worry about the car, Honey. We can take care of that. Now you just have to get well."

Just then, Norine came bustling in. "It's really wonderful to see our girl awake, isn't it! You have beautiful blue eyes, I see. I'll just take your temperature, and then I'll leave you to visit. You have lots to catch up on. And around noon, the orderly will be in to move Neenah to the second floor to a room of her own."

After she left, Doris asked, "Do you hurt anywhere, Dear?"

"I ache in a lot of places but my toes on my left foot feel like they are full of cramps. Could you rub them for me, Nash? That would make them feel better, I'm sure."

Nash just stood there. Then he said slowly, "I can't. There's something I have to tell you, and it's not going to be easy."

Neenah laughed and said, "Don't tease me so soon. I'll bet you're going to say you don't do feet or some such thing."

He took her hand and her father held the other one. She looked questioningly back and forth at them.

Nash was the one who said it. "Neenah, they had to cut off your left leg below the knee to get you out of the car alive."

She just looked at him in disbelief. And then at her mother. And then at her father. She saw the answer in their eyes, and the light in hers went out. Nash felt as though he'd blown out a candle when he had spoken the dreaded words.

"But it can't be true. I can feel my toes. They hurt. If they were gone, they wouldn't hurt!"

"It's called phantom pain. The connecting nerves are still there, and they recall funny things."

She tried to sit up. Her father bravely lifted her head, and she looked down at the flat space in the bed where her foot should have been and started to cry silently except for little moans and whimpers. The people who loved her held her and rocked her and cried with her.

It was a silent entourage that made its way behind the gurney as it rolled up to the second floor. They passed under the sign that said Surgical and proceeded to room 214. Neenah's eyes were closed, and no one knew how to break the silence that went on and on.

Hoping their daughter was asleep, the Kingmans whispered to Nash that they were going down for some coffee and quietly exited. As soon as they were gone, the girl on the bed said angrily, "Why didn't you let me die? Why didn't you stop them when they said they'd . . ." She couldn't say it.

"Neenah, I wanted you to live! I didn't care how. I just wanted you to live. What would you have done?" Now his anger rose to match hers. "If you had seen my life fading before your eyes and had to make a decision, would you have said, 'No, I want him to be a whole corpse, so let him die upside down in the cold. And then when you can get that body free of the car some day without causing the whole thing to explode. Be sure you paste back the bloodless dead piece that was his foot before it was crushed and mangled by the frame of the car.'"

The tension in the room was thick. She started to cry, and he rocked her in his arms and cried with her. When Neenah's parents came back, they found Nash collapsed in a chair, and their daughter sleeping, her tear-stained face white against the pillow. They went out in the hall where Nash told them part of what happened.

"I know it will take time for her to accept what has happened. It's so much all at once.

At three o'clock, a kindly looking, middle aged man in a white uniform went into Neenah's room.

"I'm Dr. Wilson, and I'm an orthopedic surgeon. I want to discuss with you the next step in your recovery. You are a lucky young lady to be alive," he said. "You've been through major trauma and have lived to tell about it. I'm sure it must be overwhelming right now, but I think the day will come when you'll know what I said is true. Now we have to get you back on your feet." She flinched at that expression. "We must do a surgical follow-up to the amputation, which was done well but under terrible circumstances. I'm amazed that you haven't had an infection since it was done under awful conditions. We'll clean up the site and close it so that a prosthesis will be able to be fitted to it when it heals. You should expect to be walking in a month or two. Until then, you will be able to use crutches to get around. Do you have any questions?"

"Will it be painful for her to walk?" asked Mrs. Kingman.

"Once a callus forms on the stump, it shouldn't hurt unless she stands an extraordinary amount of time. We'll be sure she has the opportunity to talk to some young people who are using prostheses, so she can ask them questions."

He took Neenah's hand and gently said, "There'll be hard times, but it will be all right. Try to believe that, and one day you'll find it is true."

Then turning to her parents, he asked, "If it's okay with you and Neenah, can we schedule the surgery for day after tomorrow? I think it should be done soon. It won't be a long operation. And then the healing can begin."

And so it was arranged.

A few days after the surgery, the Kingmans announced that since the healing was going so well, they thought they'd go back to Washington Island and go through the mail and get things ready for Neenah's homecoming, if that was all right with the two young people. Nash said it would be fine since Captain Jack had made arrangements with Jeff Randall to help on the ferry until Nash returned, which would be as soon as Neenah went home. That young lady just nodded her head.

The night before they left, when the three of them were at the motel, Stan said to Nash, "I'm really concerned about how quiet Neenah has become. I don't know what is going on in her mind. Is she accepting the situation? Will you see if you can get her to talk about it? She is so quiet and agrees to everything, but I think something is wrong. I'm glad we'll be gone for a few days, so you will have the opportunity to talk to her alone. We've tried, but we only get a gentle smile. I think she'll be able to talk to you."

Doris hugged Nash. "We are so grateful to you for your concern for Neenah. She couldn't have had a better brother, if he'd lived. I think she depends on you for strength in some way. In fact, I think we all do. Bless you!" She moved away with tears in her eyes.

There were more tears there when they said goodbye to their daughter, and Stan's handshake was hard with emotion when he turned to Nash before leaving. "Take care of her," he requested.

Since Neenah still slept much of the time, Nash found a book and just sat, reading, and was there when she woke. There was very little conversation, though the young man tried to bring up things of interest. Particularly when he talked about the future, he felt a wall go up around her.

It was the next day when he finally said, "Do you not want to talk about the future?

"I'm sorry. Right now I don't feel I have a future. All the things I thought I saw ahead of me seem to be chopped off like my leg."

"Neenah, you're a lot more than part of a left leg. No one would ever say they'd want this to happen, and it will surely take time to adjust to it, but don't give up before you give yourself a chance. You're one strong woman, and you've never had such a test before. Give yourself time."

"I can hear you, but I don't feel strong at all. Maybe you're right, though. I have always had an easy life, or so it seemed. I'm not ready for this. I'm not ready to be only part of a person. I want to dance and marry and have children and not park in the handicapped parking places. I want to be normal and whole. Was I so bad? Am I being punished?" And now the anger came pouring out. "You talk about God and His love. Would a loving God take the leg off a happy young woman on her way to college? Is that His idea of how to make her grow up and be strong? I tried to be good. I went out of my way to talk to outsiders, I was nice to old people, I didn't kick kids, and I went to church sometimes. Why would He want to hurt me? Can He be a loving God and let this happen? He could have stopped it. He could have kept the car from going over the edge. I don't think I like this God of yours very much."

"I wish I could give you some good answers, but I don't know why it happened. Do you think it just could have been an accident?

Could it have been that the deer just happened to get on the road when the surface was icy or that you turned the wheel too hard in surprise or that the trees just hadn't grown quite strong enough to hold the car back? How was it that the car just happened to fall in such a way that your foot was crushed between the frame and the engine? And a bigger question—do you think God should intervene whenever we get ourselves in trouble? And if so, what happens to "free will" and our ability to choose to make mistakes? I believe God wants good for us, and accidents happen, and we make poor human judgments that bring bad results. But I believe that He can take the pieces, put them back in a new pattern, and still make good of it. My faith is weak at times, and I have to grow into a bigger one. Life is growth, painful as it is sometimes, and it takes time and patience to grow.

"I'll tell you this—I have been so busy thanking Him for not letting you die that I haven't missed your leg. And you're probably thinking, 'He isn't the one without a leg,' and you're right." He saw in her eyes that he'd read her thoughts." He leaned over and kissed her on her flushed cheek. "I think God is probably used to people being angry with Him. But that doesn't stop Him from loving you— nor need it stop you from loving Him. I think you've had enough of a sermon for the moment. But it really wasn't that. I was just telling you what I believe, and you have to figure things out for yourself. I will be praying for you as I have for a long time—through good times and bad."

"Could you go back to the motel now, Nash? I need some time to think and to, as you said, figure things out. I'll see you in the morning."

He kissed her again and was almost out the door when he heard her say quietly, "Thanks for letting me talk and being here for me."

"Any time. I'm taking advantage of this time when you can't get away from me, and there aren't dozens of young men vying for your attention. I plan to make the most of it." And he grinned at her wickedly as he went out the door.

Three days later she was released from the hospital, and her parents came to take her home. In the car, Neenah sat by her dad in the front seat, so she'd have plenty of leg room, now that she actually needed less. She looked so white in the pale winter sunlight but was awake all the way home. She must have felt so alien and vulnerable out in the big world again after being enclosed in the white cocoon of the hospital. Nash could tell she was trying hard to control her emotions, but she hardly said a word the whole trip. Since she hadn't mastered crutches yet, they rented a wheelchair for her with the understanding that a local physical therapist, Sue Miller, would work with her, and she would return to Green Bay in two weeks for a fitting of her prosthesis.

Captain Jack welcomed them aboard the Merry Jane with obvious nervousness that he tried to hide. Nash went up to the pilot-house with him and roughly explained how things stood. "Poor kid. This is going to be one heck of an adjustment"

When they had helped install a silent, exhausted young woman into her own bed, Nash knelt beside her to say goodbye, and he saw a look of almost panic in Neenah's eyes. He had been with her almost constantly since she went over that cliff, and he realized she had grown dependent on him.

"As soon as I get my schedule figured out, I'll be over to see you. One trouble with working on the ferry is that it always ends up on the other side. If it's all right with Captain Jack and you and your parents, I'll see if I can spend the night on Washington sometimes. I'll work something out. Don't think you're going to get rid of me now that you're better. And I'll keep calling in the meantime to make sure you're behaving yourself."

She gave him a brave smile, but her chin quivered. When he got in the car with Stan to go back to the ferry, he was afraid he would burst into tears. And looking at his companion, he realized they were both perilously close to weeping.

"How do you think she's doing?" Neenah's father asked.

"She's so quiet, Stan. If she cried or shouted, she might release some emotion, but maybe her mind is working to bring some order out of the chaos to which she awakened. She'll find some resolution. I can't imagine how I'd deal with it, less how she'll handle it. How are you and Doris surviving?"

"It did us good to have some time to ourselves. Thanks for staying with Neenah while we came back here. I'm putting my business in my assistant's hands, and I'll be at home until we see how things are working out. Like you, I don't know how she'll handle it. She's been so protected."

They saw the ferry approaching. "And I am doing a lot of thinking of my own. I think the Lord's trying to speak to me, and I'll try to listen. Pray for us all, please."

"You know I do, and I will. He'll see us through, but we have to figure out what He wants us to do. If it's all right with you and Doris, I'll plan to come over two nights a week and one will be my day off. I don't know if she'll want me to come, but it will give you a little respite, perhaps."

"Whatever would we do without you, Nash?"

Three weeks later, when Stan took him to the ferry, the two men tried to evaluate the situation. Stan started the conversation. "I'm worried, Nash. She doesn't seem to be trying like I thought she would. She's a bright, energetic girl, but she doesn't seem to want to do anything. She won't have anything to do with that prosthesis, and she doesn't get off the couch very often, though she can use her crutches very well. She hardly ever laughs except when you're there. You seem to bring out the laughter that's been so absent from her life."

"Yes, but it isn't her regular laughter. It's like she's trying very hard to find some humor, but it doesn't go deep.

"I don't know what to do. I've tried anger and love and teasing and talking and silence, but nothing seems to work."

"I wonder if possibly she's very angry and doesn't know how to release it. Who would she be mad at that her whole life has changed? She may be mad at God, but she's always been too nice a person to admit that. Have you suggested she see a counselor?"

"Yes, but it wasn't met with enthusiasm."

Chapter 10

That night he thought of Neenah so much, wondering how to help her. He realized that the girl he had fallen in love with was gone. He remembered her confident, innocent, young face, surrounded by its dark curls and the tanned, athletic body that moved so gracefully. He remembered her happy gaiety and her dancing green eyes. What he saw now was a pale, quiet, emaciated woman with dull eyes and awkward movements. He asked himself how he felt about her now. It was then he realized he loved her in a deeper, more mature way. Having suffered losses of his own, his heart ached for hers. He wanted to encourage her, care for her, and cradle her. And some day he believed she would be able to give love again, and he hoped it would be to him.

One Tuesday night, Stan mentioned his reunion that was being held at Beloit College the next weekend. Nash asked about the older man's college experiences and discovered that he and Doris had met there as classmates.

"Are you going?"

"I don't think this is a good time to be gone."

"Stan, you can go and represent us both. I'm sure Neenah and I will be fine," his wife suggested.

"Are you sure you want me to go?" Throughout this exchange, the young woman at the table just watched.

Then Nash spoke up. "I'll ask Hairy if Neenah can stay with us over the weekend. She can have my bed, and it won't hurt me to sleep on the couch a few nights. She won't eat us out of house and home, so she won't be much expense."

Neenah tried a weak smile. "Nash said, you two have fun at your reunion, and Hairy and I will host your daughter—if it's all right with him."

Mr. And Mrs. Kingman looked so excited for a moment, but then Doris said, "I don't think I should leave Neenah."

Surprisingly the girl spoke. "I think you should both go. You've stopped everything for me, and it's time you thought of yourselves. My selfishness can only go so far."

"Oh, Honey, we love you and are glad to be here for you. But if you're comfortable about going to Hairy's, and if he agrees to the plan, your mom and I could go and be back by Sunday night."

Hairy did agree, and so it was decided.

Neenah was installed in Nash's spotless (he'd stayed up cleaning most of the night before) bedroom on the following Friday afternoon. She seemed to respond to her new setting. Over dinner, she and Hairy had quite a long conversation about various Door County mutual friends, and Nash had them both laughing as he told about some of the day's ferry riders. Then he lit a fire in the fireplace, set the tray of coffee cups on the coffee table, and suggested the other two join him. Neenah carefully crutched her way to the couch, and the three spent a comfortable, relaxed evening. It was the next morning when things became harder.

At 9:30, there was no sound from Neenah's room. Nash had decided during the night that if she weren't stirring by 9:00, he would get her up. He weakened for a half hour and then burst into her room and stopped stock-still. Her hair was spread out on her pillow and framed her sleepy sweet face.

"What's happening?" she asked confusedly.

There was a silence before the young man answered slowly, "I don't really know. I'm confused. When I first met you, I was so attracted to you, and I hoped we'd develop a relationship. Then suddenly I became your brother, and we did have a relationship but not the one I'd anticipated. When I see you in bed like this, part of me wants to crawl right in there with you—and part wants to get you up and going. Maybe I can find a middle road somewhere, but I'm not sure I want one."

With those words he dropped on his knees by her bed and gathered her into his arms. The kiss he gave her was definitely not brotherly, and her response was not that of a sister. They were breathless when he pulled away.

"Enough of that part for now. It's time for your brother to give you a hard time."

"What kind of hard time? I liked that first part. Could we go back to it?"

"No. It's time for you to rise and shine. I'm not about to let you sleep your life away. I want you up and dressed in five minutes, and if not, I may have to try the old mean-brother ice cube trick."

"Oh, all right. But you have to clear out and not come back in for those five minutes."

"And I'd hoped to be the timer. Phooey!" Laughingly he left the room.

She reached for her clothes that she had set out the night before in the chair beside the bed. Her blue slacks rather hung on her thin frame, but the long, striped tunic concealed the amount of weight that she had steadily been losing. She just didn't seem to be hungry since her activity level had become so low, as had her spirits. She tried valiantly to be positive for the sake of everyone else, but inside she felt that her life was over. Four minutes were up when she reached for her crutches. They weren't anywhere to be seen.

"Nash, have you seen my crutches? I can't find them," she called to the closed door.

He must have been waiting right outside the door because she could clearly hear him say quietly, "Yes, they're out by the mailbox.

"How'd they get there? Will you please go get them?"

"No. You'll have to crawl or hop out and get them yourself. Or you could walk out and collect them. Your foot is at the foot of your bed."

"Nash, that wasn't funny! Please go get them. I'll give you a big kiss," she said enticingly and made a smooching noise.

"Now why would your brother want a big kiss? Yuck!"

She was beginning to panic. "I'm serious, Nash! I need my crutches, or I can't leave this room."

"You can walk out any time you choose to. I'm going out on the porch, and I'll wait for you there."

She heard his footsteps receding and felt self-pity rising up like a tide within her. He was mean, and she was glad they weren't really related because she wouldn't want any part of such an unfeeling person. She had to acknowledge that he did kiss nicely, but probably she was just lonely. She sat back on the bed and kicked the rug with her right foot. He wasn't the one with only one foot! He didn't have to hobble along on crutches! He hadn't had to go through all she'd been through! Who did he think he was anyway?

"Hairy? Could you get my crutches for me?" she called sweetly. There was only silence. Then she remembered that he volunteered at the local rest home on Saturday mornings. That miserable Nash had it all planned, didn't he! Well, she'd show him.

She dropped off the bed and started to crawl across the floor. She'd make him feel like a worm for doing this to her! But she felt like the worm as she dragged across the floor. Maybe she could hop! But that idea had to be discarded because she knew her one leg wasn't strong enough to carry her that far.

In her life she had rarely been angry, but now all the pent up frustrations and the unfairness of her loss boiled up in a white-hot fury. Tears were running down her cheeks, but she didn't even notice. Hearing noises, she realized they were coming from her own mouth, primal screams of rage. She crawled to the end of the bed and whacked the artificial foot on the floor over and over. It didn't go away. Swearing the few words she knew, repetitiously, she put the hated object on her stump and buckled it on. She hadn't had it on much, and it didn't feel right at all, but she was too furious to care.

When it was in place, she stood on her right leg and gingerly put her weight on the foreign foot. It didn't feel good, but it didn't hurt as much as she remembered. She hung onto the bed frame until she dared launch out into the room.

It was scary. She wondered if learning to walk had been that frightening when she was a child. At least then she had been closer to the ground. Sweat was running down her face by the time she reached the door. She gritted her teeth and opened it, ready to scream at Nash, but he wasn't there. The horrible man probably really was on the porch—or maybe he'd gone to town and left her here alone. Maybe he was laughing at her as she struggled down the hallway. She'd show him!

As she neared the front door, she concentrated every muscle and stepped through it without looking to the left or right, proceeded down the steps by holding on to the handrail, and with a very straight back marched (as best she could) to the mailbox. She scooped up her crutches, put them under her arms and swung back into the house without looking around. She was through the door when she heard a loud shout. "Yippee!"

He came in the door right behind her, threw his arms around her, while her crutches went clattering to the floor, and kissed her soundly. When she could catch her breath, she sputtered, "You! You! You terrible person!"

He laughed and kissed her again. "If that's the worst thing you can think of to call me, we'd better work on your vocabulary while you work on your walking."

She looked into his shining eyes and realized the risk he had taken to help her grow up. She laughed shakily as she said, "How did you know I wasn't going to beat you to death with one of my crutches when I got it in my hands?"

"I didn't care just as long as you tried to walk. I might as well live dangerously—or die at the hands of a beautiful woman. Will you try to walk a little further?"

"I will, but I'd like to sit down for a moment. I don't think I've ever been so angry in my life, and it's an exhausting experience. I was probably too tired to kill you anyway. But wait until I've rested a while. You're not safe yet."

That morning, the crutches leaned, unused, by the door. That afternoon she was back at the prosthetist getting the fit readjusted to her fully healed stump. The man chided her a bit about not using it all along, but the glowing faces of the two young people before him kept his lecture short.

Afterward, Nash asked, "What would you like to do to celebrate?"

"I want to go to the Summer Kitchen and eat one of everything on the menu!" And she almost did. Her surprised stomach kept her awake a good part of the night, but she had so much to think about that she didn't care a bit.

When her parents came home, they were stunned to see their daughter walk fairly confidently to meet them in the yard. Her mother wept, and her father beamed. They asked her how such a miracle happened, and she answered, "A terrible person did it," and laughed. The terrible person felt it was time to appear, and there was general hugging all around.

"I knew you'd be a wonderful brother to our Neenah," the girl's father said. A look passed between the young people, and Nash responded quietly, "We'll have to talk about that sometime."

When he came for his regular Tuesday night visit, he had a glint in his eye. Neenah still used her crutches around home when her leg got tired at the end of the day, but she greeted him still wearing her prosthesis. He suspected it was easier to hug him without the crutches, but he wordlessly just enjoyed the hug.

After a delicious dinner of ham and fresh asparagus, when they were all sitting in the family room, he said casually to Neenah, "Let's go for a drive in the new car your dad got you. I'd like to try it out. I've never driven with hand controls."

She looked at him with suspicion. "I know what you're trying to do! You want to get me to drive, and you're going to try to push me into it just like you did the walking. Even I will admit that was good for me, but I'm really not ready to drive and go out. Please give me time to get used to walking, and when I'm ready I'd love to go driving with you." The smile she gave him would have melted at iceberg.

"You could be right." He smiled fondly back. "Or you could just be procrastinating," and with those words he strode across the room, gathered her up in arms that had grown strong after six months of hard water work, and carried her flailing body to the car where he unceremoniously dumped her like a sack of potatoes on the passenger side. Her parents watched in astonishment. Slamming her door shut purposefully, he strode to the other side, started the car, fiddled with the hand gas control and drove off in a shower of gravel.

She started to release her indignation but noticed the grim set of his jaw and thought better of it. They drove in silence, but the air between them was full of unspoken communication, much of it unprintable.

He stopped the car on an old lumber trail off the road and turned to look at her. She braced herself and was composing her rebuttal when he unexpectedly said, "I have been wanting to hold you and kiss you so desperately that I was going crazy. We were never alone, and even though I love your parents dearly, I wanted to have time just with you." He gave an unconvincing leer and said in a Draconian voice, "And now I have you all to myself, in the woods, with no one around to hear your calls for help while I smother you with kisses. And since these bucket seats aren't conducive to that . . ." He went around to her side of the car, opened the door, gathered her up, and deposited her in the back seat where he joined her.

For a moment she was almost frightened by his intensity, but then he kissed her, and it was so gentle and loving that she pulled back and whispered, "Help," before pulling his face back to hers.

When they had satisfied some of their longings, he leaned back and said, "We should be getting back, or your folks will worry." He smiled roguishly. "I'm worn out from all this kissing, so I'm afraid I won't be able to drive home."

"Oh, no, you don't! I'm not ready to drive yet. Please take me home," she pleaded.

"It will be cold tonight, and I didn't bring a blanket. Since you probably won't be speaking to me, we'll each freeze alone. Or maybe your dad will find us in the middle of the night when he comes looking for me with his shotgun. Either way, it could be a long night."

"You *are* a terrible person!" she said emphatically.

"What a way to speak about your brother!"

She sighed. "Will you put me in the driver's seat, or do you want me to crawl there?"

"I will valiantly try to get you there with the last of my remaining strength."

His ease in her replacement belied that statement, and laughingly he dragged himself around the car to the passenger side. He showed her what he had learned on the drive up, and with a minimum of lurching, she accomplished the drive home.

Her parents were waiting, as casually as possible, on the porch. When Nash deposited their precious child in a chair next to theirs, they looked innocently curious as they asked her, "How did it go?"

"Amazingly well. It's not nearly as hard as I'd anticipated. I haven't thanked you for getting me that car. You were wonderful to do it, and I'm sorry I haven't been more appreciative. It will be great to be able to run errands and help a bit instead of lying around here like a sponge." She hopped up and gave each of her parents a big hug. They beamed at Nash like he'd invented the sun.

The object of their gratitude gathered up his courage. "I need to talk to you. I'm in love with your daughter. That sounds almost incestuous because I really think of you as my parents, but would you mind if Neenah wasn't my sister?"

Mr. and Mrs. Kingman looked at each other as though what they had suspected had been confirmed. "Dear Nash, we love you and are glad you love Neenah, but whatever happens about that we will still love you. Our only concern is that you not hurt each other. Then we'd be doubly sad. Please go slowly. You've already been through a lot together, and maybe the rest will be easy. The old saying 'The path of true love does not run smooth' may not apply to you."

Now it was his turn to hug them, and his eyes were suspiciously shiny as he said goodnight and drove off to catch the ferry.

Chapter 11

Nash was whistling as he secured the last chain after the ferry left the dock for Washington Island. Neenah was getting ready to go back to school for the last block, and she was fast becoming the girl he'd first met. Spring had come slowly to the northern part of Wisconsin, but its promise was sure, and he was in love. As he started to go up the stairs, he heard someone call his name. He turned back, expecting to see some Door County friend and instead, looked into the astonished face of Ed Hanson, his families' lawyer from Cedar Rapids.

"Thank God you're alive, Nash! We thought you were dead when you disappeared almost eight months ago. Where have you been? You look great! I'm so glad to see you!" And the usually calm, unemotional lawyer threw his arms around the surprised young man.

"It's a long story, Mr. Hanson. Are you up here for long? If you have time, I'll come and tell you about it," Nash said, disengaging himself.

"Great! Edith and I are staying at the Smith's resort. Can we take you out to dinner tonight to the Summer Kitchen and have the evening to hear it?"

"I finish about 6:00, and I'll get there as soon as I can. It shouldn't be a problem."

"You look great, Nash! Different though. You're a man now, aren't you? I have some things to tell you, too. I can't wait to get back to the resort and tell Edith I saw you!"

As Nash turned to go up the stairs, he said, "See you tonight—about 6:30 at the Summer Kitchen."

He was showered and freshly shaven when he was ushered to a corner table at the restaurant where an excited Edith embraced him with tears in her eyes. She had been one of his mother's best friends, and for a moment he felt the intense pain of his loss again. Then he straightened up emotionally and shook hands with Ed.

"It's very nice of you to give an evening of your vacation to me, Mr. Hanson."

"For goodness sake, Nash, call me Ed. You're not a little kid anymore, and I hope you consider me a friend."

"Fine, Ed. And I always called you Aunt Edith," he said, turning to Mrs. Hanson. "My mom really valued your friendship highly."

Her eyes filled with tears again. "I miss her every day. I'll never have another friend like her."

They sat together in the silence of memories.

After ordering, they asked Nash to tell his story.

The restaurant was almost empty by the time he brought them back to the present. It was the first time he'd really put it all together, and even with the sadness, it brought back it felt good to get it all out.

"Let's go back to our cabin because I have some things to tell you, too, Nash."

There was an air of excitement in Ed's manner as he laid the fire while Edith made cinnamon-flavored coffee for the trio. When they were all seated, Ed looked like he could burst, and he started to talk immediately.

"Well, Nash, when you left I gather that you felt there was no future there; in fact, after hearing your story, you thought there was no future at all for you. But now things seem to have changed a great deal in your outlook, and I'm so glad.

In our last conversation, shortly after the accident, I mentioned that Sam Wentworth was planning to sue your parents' estate over Beth's death, assuming negligence of some sort on your father's part. I'm happy to tell you that it never happened. When you left and didn't return, I think it woke Sam up to your losses. He came to me one day, very apologetically, to tell me that he'd been blinded by his grief, and in his anger had turned it on your dad. He realized your family would never have hurt Beth, and he said he was sorry about the whole thing."

75

Nash was trying to take it all in. He felt guilt still about hurting Beth that day, but in his heart knew he had been right, and if she'd lived she would have come to realize it, too. He suddenly thought of another ramification of Ed's news. His inheritance would come to him! His house would be his! He could marry Neenah and have a home even if he didn't decide to stay in Cedar Rapids. He looked over at his host and saw his own joy reflected.

"Does it really mean that I'm not penniless and I have a home? Can it be true?"

"Absolutely! And there's a bit more. When the Civil Aeronautics Board investigated the crash, they found no pilot error, so your dad was completely cleared of any blame. What they did find was that when the plane had been assembled, a part had been installed backwards, and that's what caused the crash. It hadn't shown up under regular flight conditions but the combination of wind and altitude had caused it to malfunction when your dad took off that day. Sam did get his chance to sue, and he did it for you, too. So you now have a sizable estate, which I have been investing but didn't know what would happen to it. I've kept the house cleaned and maintained, too. When I saw you earlier today, I was glad to see you for a number of reasons."

He put his hand on the younger man's arm and added, "But mostly I was happy to see you alive and well again. I'd feared for you ever since I left your house, and even though I was back an hour later, you were gone."

"Thank you, Ed, and you, too, Edith, for caring about me. This conversation changes my future plans a great deal. I'd thought I could work for a few years until I had enough money to go back to school, and now I think things can speed up a bit for my education. Wow! I'm in a state of shock."

They sat quietly, watching the fire.

Suddenly Nash jumped to his feet. "Will you excuse me for a little while? I'd like to take a walk by the bay for a bit, just to try to adjust to this good news."

"We'll be right here. You take as long as you want. We have some happy adjusting to do, too."

Nash wanted to shout and sing, and he did do a few dance steps on the darkened beach. And then a very deep sadness engulfed him as he thought that he would have to go on with his life without his parents and sister and that he was the only one remaining to live in that house of his childhood and happiness. He prayed to the Lord for peace and hope. Then he thought of his life at the present and how happy he was with Neenah and how comfortable he felt with her parents after all they'd been through together. But he also felt guilty to be happy and to love her parents. Was he being disloyal to his own? Had he forgotten them or tried to replace them?

He sat on the beach and listened to the waves break peacefully and endlessly on the shore. There was an inevitability about them. He thought pensively:

> Does life move on like those waves? They keep moving forward all the time. Have I finally begun to accept what has happened? Am I beginning to move on in the rhythm of life? Oh, Lord, let my family know how much I love them and miss them! If I could reverse things and stop that horrible accident from happening, I would give almost anything. But like the tide, I can't make time go in reverse. Please give me the wisdom to move into the future in Your love. Help me to accept this unexpected news with wisdom and gratitude. All of a sudden I'm on another new path of responsibilities and decisions when I'd just been enjoying each day without plans for the future. Hopes and dreams were far ahead, and now they can become real. Am I ready? Oh, Lord, I need you guidance now more than ever.

As he prayed by the water, a kind of peace crept into his heart, and he fell silent. When he rose to his feet at last and started walking back to the resort, he felt comforted and ready to meet the future.

His first request of Ed was, "Can I get $150 from my account? I'd like to take you out to dinner tomorrow night with four of my friends from up here, and I'd like you to share my good news with them. Every one of them is special to me and has been responsible in some way for my return to hope and health."

It was arranged that he would meet the Hansons the following night for another dinner at the Summer Kitchen and he would bring his four friends. As luck (?) would have it, the following day he saw the old VW ease on board the Merry Jane. After releasing the boat from her southern home, he hurried to find Billy. They hugged each other with obvious pleasure, and Nash immediately invited him to the dinner that night.

"I've so much to tell you! Come to Hairy's early, and we'll get caught up a bit before we go to dinner. Hairy's going, too, and a girl I'm crazy about and her parents. It's a sort of celebration dinner. Wear your best tee shirt."

"My goodness, Nash, I can hardly wait to hear all about it. It must be good news if the smile on your face is any indication. I thought I'd drop by this afternoon to see Hairy and wait for you to get off work. I'll see you later."

Nash returned to his work, thanking God for his friend's appearance.

The day seemed to drag by since he was so eager for the evening. At last, the Kingman's car drove on the boat the last trip of the day. They waved at him, and he did his best to concentrate on his job, but he could hardly wait for the evening to begin.

He went home to shower while the Kingmans did their grocery shopping at the store south of Sister Bay. They agreed to meet at the restaurant.

Nash dressed in his best jeans and a new long-sleeved white shirt that he'd acquired. Now he wore a size 18 shirt since he'd been doing such heavy work. It gathered at his slender waist but that couldn't be helped. When he stepped into the living room, he could hardly believe that the two well-dressed men who stood there were Hairy and Billy. Hairy was wearing a sport coat that Nash had never seen, and Billy had on a dark suit and tie!

"Are you two fashion plates willing to be seen with me, your country cousin?"

They looked at each other questioningly. "Maybe he could eat out in the kitchen while we dine," suggested Hairy. Then Hairy took Billy's arm, and the two men marched out the door, with Nash following docilely behind.

They were early, so the table in the corner was all set up with seven places when the Kingmans arrived. The three men stood up as they approached the table. Nash introduced Billy, and Neenah said, "I've heard so much about you and all you did for Nash. I'm really delighted to meet you at last." Billy grinned.

Everyone stood again when the Hansons arrived about five minutes later. After Nash made the introductions, the guests sat down but he remained standing.

"At this table my past, my present, and my future meet. I want to thank you all for what you've done for me. Ed Hanson has been our family lawyer for years and his wife, Edith, was one of my mother's best friends and dear to me." He lifted his water glass to the Hansons.

"Billy gave me a lift, in more ways than one, when I was at the end of my rope. He offered me compassion and a blanket and kept me going. He has also taught me a lot about life and what's important." He lifted his glass to Billy.

"Hairy literally saved my life. He dragged me out of the snow, sat in the hospital with me, took me to his home where he gave me a bedroom and meals—and he hardly knew me. Then he dragged me out of my self-pity and brought me back to life. He is a wonderful father!" And he raised his glass to that generous man.

"Neenah forgave me my immense rudeness and brought love back into my life. Her innate goodness and sunny disposition could charm a hibernating bear out of his cave—and did." He lifted his glass to her. "And she's a brave and courageous lady."

"Stan and Doris Kingman have let me be part of their family and have filled some of the void that my parents' death created. We have been through a lot together, and I've seen what truly fine people they are." Once more his glass was raised.

"I hope, and pray, that all of you will be part of my future. I especially want to mention Neenah again because my hope is that she will be beside me in whatever that may bring." The young woman's face was tear-stained but radiant.

"And I cannot express my gratitude without thanking my Lord, who has blessed me with all of you and in more ways than I can imagine. I pray that I may use the life he has restored to me in his service. I'd like to say grace and then we can eat.

"Dear Father, please bless all of us gathered round this table and bless the food we will soon order. May it nourish our bodies as you nourish our souls. Amen."

"Now let's get ready to eat!" He sat down.

There were many questions and answers during the meal, filling in the unknown spaces. It was a happy group who finished their dessert and was sipping their coffee.

"Ed, will you tell them the good news that you told me last night?"

"I'd be delighted to do that, Nash! As you may know, when Nash left Cedar Rapids, he thought everything was lost—his family, his home, and his future. You," he looked at the people around the table, "showed him there was a lot to live for and gave him a reason to do that. It's true that his family was gone, and I hope they are here with us tonight, but his home is still his own, his parents' estate is his, and the investigation of the crash which proved the plane manufacturer at fault added a substantial amount to that estate. Nash is now financially able to pursue whatever career he desires and is quite an independently wealthy young man."

Nash tried not to look at Stan, but when their eyes met the older man gave him a rueful smile and winked. Nash winked back in understanding. Neenah looked astonished but happy. The rest expressed delight at Nash's good fortune.

"And that's why I'm able to take you all out to dinner tonight," he quipped.

At the end of the celebratory meal Nash stood again and lifted his glass. "A toast to the future!" and everyone stood and joined him.

Chapter 12

His restored fortunes made Nash anxious to see his home and get things straightened out in Cedar Rapids. He talked to Captain Jack about his desire to go south and then to Jeff Randall to see if he would work until young Ben McGrath was out of school for the summer. Jeff agreed because his lawn care business hadn't started yet and snow removal was over for the winter—he hoped. And so it was agreed that Nash would finish out the week and be free to go.

The last day was difficult. He was so grateful to Captain Jack for taking on such a landlubber and a sullen one at that. Many of the regular riders knew him now, and they seemed to know he was leaving and pumped his hand and wished him well. It gave him a sense that the whole county had taken him under its wing. There seemed to be a large lump in his throat throughout the day.

When the Merry Jane docked at the end of the day, Nash went up to the wheelhouse and thanked the captain. "I can't ever thank you enough, Captain Jack, but I want you to know that I'll always be grateful to you, and I'll strive to pass your kindness on. You are truly a Christian man!" Unable to say more, he threw his arms around the big man and then hurried out the door. He heard the captain blowing his nose as he hurried down the ladder.

It was even harder to say goodbye to Hairy. Nash just wanted to keep his arms around the frail older man. "You will eat better, won't you? Can I trust you to have three meals a day? You've been my family, and that won't stop now. As soon as I get things straightened out down south, I want you to come and stay with me for a while. Goodness, I'll need someone to cook for me, and you're pretty good at that. And I'll call you as soon as I get there. I can't say goodbye to you!" Both men needed handkerchiefs after that speech.

Neenah had suggested that he drive her back to school in her hand-operated automobile when she went back for the last block of the year, and he was delighted to do that. Her parents came over to the mainland to see them off. Nash began to think that he couldn't say goodbye to one more person, but he managed to keep some semblance of control. He knew he'd see them soon.

It was a different young man who left Door County in early April from the one who'd arrived in the fall. The tragedy that brought him there had not gone away. Instead he'd found a new life, a new love, and a new purpose. As he drove by the bay overlook where he'd met Billy, he realized how much his life had changed, and he thanked God.

He was driving and enjoying Neenah's company when they saw the sign for the upcoming Neenah-Menasha exit.

"There's my name," the girl beside him said. "My parents decided on it when they saw it on their honeymoon. I always have to explain about the spelling."

Nash turned the car sharply just in time to get onto the off ramp. "Is something the matter?"

"I just need to stop for a minute."

He drove until he found a parking lot, pulled the car into it, and turned off the engine. Turning to her he asked, "You truly are named for Neenah? N-E-E-N-A-H? I have never seen your name written, and I assumed it was N-I-N-A. I had it wrong the whole time."

She laughed uncertainly. "Does that mean you don't love me anymore now that you know my real name? Does it matter?" She was puzzled by the intense expression on his face.

"Oh, my Darling, I'd have to say I love you even more." He took out his wallet, opened it to his driver's license, and handed it to her. Her eyes widened as she read "Menasha James Williams."

"My parents saw that same sign when my mother was expecting me and they thought it would be a good boy's name if the baby turned out to be a boy." He gathered his girl into his arms as he said, "Apparently we have more in common than we knew. Our names have been linked for a long time. We're the right combination!" Their kiss sealed it.

A GARMENT OF SPLENDOR

Chapter 1

"A garment of splendor for a heavy heart"
(Isaiah 61:3b).

"Talk to me!" the woman hissed.

Startled, Sophie jerked around to look into a pair of brown eyes, wide with terror. She'd hardly noticed the woman next to the window when she skidded into the aisle seat after her mad rush through the terminal due to the tardiness of her connecting flight. She found herself looking at a lined, anxious face crowned by graying hair so tightly curled that it carried its own impression of fright.

"Is this your first flight?" Sophie asked gently.

Tears rose in the terrified brown eyes.

"Try to relax. We're taxiing out on the runway now, and this may be the roughest part of the trip. As soon as we're in the air it's usually very smooth."

In response, the woman grasped Sophie's arm so tightly that the younger woman winced.

"Just talk to me. Tell me a story. Tell me why you're flying to Czechoslovakia—anything to get my mind off the fact that I can't get out of this room that will soon be flying through the sky."

Sophie thought quickly. Should she tell *her* story? Did she want to relive it? Perhaps it would be wise to say it out loud and face it before she was actually back again. The pain in her arm helped her make the decision.

"My story is quite long, but it's about Germans, lost love, and escapes."

"Please tell me. Please!"

The engines were revving for takeoff. She'd better start now.

"My father owned and ran a glass-making factory in a little town in the western part of Czechoslovakia where I grew up in a comfortable home with love and security. My grandfather had started the business and, due to its success, had been able to invest and accumulate a substantial estate. Since my father was his only child, he managed it after his father became too old and then inherited it. Because of his position, we were considered "important" people in the village. The only thing that was different about my family was that my mother was "a foreigner." Her father had immigrated to America from Czechoslovakia, married there, and had a daughter and two sons. When the young people were almost grown, the family came to Czechoslovakia for six months, so the children could understand their heritage in its actual setting. My father fell in love with the American daughter, and when it was time to leave she begged to stay and marry Father. Thus, my brother and I learned to speak American (English) from the time we were little. Mother was lovely and due to that and my father's position in the village, she was welcomed into the community. She made every effort to become part of the life she had chosen, but she insisted that her children know English, just as she had learned Czech as a child and now found it so useful.

Life was fun and exciting in our small town of Pusta Kaminsty until the day in 1939 when the Germans came marching in. Then, even my father's position did little to protect us from their demands and subjugation. I was seventeen when my life changed forever. I remember the very day . . ."

And in her mind she was that seventeen-year-old girl again.

It was a clear morning that welcomed the sun, giving it the opportunity to warm the day quickly with its rays. She looked in the mirror and saw her familiar face with its large, gray eyes surrounded by dark lashes, its high ruddy-colored cheekbones, and the happy mouth that turned up at the corners. No, the mouth was wrong! It almost turned down, and the even pink lips quivered. She hardly recognized herself with the flowers woven into her dark, plaited hair. She saw behind her, in the reflection, her wedding dress; the *kroje* she'd begun to work on at eight which she had continued to embroider, trim, and sew over the years in preparation for her joyous wedding day when the villagers would escort the groom to her door and they would walk to the church. She had hurriedly finished it in the small hours of the morning, numbed by the news of her impending marriage.

"To whom?" she had asked incredulously when her father solemnly announced it after dinner the night before. She whirled to look at her mother and saw the tears rolling down her cheeks. This was no joke! Her father's voice broke as he explained what had happened. .

"Two things have made this necessary. We heard from your cousin, Hilda, who works where the German officers eat that Leftenant Krosser was bragging that he would have you in his room when he gets back from Berlin in a week. He explained how he would get an order from Field Marshall Goering since he was a family friend and the commandant would not refuse. He left this morning, and we must act now. We have tried everything to keep him away from you, but we have no power."

She shuddered at the thought of the cruel, arrogant German who delighted in frightening her and took her aversion to him as a challenge which he swore to overcome. She never went out alone anymore and was beginning to stay at home, out of sight, living in fear that she would hear a pounding on the door and see his smug face, waiting for the invitation to enter that he knew they dared not refuse to extend.

Her father sadly continued. "We cannot travel freely, so you cannot visit a relative in another village and the Leftenant has the power to have you brought back even so. The second thing that has come to light is the presence of an American who has been sent by his government to find the exact location of the airplane factory that has been turning out so many Messerschmitts. He grew up in a Czech home in America so he could easily pass as one of us, but the Germans found out about him through a betrayer and tortured and starved him trying to get him to admit he was a spy. He remained silent and fortunately the underground was able to get him out and hide him before the Nazis killed him. He is now hidden in your Uncle George's attic. We had to come up with a desperate plan. You are to marry him tomorrow, and then we will all see you off to a distant village which he will claim as his home. We had to plan this quickly because both of you must get away immediately. We have invited the commandant to participate in the wedding. It must be legal, and Father Thomas cannot know what is happening since there is great danger to anyone who knows the truth. Somehow we must convince him and the town that this has been a secret romance since the young man's parents did not approve, or he was engaged to someone else or something."

He looked at her hopefully, but she was too stunned to respond. He continued. "When you get beyond the checkpoint to Austria, the underground will send someone to guide you through that country to Switzerland. It breaks my heart to send you off like this, but it seems to be our only hope to save you both."

Her memories of the evening before were interrupted by the sound of pounding feet on the stairway and the door was flung open as Sylvia, her best friend, burst into the room.

"I heard the funniest thing from old Granny Lievski! She said that you were getting mar . . .," and she grew silent as she saw the wedding dress hanging there and Sophie's tear-stained face.

"It can't be true," she whispered. She ran to her friend and threw her arms around her as they both wept. Sophie swore her to secrecy and told her why the marriage was to take place.

"No one must know the real reason, or it might get back to the Germans. We must take advantage of every day that Leftenant Krosser is gone, and there must be no suspicions."

"Are you really going through with this farce?" Sylvia asked incredulously.

"What else can I do? It is not just my happiness at stake. It is the American's life—and perhaps mine, too, having seen evidence of Krosser's anger. I have been praying and trying to find some peace, but it all happened so quickly that my head aches. I will have to leave it in the Lord's hands and trust that things will work out for good." She paused and then burst into tears again. "I'm so afraid!"

Somehow the morning passed, and with her mother and Sylvia to aid her, Sophie donned the dress of her hopes that had now turned to ashes. Nothing seemed real, including the girl in the mirror with her gorgeous wedding cap, sparkling with sequins and glass trinkets to ward off any evil spirits that might make trouble. The dress fitted her beautifully, and the skirt frothed out below her slender waist. It should have been so different. At seventeen, she felt that her life was over.

Then she heard the music as the villagers moved toward her house in the procession escorting the bridegroom to claim his bride. She tried to catch a glimpse of him, but there were too many people in the way. She almost felt the knock on the door as though it was on her heart that it pounded. Her father opened it, as was proper, and she knew what an effort that must have been for him. He offered her his arm and led her out into the sunlight while her mother followed behind silently.

She was unable to lift her eyes from the ground in her apprehension of what lay ahead, so it was not until they were at the door of the church that she met the eyes of the man who was to be her husband.

He was quite tall and very thin and did not appear well, but the look he gave her was so full of compassion that she caught her breath. He knew what she was going through and understood! For the first time she wondered what *he* felt. Did he have a sweetheart at home? Or a wife! She forgot some of her own worries and looked at him with real interest. His eyes were brown as was his thick straight hair. He looked like he could have grown up in her village. Thank goodness for that! How could they hide someone who looked completely foreign? Something about him spoke of another culture, but she didn't know what it was unless it was his firm jaw and the determined look in his eyes. Someone had lent him a festive wedding shirt so that the two of them looked like bright birds of plumage. Then they were in the church, and Father Thomas was saying the words she heard so often before but never involving her. The service passed as though in a dream that ended in a gentle kiss that woke her to reality. People smiled and murmured. They turned and walked down the aisle, followed by all the observers, as they walked into the bright sunshine.

It was a warm day in early spring, and it had brought the whole village out in their Sunday clothes to celebrate. There had been so little cause lately, but their spirits rose as they realized that marriages still went on, even if unexpectedly. Some of the old men had brought out their accordions and began playing familiar melodies that soon had shoulders swaying and feet tapping. Sophie's husband (!) led her out into the square, and they danced together. She could feel his weariness and was careful not to droop in his arms. Fortunately it was a short dance, and after the clapping, other couples joined them. Soon they could go sit down on one of the benches under the trees where they could watch the dancers. She shyly said, "I don't know your name. What shall I call you?

"My name is William, but my friends call me Bill. I know this is very hard for you, and I wish I could have done this some other way, but there didn't seem to be much choice in the matter." His eyes closed for a moment, and he seemed to sway.

"Are you all right?" she asked anxiously. He straightened up and gave her a weary smile to reassure her. Fear showed in her face.

"Don't worry, Sophie. We can do it."

There wasn't much food to be had, but she managed to gather a few things in her scarf, and finally her father announced that it was time to go. The commandant had been in attendance the whole time, and now he stepped up to the newlyweds and handed them an envelope. Sophie opened it and found forty guilders which she held up for the crowd to see. There was scattered applause, and everyone laughed as the couple climbed on the back of an ox cart hitched to an ancient animal, and the villagers escorted them out of town. She knew her father must have thought of the cart since there was no other transportation available, and "her husband" was in no condition to walk far.

It was almost dusk when the procession arrived at the German checkpoint, which marked the border of Austria, and one it was not allowed to enter since nationals were not permitted to travel outside their own country. Bill showed his fake identification that claimed he was an Austrian citizen, the commandant pointed to Sophie in her bright dress, and the soldiers stepped aside. There were shouted goodbyes, hugs from relatives, and brave attempts to control tears.

Sophie sobbed as she hugged Sylvia, but with her mother and father the pain of parting was too great to be expressed. Her father held her gently as he whispered, "Turn right at the first street in the next village. Knock on the door of the house with the blue shutters and ask for Marcus. They will be expecting you. And be careful, my darling girl." He stepped back, and she saw tears sparkling in his eyes. Then Bill touched her arm, and she turned away to the unknown future.

Chapter 2

The tall, thin man and his gaily-dressed wife trudged down the road. She occasionally looked back to see her past fading over the horizon, and even when she could no longer recognize individual figures, she was able to picture them in her mind—the fabric of her whole life. But now a new pattern must be woven, and she resolutely turned her face forward and straightened her shoulders.

Once out of everyone's hearing she repeated what her father had whispered. Bill had roughly the same directions, so she felt a bit more confident. It was hard to go into the unknown, but at least they had a name to ask for and blue shutters somewhere ahead. The man beside her was silent, and when she looked more closely she saw he was making a determined effort just to stay on his feet. Rather than show her pity, she announced that her shoes were tight and she wanted to rest on the stone fence paralleling the road. He agreed, trying not to look relieved. Observing that he was perspiring and that his hands shook visibly, she asked, "Are you well?"

"I had a little difficulty with the Germans when they captured me and again when I escaped. I'll be all right with a little rest. I have to be all right!" Again she noticed the determined jaw and the light in his eyes. "You are the one who got the bad deal," he said gently. "Suddenly you're the legal wife of a man you never saw before today, you've been removed from your village, and you're going God knows where and in danger. I'm sorry you got sucked up in this, but if it helps at all, the facts tucked in my head will help to defeat those dirty Nazis." Then with a twinkle in his eyes, "The folks back home will really be astounded at how I acquired such a beautiful wife on such a short acquaintance. I'll just tell them it was my natural charm." Then he shyly touched her hand, all laughter gone from his eyes, and whispered, "I am sorry."

"I don't know if anyone told you, but it was necessary for me to leave, too. There was a German officer . . ." Unconsciously, she shivered.

Straightening painfully, he took her arm, and they continued their journey. She was relieved when they reached the village and swung to the right. Sure enough, three houses down was one with blue shutters. Bill bravely walked to the door, which opened a crack as his knuckles touched it. Someone had been watching for them. He asked, "Is Marcus here?" and the unseen person within whispered, "He's waiting in the barn behind the house," and gently closed the door.

Sophie realized she was hardly breathing and felt light-headed until she took a deep breath as they walked around the house as casually as was possible under the circumstances. There was a barn that looked completely deserted and unused, but Bill knocked gently on the door and said quietly, "Marcus?" as he pushed it open.

It was dark inside, but the light shone on them from the opening behind them. Then they heard a stream of cursing coming from the dimness to their right. A bitter voice hissed, "I agreed to lead one man and instead I see a couple dressed in the most conspicuous clothing possible. I can't believe it!" And the curses flowed freely again.

The angry man stepped from the gloom and stood before them with his hands on his hips, his eyes narrowed, and his forehead furrowed in an unpleasant frown. "If you carried candles, you could pass as Christmas trees."

In the silence that followed, as the couple and the furious man stared at each other, they heard a soft knocking on the side of the barn. "Hide quickly! The Germans are coming!" warned an unseen ally.

From the desperate look on the man's face, Sophie realized that there really was no place to hide and she thought quickly, motivated by both fear and anger. "Get back in the corner, whoever you are. Roll in that hay on the floor, Bill." He looked puzzled but lowered himself to the ground. She threw herself down beside him, taking handfuls of the stuff and sprinkling it over her hair as she quickly unfastened some of the tiny flowered buttons on the bodice of her wedding dress. Suddenly the door was thrown open and the couple sat up in astonishment as four German soldiers rushed into the barn.

"Who are you, and what are you doing here?" demanded the sergeant in command. "Someone was seen coming in here, but I didn't know it was *two* people."

Bill had caught on quickly and he put his arm around Sophie and tried to cover the opening in her blouse. He looked properly frightened as he answered, "I am Peter Sedlecek from— — —and this is my wife, Sophie, who I married this morning. We are going to live with my parents and . . .," he paused and gave them a sly smile while Sophie looked embarrassed and helpless. "My parents live in a very small house, and I didn't know when we'd have a chance to be alone, so when I saw this old barn . . ." He let the sentence trail off.

As Sophie looked up at the leering faces above her, she felt a sharp tremor of fear. She knew they were thinking that they might celebrate the wedding also, and she clung even harder to Bill. Then the sergeant spoke, "I believe you because I've been here long enough to have seen some weddings, and no one else wears those outfits. Go ahead and finish what you're doing," he smirked, "and we might just stay and watch to be sure you're not lying." Then he laughed and said something in German to his men who laughed loudly, too. Bill pulled a trembling Sophie to her feet and said with dignity, "I think we will go to my parents now," and he gathered their packs and walked with her to the door.

The sergeant laughed again, walked over and slapped Bill's shoulder as he motioned to his men to leave the barn. "Good luck, friend. That was just a little wedding joke. Stay here for a while and enjoy your honeymoon, but be on your way before dark. Not everyone is as romantic as I am, and you could get in trouble on the road." He looked Sophie over very carefully and said to her husband," You should have a very good time." Then he leered and walked through the door.

Sophie just stood in Bill's arms and shivered uncontrollably. He comforted her gently until she stepped back and straightened her shoulders.

They heard a rustle in the hay and the man stood beside them. He looked calmer as he said grudgingly," I guess those bright feathers turned out to be useful after all. I'm Marcus, and I'm here to try and get you out to Switzerland. You must be Bill, and you picked a really unique way to get through the border."

Sophie had time to study him now. She had heard of the legendary Marcus but assumed he would be an older man. It was rumored that he had smuggled many influential people out of the country after the Germans took control. He was taller than most of the men she knew, but his shoulders were so broad that he appeared to be short. His slenderness was emphasized by the dark clothing he wore, which made him look like a burglar and kept him from being evident in the shadowy barn. His features were regular under his very curly black hair, and he might have been quite handsome except for his angry face with its hard brown eyes.

Turning to Bill, he began to tell him of the plan to get out of the country. Sophie stood there feeling invisible. She finally cleared her throat to remind them that she was still there. Marcus turned slightly toward her and said, "I assume you have a way to get home, and you should be on your way before it gets much darker."

"But I'm going, too," she started to explain.

More curses met that statement, and his face became even angrier as he hissed, "Not with me!"

She was about to retort when Bill said quietly, "She is going. We are married, and I won't go without her. She is part of this whole escape. She is going!"

There was electricity in the silence that followed, and Sophie felt rather than saw the rage generated by that quiet statement. It made her unconsciously step closer to Bill.

Suddenly Marcus started to cough, not a casual cough but a choking spasm out of control. He leaned forward against the side of the barn with his upper body perpendicular to the ground and lowered his head. Gradually the sound stopped. When he finally regained his breath, he straightened and grudgingly nodded his head. "We probably won't make it anyway," he muttered ungraciously, and with a curt "Let's go," he started toward the door.

Bill said firmly, "We have to change our clothes. You're right about attracting attention in these, and we brought some much quieter ones in our bags."

He and Sophie moved quickly to dim corners of the barn and slipped into dark slacks and jackets. She carefully folded her wedding dress and placed it lovingly in the backpack she'd folded in her satchel. It was the only material thing she could take from her past, and it was permeated with memories of her childhood, her mother's tender help, and the whole atmosphere of her village life. She was determined to take it, even though it made a somewhat bulky lump in her silhouette.

Chapter 3

The night seemed endless. They had fumbled their way through fields and over fences until they were far enough away from the village to take a chance using the road. Marcus knew his way, but he moved quickly and made no effort to help them avoid obstacles. Once on the road, they moved with so much speed that Sophie found she was perspiring. Young and used to physical activity as she was, she knew she'd be a little sore the next day.

She became aware gradually of a strange sound, almost a hissing. Marcus was far ahead (he seemed to want to put as much distance as possible between himself and them), so she tapped Bill on the shoulder. He stopped and turned to face her. She was shocked to see his face, even in the dim light, was twisted with exhaustion.

"Are you all right? This must be too fast a pace for you."

She heard the hissing sound again as he tried to gather enough air to answer her.

"Sit down on this stone beside the road and catch your breath," she suggested. He collapsed on the hard, cold surface gratefully. She sat down beside him.

"Why didn't you say something? I would have been glad to stop because I thought we were really setting a terribly fast pace."

"I . . . didn't . . . want . . . to . . . slow . . . you . . . down," he gasped.

Marcus appeared suddenly out of the darkness and snarled, "What's wrong? We have to get to the next safe house before dawn, and we barely have time to do it without stopping to chat."

Sophie spoke before Bill could and announced, "I was tired, and since you were so far ahead I asked Bill to stop with me." That gentleman looked at her gratefully. Marcus did not.

"I knew it would be trouble to bring you along, and if you don't keep up, I swear we'll leave you along the way. Now if you will kindly get to your feet," he said sarcastically, "we will continue on our stroll to Switzerland."

Bill seemed to be breathing more evenly, and he managed to stand without help, so they plunged on into the night.

The sky was just starting to lighten when they finally approached a dark house tucked back in some trees outside a small village they had skirted. Marcus was ahead, as usual, and must have given some signal because an even darker rectangle appeared in the side of the house, and they all passed through it into the interior. Sophie couldn't see anything, and she stopped, fearful that she would fall over something. Suddenly a match scratched into light, and after the lamp was lit, she saw a sparsely furnished room without any personal features. The woman holding the lamp had those same qualities. She said very quietly, "There is some porridge and bread in the kitchen, but you must eat quickly before the others get up. They don't ask questions, but the less they know, the better."

Moving into the next room, Sophie saw that it, too, had just the bare necessities, which consisted of a table, some chairs, an old cook stove, and a cupboard. She was suddenly ravenous as she smelled the porridge and realized she hadn't eaten since the wedding reception, and it had been very little then. Perhaps that was the reason Bill had been so tired.

They fell on the food with no reminder for silence necessary. Swallowing is not a noisy occupation. As her hunger began to be assuaged, her eyelids became increasingly heavy. Marcus was carrying on a whispered conversation with their hostess, which she couldn't hear.

"You and your wife can have the double bed in the back room," the woman intoned emotionlessly. Sophie's lifted startled eyes to Bill's face. He smiled gently and reassuringly at her, so her exclamation was only heard inside her head.

A light was held briefly in the door to a room that contained a double bed, as promised, and a chair. As soon as the newlyweds had passed through it, the lantern moved on to other places and left them in a lightening grayness. Just as the woman turned away, Sophie had seen the cynical half smile on Marcus' face as he looked at them. She blushed in the gloom.

When Bill stepped close to her, she unconsciously stepped back. It was her wedding night—no, morning—and she didn't even know this man's last name. Tears began to roll down her cheeks. He gently wiped them away and stepping close again, whispered," Don't worry, Sophie. I have to talk quietly, but you have nothing to fear from me. I think we should both get some sleep because we are going to need all the strength we can muster for tonight."

Even in the pale light, Sophie could see that Bill looked almost ill with weariness. She touched his arm gently and whispered, "You don't look well. Are you all right?" He just smiled and turned toward the bed.

In less than a minute she heard his even breathing and gingerly lowered herself onto the bed beside him. She thanked God for seeing them through the day and the night. Belatedly, she remembered she still had her shoes on, but by then it was too late. She was asleep.

Chapter 4

After a hearty meal in the kitchen of tough meat, boiled potatoes, and shrunken apples, the light was extinguished, and they felt their way through the door. They waited for their eyes to adjust to the darkness before they set off at a brisk, but occasionally blundering, pace.

The second night became a repeat of the first, but since Bill was more tired, the first rest stop confrontation came earlier. Again, it was Bill who almost fell, and Sophie who suggested stopping. And again, it was Marcus who sarcastically "suggested" they move on. Sophie patiently explained that they were weary even though she was barely breathing hard.

It was the pattern of the night and kept getting more difficult. Bill was tiring more quickly. Marcus was angrier, and Sophie felt caught in the middle. She didn't want to embarrass Bill nor irritate Marcus, but she was clearly the target of his anger. It seemed like an endless procession of stops and enforced starts before they reached the next haven.

It was a hut on the foot of a mountain, and no one was there, though they were clearly expected because there was food on the table and blankets on the three cots against the walls. They fell on the food eagerly and soon were ready to sleep. That was when Marcus said to them, "I'm afraid this isn't a honeymoon cottage, so unless you two want to sleep together on a single cot you will have to sleep apart today." He said it in such a hateful way that Sophie began to wonder what had happened to him to make him so bitter. She really was too tired to care, but she lifted him in prayer and thanked God for another day. Then she lay down on the bed nearest to the stove and fell instantly asleep.

She woke suddenly in flight from a nightmare in which Marcus had killed Bill and then turned to her and said grimly, "You're next!" It had seemed so real, and in the darkness it was hard to tell reality from dreams. In the darkness! It couldn't be dark unless she'd overslept. She was supposed to wake in the evening, long before the sun went down. Why hadn't the men wakened her? A chill ran through her. Had they left her there alone and gone on without her? She was sure that Marcus would have done it, but could he have talked Bill into leaving her behind? She didn't even know where she was because she had just followed Marcus like some stupid sheep. Panic rose within her, and she wanted to call out but was afraid if she did, she would hear no answering voice, and she would *know* she was alone. She rolled over and reached a trembling hand out to touch the cot beyond her head. She felt the end of it and then the mattress, and there was no leg or foot or person.

Marcus must have been sitting on the side of the bed because he said very quietly, "What are you doing?" She was torn between relief and embarrassment and settled on tears. Once they started, they seemed to come from an endless reservoir, and even though she wouldn't allow a sob to escape, the cot shook with her anguish. She finally had to blow her nose and, much to her surprise, someone handed her a handkerchief with a gruff, "Here." That deep voice could only be Marcus's. She blew as quietly as she could in order not to wake Bill.

A shutter was quietly opened a crack, and she saw it was daylight outside. With the light came the assurance that she was not abandoned, and her tears stopped.

"I had a nightmare," she whispered, "and I thought you'd left me here."

Silence was the only response, and she wondered if he would have had any qualms about doing it. Thank goodness, they should reach the border before many days and hopefully that would be the end of their association.

She rose from her bed, too awake now to think of sleep, and peeked out the shutter crack. She saw a mountain range, snow covered and pristine, with green valleys like ruffles at their feet. The sun was low enough that the peaks were beginning to turn gold in the twilight. She felt that God had made that beautiful scene just for her to enjoy and to reassure her that He was in control and would take care of her. She felt so ashamed of her panic and lack of faith.

Marcus opened another shutter, and the room was flooded with light. Bill stirred reluctantly, and Sophie felt pity for she knew how much he must dread another night of walking.

A tiny creak was the only announcement of their dinner. A young boy stood inside the now-open door and handed a basket to Marcus. From the look of awe on his face, Sophie remembered that their leader was a kind of legend. What had made him so bitter? She'd never know, but she hoped he wouldn't have to go through life bearing that kind of anger.

They ate quickly because the sun's decline behind the mountains made dusk come to the valleys early and suddenly.

As they prepared to leave, she wiggled into her backpack. Behind her Marcus snarled, "Why don't you leave that useless baggage here? It's stupid to haul it with us—and it might even be dangerous!"

She almost responded with the anger she felt, but she turned and said calmly, "I haven't asked you to carry it. It's all I have left to remind me of my beloved home, and I intend to keep it!"

His frown became a scowl, and he brushed past her to go out the door. Bill, looking very pale, rested his fingers lightly on her arm in understanding. And they started on their flight into the darkness.

It was as though her tears had washed away some of the inertia in her mind, and instead of following mindlessly, she pursued her own thoughts while keeping an eye on Bill's back.

Her sense of humor even reappeared, and she chuckled to herself as she pictured the odd procession of which she was the rear: Marcus, angrily silent as he moved like a cat through the night, and Bill, trying to be silent but wearily stumbling and occasionally crashing into obstacles, and then Sophie, trailing quietly behind like the tail on a dog. She wondered if either man would notice if the tail dropped off. Tails weren't really necessary for survival.

The first leg of their journey was downhill, and even Bill moved easily but began to lag when they came to level ground. Sophie feared for the journey and found Marcus immediately impatient at their first rest. It did not bode well for the night!

It was a living nightmare when they started to climb to one of the mountain passes. Bill was finally leaning on her and staggering when Marcus came back to see what had delayed them. At last he saw the situation as it was, and he got on Bill's other side as he asked him, "Are you ill?"

"The Germans wanted some information from me and they urged me to communicate by not giving me any food and a few other inducements. I have to get to the border, and I will, but I'm afraid I won't win any prizes for speed. I'm sorry to hold you and Sophie back." At this comment, she noticed Marcus looking at her strangely. She hoped he felt guilty for some of the things he'd said to her on previous nights.

They almost carried Bill over the pass. It slowed them down immensely, but there was nothing that could be done short of leaving him, and Sophie would never do that. Marcus did not suggest it, fortunately, so they plodded on. Downhill was better, but she sensed the worry in their leader's mind because she knew the night was hurrying by.

When they stopped to rest, Marcus shared his concern with them. "It's imperative that we cross the river before dawn. There are all open fields on this side, and our safe house is across it. Bill, it won't be easy for you to swim in the strong current, but I'll stay right with you and the safe house isn't far from there. Now we'd best move on as quickly as we can."

Sophie was aware that the group dynamics had changed. She and Marcus were now working together to get Bill, and thus all of them, to safety. The three of them were suddenly a team, and somehow in spite of the worry, it heartened her.

Unfortunately, all their efforts could not slow down the passage of time, and the sky was lightening as they came in sight of the river through a stand of trees. Marcus looked openly worried now.

"There's no cover on the riverbanks. That's why we have to cross in the dark. We'll have to stay here in the trees through the day, and that's chancy because the Germans patrol the area with dogs. It's a natural boundary, and they guard it well. There are only two guards on the bridge this time of day, but we have no way to get by them. There's nothing to do but wait, so we may as well sit down and rest."

Bill looked anguished. "It's my fault," he said. "We'll all be caught because I've been such a weakling!"

Sophie leaped to his defense. "You can't help it that you're ill. No one blames you at all." She looked defiantly at Marcus as she spoke, and for once, he shook his head in agreement. He certainly wouldn't have been agreeable if she'd been the one who was slow.

Suddenly she had an idea. "Do you have any alcohol or any way to get some?" she asked Marcus. In reply, he pulled a small, flat flask from his back pocket and looked very puzzled. "If you two are willing to take a chance, I think I can get us past the guards on the bridge."

She explained her plan to two dubious faces, but as the sky lightened, it was obvious that the underbrush had been cleared under the trees where they sat, and there was really no hiding place for them. They turned their backs as she changed her clothes.

The two tired young Germans were thinking about getting some sleep soon, when one nudged the other and pointed at three figures coming across the bridge toward them. They could see that the middle person was being guided and supported by the other two. As they came nearer the bright colored outfit of the woman caught their attention. "What is this, Hans?" the younger guard asked.

"It looks like a wedding party . . . or the end of a wedding party."

The trio walked up to the guards who aimed their guns at them and told them to stop. The girl, who they couldn't help but notice was very pretty and very angry, spoke first.

"I hope you aren't going to stop us! I've had enough trouble today. It was my wedding day yesterday and what do I get out of it? A drunken husband and I'll be late to work because I had to haul the fool home." She gave Bill a shove that would have knocked him off his feet if Marcus hadn't made an awkward grab and caught him before he fell. "She looked appealingly at the young guards and glared at Bill and Marcus. "Dummkopfs!" Her face screwed up, and tears threatened as she asked the Germans, "Do you think it's fair? He courted me and was so romantic, and now I'm married to him, and do you know how we spent our wedding night?" The men unconsciously leaned forward as if to hear better. "Sitting in a bar, watching him get so drunk that he couldn't raise his (she giggled) . . . glass." The guards grinned at each other. She lowered her voice, and it quivered as she said, "We haven't even gone to bed yet!" The soldiers looked in mock horror at her. The younger one boldly suggested, "We could help you out if your husband can't." She peeked up at him. "I should have married one of you strong fellows instead of this drunk. And I'll be late to work at the dairy, and Frau Schneider will box my ears, and I haven't even had my wedding night!" This time she burst into tears, and Bill and Marcus looked down at the ground guiltily.

"Who is the other man?" one of the soldiers asked suddenly.

"My cousin, Emil, who is almost as stupid as my husband. I asked him to help me because he's so dumb that if he opens his mouth to tell anyone, no one will believe him. And," she glared at Marcus, "if he so much as breathes a word of this, he will never tell anyone anything again."

"But everyone will know if you don't let us cross right away. I must get the dummy home before anyone sees us. Please let us go past."

She looked so entreatingly at them and with such hope in her eyes and admiration that after a short conference that included smothered laughter, the guards stepped aside. As they passed, the younger guard took hold of her arm and stopped her. "Remember me if he has this trouble many nights. You might get lonely, and I'd be glad to keep you company." She looked up into his eyes and gave him a wicked wink just as Marcus mumbled, "Come on, Hilda. He'll fall over again if you don't help." The soldier laughed and gave Sophie a pat on the rear to help her on her way. She giggled again and scuffed her toe in the dust before putting Bill's arm carelessly around her shoulder and continuing across the bridge.

"Get over to the side!" she commanded as she gave her companions a shove toward the graveled edge of the bridge. "You'll get us run over by a truck, Stupid." Under her breath she whispered, "He's bleeding, and we mustn't leave a trail down the concrete." Marcus' scowl deepened.

"What's wrong with him?" he hissed.

"I don't know, but he's barely conscious, so he may have been losing blood for a while."

"You're his wife! Why don't you know what's wrong with him? Are you too busy thinking of your new German friends?"

"Goodness! I must be a more convincing actress than I thought. You seem to have been taken in, too," she said evenly, trying hard to control her anger at his unfair attack.

A cool silence reigned as they slowly dragged a limp Bill across the bridge. "It's getting too late! There'll be traffic on the road soon. We have to move faster!" Marcus said anxiously. "I can carry him faster alone, so can you do your 'act' and walk away from us. Wait for us inside the tall hedge at the fourth house on the right."

She couldn't resist. "I'd gladly walk away from you, but be careful with him." Then she shouted, "You drunk! You aren't going to lean on me anymore and make me late to work. I'm going on, and you can get home any way you want!" and she walked out from under Bill's arm and marched ahead, leaving a befuddled-looking Marcus who finally managed to balance the unconscious man on his broad shoulders. He carefully staggered under the weight and slowly proceeded to the end of the bridge and around the bend in the road while the soldiers cackled with laughter.

Once out of sight, he straightened up and began a shambling run, trying not to jar his burden.

Sophie had waited only a few minutes when a red-faced, sweating Marcus hurried though the opening in the green, leafy wall.

"How is he?" she asked anxiously. "You must have flown to get here this quickly."

"Disappointed? Did you hope we wouldn't make it, and you could go back to your 'friends'?"

"I don't know what's wrong with you, but whatever she did, you probably deserved it!"

His face reddened to a deeper hue, and he growled, "We'll have to find out why he's bleeding, and we'd better get inside right now."

A frightened, middle-aged woman opened the door a crack at his coded knocking, then stepped back as they slipped in. "You can use the rooms downstairs," she said and opened the door to a dark stairway as she handed Sophie a lantern.

Marcus let out a sigh of relief as he lowered Bill to the double bed in the first dank room. "Take his clothes off and see what's wrong," he ordered Sophie.

She shrunk back from the bed and whispered pleadingly, "Will you do it?"

"What's the matter? Don't you want to touch him now? You must have undressed him before," he growled.

It was too much for her! She spoke slowly, quietly, clearly and with such venom that each word was like a dart directed at Marcus' scowling face. "I never laid eyes on Bill before our marriage. It was the only desperate plan that could get us out of the village. The priest couldn't even know, and it had to be completely legal since the commandant was standing right beside him. I've known Bill two hours longer than I've known you. And it's none of your business, but Bill and I don't know each other . . . not in any sense of the word. I trust you will keep your nasty thoughts to yourself in the future. You may have been disillusioned, but that doesn't give you the right to paint everyone else black. Now you leave me alone and look at that man to see if you can help him!"

He looked chastened and mumbled something under his breath.

"What did you say?" she spit at him.

"I'm sorry," he whispered.

Chapter 5

An angry hole by his third rib was revealed under a very dirty cloth binding upon the removal of Bill's shirt.

"He's been shot!" Marcus groaned.

"Is it infected?"

"It doesn't look good. See the red area around it? I'll go up and ask the lady of the house for some food and soap and hot water. We'll see if she'll wash this nasty bandage, too. I'll be back soon."

She moved to take Bill's pulse as Marcus started up the stairs. It was slow but steady, and she rubbed his face gently with her right hand while she put her left on his arm. His eyes blinked open, and he struggled to focus on her face in the dim lamplight.

"I'm sorry, Sophie. I couldn't tell anyone about the bullet wound because I was afraid no one would take a chance on getting me out. They shot me as I escaped, and the bullet went on through but the wound keeps breaking open. You surely didn't get any bargain in this arrangement. I've slowed you down, and I hope I haven't brought disaster on you and Marcus. I'm so sorry!"

She leaned over him and looked straight into his eyes. "I think we're going to make it. I know the information in your head is so important that you'd give your life to get it delivered. But I'm confident that it won't come to that. We're all working together, and Marcus will get us out. Now you try to get some sleep. We'll wash that wound and get you some food, and you'll feel better; I'm sure."

He smiled weakly and took her hand.

When Marcus returned Bill was sleeping peacefully, clutching Sophie's hand as if it were a lifeline. They woke him and got as much soup down his throat as possible. The hole was washed carefully and gently by Marcus who applied a hot, wet cloth to both the exit and entrance of the Nazi bullet. The wounded man slept again.

"I'll go up every hour and get hot water if you'll lend me your watch, Marcus. You get some sleep. You're our leader, and if you get too tired we're all lost."

"When will you sleep?"

"I can doze between trips," she suggested.

He looked doubtful but handed her his watch before borrowing the lantern to find his bed in the next room. He then returned the light to its hook before groping his way into the adjoining darkness.

Three hours and trips later, Sophie went upstairs again. She must have looked exhausted because the woman offered to wash her clothing and hang it in the kitchen to quickly dry.

"Would it be too much trouble to wash my husband's clothes, too?"

The woman nodded in agreement, and Sophie hurried downstairs with her hot poultice. She steeled herself and emotionlessly stripped off Bill's travel-dirtied clothing, slipped out of her own, and after gathering an old gray blanket around her, she carried them up the stairs. She must have looked uncertain, knowing how helpless she'd be without clothes because the woman touched her arm and said, "You can trust me, Little One." Sophie blinked back her tears.

She must have dozed because when she looked toward the door, she saw the motionless shadow of a person standing in the hallway though she'd heard nothing. Someone must have followed her! Panicked, she picked up an old shovel leaning against the wall and stood at the end of the bed, clutching her blanket and the tool, prepared to defend herself as best she could. She raised her weapon in the air, ready to lower it on the intruder's head, when Marcus walked into the room.

"Was it something I said?" he asked drily.

She was shaking with fright and almost stuttered as she asked, "Why were you just standing in the hallway? I could see your shadow!"

"I was trying to think how we could get Bill moved tonight. I may have an idea. Meanwhile, I want you to get some rest. I'll change his dressings since I'm up, and you go crawl in my bed and get a full hour of sleep. I'll lie down on the bed and if Bill wakes up, he'll just think he's having a nightmare." She wasn't sure how to react to that, but when she saw him grin, she realized he was being humorous.

She turned away to put down her spade, feeling ridiculous that "crawl into my bed" had made her turn quite pink. As she walked by him, he said, "Sweet dreams" so quietly that she wondered if it was her imagination. By the lantern light from the hall, she saw the bed had been neatly made with the sheet turned down invitingly. Gratefully she slipped into its cool embrace only to find some areas of warmth remaining from its former occupant. It was comforting but in some way disturbing, and it was almost half an hour before she fell asleep.

She was dreaming that her mother was trying to wake her, and she said, "Let me sleep a little longer, Mother." Her mother cradled Sophie's face between her hands, kissed her on the forehead, and said, "You have to get up now." But it was Marcus' voice, and she opened her eyes in confusion and saw him. An unidentifiable emotion flickered across his face, like sunlight between clouds, and then his countenance was impassive again.

She was befuddled between dream and reality and tried to explain. "I dreamed my mother was trying to wake me and she ki . . ." Her voice trailed off while she looked into Marcus' patiently inquiring face. "Have you thought of a way to move Bill?" she asked instead of finishing her earlier sentence.

"They are going to take a chance by letting us ride on the milk truck that goes every night. The soldiers like milk, so it is allowed and now they are used to it. The driver thinks the bride story may work if he's stopped. Could you get dressed in your "bright feathers""? And would you mind a new bridegroom for tonight? My German is better than Bill's, and I'm not sure he's strong enough to be questioned anyway. He can be a helper tonight."

She nodded a mute assent as he handed her the bulging backpack. She had been defensively leaning against his constant anger for so long that she felt she might fall over emotionally now that he had become kind and supportive. The absence of the resentment that had kept her back straight left her feeling very off balance. Things had changed.

Chapter 6

The Germans only checked the back of the truck once as the driver called out the nuptial story from his cab window. The embarrassed couple were discovered in a corner in the back of the truck, made to climb down to the road, and became the subject of some lewd remarks that brought even more color to the already rose-colored face of the shy bride. Then, with good hearted laughter, the soldiers helped them back on the vehicle and waved them off into the future.

It was almost dawn when the three climbed down from the truck at a faint track leading back into the fields. All were stiff but delighted to have covered two nights travel while seated. After only a few steps, Sophie and Marcus were on either side of Bill, supporting him gently. He was better, but his face was flushed with an impending systemic infection they had no way of stopping.

The farmhouse they surreptitiously approached was large and prosperous looking. Bright boxes of flowers underlined its windows and its whitewashed surfaces were glowing pink in the sunrise. Looking around carefully, Marcus knocked four times and then two more on the heavy wooden door. A young woman opened it and they scurried inside. She led them along a flag stoned hall into a large kitchen whose warmth and normalcy seemed light years away from the world they'd been living in. Only then, did the girl throw her arms around Marcus' neck with a cry of delight. He gently disengaged himself much to her obvious disappointment.

"How have you been, Emma? Are the young men still swarming around you?"

She managed to look into his eyes soulfully and pout at the same time as she said accusingly, "All but the one who matters to me, Marcus."

She had ignored Sophie and Bill but was allowed to no longer as the center of her attention turned to introduce them. Her glance flicked over a flushed, exhausted Bill to settle sharply on Sophie in her bright wedding dress. She whirled toward Marcus and shrilled suspiciously, "Who's she married to?"

The object in question spoke. "Bill and I were married a week ago."

Emma's narrowed eyes turned wide with innocence as she gazed at Marcus. "For just an instant, I thought you might have finally been caught," and as her eyes passed over the other girl she added, "But it was just for an instant. I know you're waiting for the best." Her tone made it obvious who she believed that perfect one to be, and she stepped close to him possessively, managing to brush her ample bosom across his chest.

He looked slightly embarrassed as he asked, "Could we have something to eat? And then we'd like to get some sleep. It's been a long night."

Sophie found herself bristling. First, this obnoxious young woman drooling over Marcus, and then her juvenile remarks. "Silly goose," she chided herself. It all had nothing to do with her. But the irritation surfaced again when Emma dismissed her and Bill with a wave of her hand to a tiny dark room behind the fireplace while she coyly told Marcus that he could sleep in her room and she'd show him the way in case he'd forgotten.

Sophie took Bill's arm and fairly yanked him into the room. He looked startled, but his surprise was overcome by the sight of the bed, and he flopped onto it with relief. She helped him get his shoes and shirt off, then went back into the kitchen in search of towels and hot water. Much to her surprise, Emma was there, pouting over the dirty dishes. Sophie volunteered, "I'll dry!" and asked for a towel. The girl looked at her suspiciously but handed her one.

"First I need some warm water and a cloth. My husband was wounded while escaping the Germans, and it seems to be infected. We need to keep some hot compresses on it." Emma looked irritated but managed to thrust a pan of hot water at her and almost threw the cloth in her face. Sophie felt like throwing it back but instead left the room and went to minister to Bill. After applying the warm heat to the wound she returned to the kitchen.

When she tried to draw Emma out by asking about her family and life, there was very little response until they got to the subject that really interested her hostess.

"He's changed! He and his father used to come here selling their nursery stock, and he knew I liked him and he liked me, too—I thought. I told him I wanted to marry him, but he just smiled and teased me. Lots of other men are interested, but he's the one I want. And I'm going to get him!" she said determinedly.

Sophie was silent in the face of this declaration. Most men would be very excited by Emma with her voluptuous figure, long dark hair, big blue eyes, pale red-lipped face, and provocative ("Be honest—sexy," she thought) affect. She assumed that Marcus was no exception.

"He told me to go back downstairs!' she said indignantly. "I was going to stay with him for a while . . . and he told me to go downstairs! He can't do that to me!" she declared.

"We've been on the road for almost a week, and he must be tired. He didn't get much sleep yesterday."

"How do *you* know that?" Again the narrowed eyes.

"We took turns putting hot packs on Bill's infection all day, so no one got much sleep."

"Well, I'm the girl for him, and he'd better find that out soon." Her voice changed as she said, "I think he's so handsome and sexy and brave and strong, and when he looks at me with those mysterious brown eyes, I melt. But he hardly looked at me today!"

Sophie tried to change the subject, but Emma's mind was on only one thing, and the conversation, if it could be called that, ground to a halt. Dishes done, the traveler excused herself, changing into her drab outfit before crawling into bed next to an unconscious Bill.

She slept fitfully, waking occasionally to replace the hot cloths and then resting again. In midafternoon, she decided she might as well get up, and when she took the compresses into the kitchen, the older woman was there. She asked if she might heat some water and was answered with a courteous nod. She noticed Emma sitting at the table looking at magazines when she returned, but the young woman didn't even bother to look up, so Sophie introduced herself to Emma's mother. She was peeling potatoes, and Sophie offered to help. She spent a pleasant hour preparing food, washing dishes, and doing normal kitchen work just as she'd done at home. The two workers chatted while Emma ignored them, but Sophie saw how the plain, work-hardened mother watched her daughter as a hen might watch a swan she had hatched by mistake. "Poor woman" she thought. "Her swan seems to want no part of the mother hen."

Suddenly the swan spoke. "Marcus wants to see you," she grumped. Sophie was startled by this piece of information and asked, "How do you know?" Did they practice mental telepathy?

"He told me to tell you," was the surly reply.

"I'll talk to him when I get the hot pack on Bill," and she walked into the little bedroom. After that was done, she had to ask, "Where is he?"

"Upstairs in my bedroom," she smirked.

Her mother said softly, "I'll show you the way."

Sophie followed her up the scrubbed wooden stairway and knocked on the indicated door.

"Come in."

She opened the door to a feminine pink room decorated with lace and luxuries, obviously the setting of the family jewel. Tough Marcus looked like a being from another world as he sat in a chair facing the window. He rose when she entered. Standing stiffly in the doorway, she asked, "You wanted to see me?"

He stood up and said, "Yes. Please come in and sit down." He turned the chair toward the bed and indicated he wanted her to sit in it. Reluctantly she entered the room and sat down primly.

He had a quick, fluid way of moving, and swiftly he had closed the door and returned to sit on the bed, not quite looking at her. She waited uneasily.

In a quiet, emotionless voice he said, "I owe you an apology." Now he looked directly, earnestly at her. "You were right about a woman hurting me, and you deserve to hear the story if you are willing to listen."

Startled, she replied awkwardly, "You don't owe me any explanation. I accept your apology, and it's quite possible that I did something that added to our differences. I sincerely hope we are beyond them now."

"Please let me explain."

She nodded helplessly and sat back in the chair.

"I grew up in a town much like yours but on the other side of Prague. My parents had two boys, but we were nine years apart. I almost worshipped my older brother. He was tall, handsome, athletic, smart, gentle, and good. We didn't even look at all alike. He was blond and blue eyed and tall and I was dark and very average. I tried so hard to copy him. He must have thought he had a dark shadow when I was growing up. At twenty-four, he married the most beautiful girl in the area. Everyone came to the wedding, and it was like a fairytale romance. They moved to her village because she wanted to be near her friends and family. We went to see them fairly often at first, but after a while it seemed that she had always made other plans and didn't have time for us. He was still his gentle, kind self, so we assumed he was happy, and we all rejoiced when a baby boy was born to them and then a baby girl. This was the start of a happier time when he would bring the children by himself over to our house, and we would be a family again, laughing at the old jokes and playing with little Emil and Libbie. My brother, Emil, never said anything against his beautiful Greta, but there was a tension when he spoke of her.

One day I was in their village and I stopped at their house to see Emil, but after I was inside, Greta told me that he had taken the children to see my parents and wouldn't be back until evening. She invited me to have a cup of tea and was so friendly that I began to hope her feelings toward us might have changed. I was so pleased that when she put her arm around my shoulders, I thought nothing of it. Then (I've never told anyone about this, but you don't know her and I want to get this out) she threw her arms around me and tried to kiss me. She was talking about going in the bedroom before I realized what was happening. I rushed out of there as if the devil himself was pursuing me, and I'm not sure he wasn't.

I really knew then that Emil's marriage was very troubled. I have no idea why she threw herself at *me*, but I was always in awe of her beauty and maybe she needed someone to adore her.

Life might have gone on that way, making do, but the Germans came and everything changed."

He paused—then went on in a rush.

"We were not allowed to travel, as you know. Some men were taken away to work . . ."

"My brother was sent to Germany," she interjected.

"But I was put to work building barricades and fences, so I stayed at home. We heard about my brother via the milk truck and other tradesmen. He, too, was working locally.

When the underground began to function, I was able to see him occasionally, and my admiration for him increased even more as I observed his wise council and lack of hatred. I tried to be like him and not hate the Nazis, but I sometimes felt I would burst with anger. He began to have an air of gentle sadness that puzzled me.

One day a close friend of his spoke to me in concern to tell me that Greta had been seen with a German officer. I didn't know what to do! I had no idea what the circumstances were, but after my experience with her, I feared the worst. I tried to draw Emil out about the children and Greta, but when I mentioned her, he became vague and distant.

It was three weeks later, the third of August, when word reached us that he had been arrested and was being questioned about his connection with the underground. I thought my time had come when the soldiers came banging on our door the next day. They threatened my parents and searched the house, but my brother and I had been careful not to let them know of our activities for their safety, so they had nothing to tell. I had just come home from work, and they took me outside in the backyard. Fortunately, I had worked under the direction of one of them and had never given them trouble as many of my fellow workers had done, so he spoke up for me before they got really rough in their questioning. They left us all shaking and desperate with fear for Emil.

Word reached us the next day that one of the cleaning ladies at the German headquarters had overheard a conversation between two officers, one of whom seemed to know Greta very well. He was bragging about his great appeal to women and about how Greta had even betrayed her husband for him. We were horrified, but our thoughts went to the children, and I managed to get a work assignment in their town, so I might find a way to see them. The children couldn't understand what had happened to their family, but they seemed well cared for. It was little Emil who told me about the night when his mother was so angry with their father. She said he should be home more and should get her pretty things, and his father just smiled sadly at her without saying a word.

Little Emil said, 'I had never seen her like that. She didn't even look pretty. And then she ran out of the house. In a little while, the soldiers came, and Daddy went away with them. Mommy was there, and she was crying, and one of the soldiers with shiny buttons put his arm around her. I tried to go to my dad, but that man wouldn't let me, so I kicked him and Mommy screamed and I cried.'

When I asked him if he'd like to bring Libbie and come to Gramma and Grampa's to live, he looked relieved. 'Mommy will be there, too, won't she? And Daddy?'

I didn't answer his questions. I couldn't answer my own. I talked to my parents, and we decided to ask Greta if they could come and stay with us since she might feel they were better out of the miserable situation in which her pride and anger had placed them. But it was not to be."

Marcus put his head in his hands. His voice was muffled and broken as he went on. "They could not get him to betray the resistance, and it was the broken shell of a man that they hung in the town square as a warning to everyone. Neighbors reported that Greta was hysterical when the German officer loaded her and the children into a staff car and drove off. It was two days later that I met you in that barn."

Sophie's kind heart ached for him as his shoulders shook with silent sobs, and he muttered, "My gentle brother. And I never got to say goodbye or tell him how much I loved him."

Impulsively she moved to the bed and put her arms around the grieving man. Holding his head against her chest, she rocked his hard body as one would a child. She felt the wet tears on her blouse and called in her heart on God's love for this poor, tortured man, and she pictured it flowing through her into his sob-wracked soul.

After a few minutes, he pulled away and turned his back to her. She managed to find a handkerchief in her pocket and handed it to him. She wanted to go back to her chair but was afraid to move for fear he would think his tears repulsed her. He wiped his eyes, blew heartily, and straightened his back. She gently put her hand on his shoulder and said quietly, "I'm so sorry! I only hope I haven't added to your troubles. No wonder you were so angry. Thank you for helping me to understand, but I feel so sad about your brother." Her own voice broke on the last sentence, and handkerchiefless, she could only sniff.

He turned suddenly and gathered her into his arms, and they held each other in common grief. That was when Emma opened the door.

Her face turned all colors as the two sprang apart, and in her anger she did not notice the tears. "Well, I'm so glad you could use *my* bedroom for your lovemaking. No wonder you didn't want me to stay, dear Marcus! You had someone else in mind to bed. And you," she spat at Sophie, "were so innocent. 'I'll talk to him when I'm ready'" she mimicked. "Talk wasn't what you had in mind! You may think you can do this behind my back and laugh at me, but I'll have the last laugh."

Marcus opened his mouth, but the sound of the door slamming drowned out anything he might have said. He and Sophie looked at each other in alarm. Sophie leaped from the bed and stammered, "We'd better go right down before she becomes angrier."

He stood, too, but reached for her hand before she could move to the door. "Before we leave this room you must know how much I admire you. You've listened to me tell you about my anguish and shared my grief. I thought that when you were protecting and caring for Bill, you were doing it because you were married and also because it was through him that you would be able to get out of the country. I looked for the worst motive in everyone. When I found that you didn't even really know him but that you're a kind person, I really felt small, and I began to see what I had become. You have given me hope, and I'm grateful to you, Sophie." He kissed her gently on the cheek.

Her eyes were shiny with unshed tears as she spoke. "I'm thankful that I could help you. I've been praying for you and asking the Lord to heal you of any hatred that you may have. May He give you peace of mind and faith and not let the goodness within you be overcome by what you've experienced. I want you to know that I will continue to pray for you until you tell me you're all right."

Now his eyes were shiny, but his voice was steady as he suggested, "We'd better go and face the music."

Actually, it was silence they faced as Emma, her mother, and Bill all watched them come into the kitchen. Sophie broke it by asking Emma's mother if there was anything she could do to help, and soon she was carrying food to the table while Greta watched through narrowed eyes. Bill just looked puzzled at the feeling of impending storm that permeated the room.

"How are you feeling?" Marcus asked him.

"Better, I think. I really slept well, and the hot compresses seem to soak out some of the pain and redness." In spite of this brave talk, his face had a red flush about it, and his eyes looked too bright. Sophie thought, "I don't believe the infection is gone. It's just gathering force in that wound."

After an awkward dinner of potatoes, a small piece of meat, turnips, and plenty of milk, Sophie started clearing the dishes. Greta shrugged into a "snow princess" coat and started toward the door when Marcus moved smoothly to her side and said, "I'd like to talk to you."

She snapped, "You'll have to talk quickly because I only have a few minutes to listen."

Sophie wondered how that conversation would go, and she soon found out. Apparently they'd gone around to the side of the house because she could hear the sound of Marcus' low voice as she stood wiping dishes by the window. She caught only phrases like "brother," "talked," and "Emma" but she heard every word of Emma's angry reply.

"If you needed someone to comfort you, why didn't you come to *me?*"

Sophie couldn't hear his reply. When the girl spoke again, her voice had become slow and sensual as she said, "You can see how I could make you forget your brother and that woman and everything else. Come out in the barn with me now. No one is around."

Again there was just the low vibration of Marcus' inaudible response.

Sophie realized that she was holding her breath, waiting to hear what would happen next. She let it out suddenly when she heard Emma say shrilly, "You'll be sorry that you weren't nice to me!"

When Marcus came in, he looked angry and tense, and his voice reflected it as he ordered, "Hurry and get ready to leave. We have to go right now!" As he moved across the room on his way to the stairs, he gave Sophie's shoulder a quick squeeze. She didn't know if it was to reassure her or to hurry her. Either way, she laid down the dish towel and walked quickly toward the little bedroom, telling Bill, over her shoulder, "I'll pack up and you rest as long as you can."

She quickly took some of the heavier clothing from his pack and stuffed it around the wedding dress in her own. It now looked like a large ball. She was carrying it to the kitchen when Marcus came through the doorway. He almost filled the low opening with his broad shoulders.

"Are you ready?"

"Yes," she answered. He just stood there. Hesitantly she touched his arm. "Please don't let Emma disturb your peace," she pleaded softly.

"I won't," he replied. She was amazed to see his expression of almost fierce joy. He took her face between his hands and very gently kissed her before quickly moving from the room. In her confusion, she dropped both back packs, and her face was flushed as she handed Bill his burden.

"Sophie, why is mine so much lighter than it was?" He picked hers up and knew. "You can't carry my things, too," he argued.

She smiled at him. "Let me try it for a while," and as she shrugged into the heavy pack, somehow her light heart made it seem unimportant.

She saw Bill to the door, then turned to cross the kitchen and hug the woman at the sink. "I'd have helped finish up, but we must leave now. Bless you for hiding us!"

The woman's eyes filled with tears as she whispered, "Can you forgive her?"

"Yes, I think so . . . and I pray that someday she can forgive herself." Another hug and Sophie hurried out the door into the twilight.

Chapter 7

They were climbing steeply when Bill finally spoke the question he'd been pondering. "Why are we back in the mountains when it's so much easier in the valleys? I thought we were done with the hard part when we reached our last stop. I'm not complaining, but I know I'm slowing you down lots more than if we were on the level."

Marcus spoke over his shoulder. "Our plans changed rather quickly, and I'm still not sure whether it was necessary or not." He paused. "I'm afraid Emma's stroll may have been to the Germans."

From the rear Sophie said, "I think her mother suspects that. She asked me if I could forgive her daughter."

Marcus stopped so abruptly that Bill walked right into him. "How did you answer her?" he asked without turning around.

"I told her I thought I could, and I hoped she'd be able to forgive herself someday." She wished she could see his face.

"I want you and Bill to follow this path to the saddle up there where the shepherds have a hut. Wait for me there. I have to go back and find out if the Germans are really looking for us."

"Don't go back!" Sophie pleaded.

"You're our leader, Marcus. What would we do if you don't come back?" Even Bill was agitated.

"I'll be careful. And I'll be back! You're too important to me to take any chances," and he touched Sophie's hand.

They both hugged Marcus when he appeared in the doorway of the shepherd's hut, and he enjoyed it even though he knew some of the welcome was because they needed him. He kept his arms around them for a few seconds just to hold the feeling of companionship but suddenly he started to cough, with the same overwhelming force that they'd seen once before. Again he leaned toward the wall and hung his head until the noise subsided. After a minute, he stepped back to tell them that their worst fears had been realized. The farm had been swarming with troops.

Sophie thought of the tired, worn woman at the sink and wondered sadly what would become of her. And Emma would have to explain her part in the whole thing. What would be the end result of her selfishness?

"We'll have to move on quickly. I fear that Emma may have some information on our next stop. We can't take a chance, so we'll have to sleep outside tomorrow. Since we're taking the long way around, we'll be ready for sleep. I fear I have put us all in danger. Let's get started," and he sighed as he turned toward the door.

By the end of the long night, as the sky was beginning to brighten, Bill was stumbling forward, supported by his two fellow travelers. Where their bodies were in contact, they could feel the heat generated by his fever. Unspoken was the growing fear that he would not be able to get to the border.

A thick-looking grove of trees was dimly visible to their left, and with relief, they made their way to it. After picking their way through the dense underbrush, they carefully laid down their packs in a small clearing before collapsing exhausted on the ground. Marcus was the first to recover and slipped off through the bushes to return shortly with a canteen of water. Sophie gratefully let the cool liquid run down her throat. Bill wolfed the rest down in great gasping gulps. When Marcus returned with more, Sophie poured some on an extra shirt and laid it on Bill's burning forehead. She and Marcus lay down beside him, and the last thing she remembered was her hand resting safely in Marcus's hard one.

They awoke when the sun was high, but all seemed quiet, so they ate in silence the little food Sophie had thought to gather before their hurried departure. Bill lay down again, his eyes glassy in his flushed face, uttering small fragments from his fevered mind. Marcus had that tight, hard expression on his face, and she wondered what was going on behind those dark eyes.

"Come with me to get some more water," he invited Sophie. Surprised but willing, she rose and followed him. When they were out of Bill's hearing, he motioned her to sit down. He looked openly worried now. "I don't think he can go tonight without help, and even if we could carry him, we'd be sitting ducks in the many open fields ahead. We have to communicate with the underground to see if they can provide some form of transportation. I'll have to go into the town alone and meet our contact." But the worry lines were still there.

"What's wrong, Marcus?"

"I don't like to leave you and Bill here, and we can't leave him alone." He paused. "And I'm afraid they will be looking for me everywhere. The Germans know roughly where we're heading, and with Emma's help, I'm sure they have an excellent description of me," he said bitterly.

She reached over to put her hand on his arm, so he'd know he wasn't carrying such anxiety alone. He covered her hand with his, and they sat silently, each with their separate thoughts but together.

She spoke hesitantly at first. "There's another possibility. *I* can go. They wouldn't be looking for a woman alone and," she smiled, "I don't think Emma was too interested in *my* looks. You'd have to tell me where to go and what to do, but I think I'm the one to go," she finished with assurance. Looking very serious, she added, "And I am the most expendable. Bill must get his information delivered, and you are the only one who can get him out." She saw the protest in his eyes but stopped it before it found a voice. "Just think about it." They sat silently for a few minutes. "We must get back to see how Bill is doing. Then we should get more rest because one of us," she smiled at him, "will have a long night."

They rose, and as she turned to go, she was stopped by his hand on her shoulder. She turned partially around and was drawn firmly into his arms. He held her gently but she was aware of the hardness of his arms against her ribs. He kissed her hair and when she lifted her face, their mouths sought each other desperately, urgently. Tomorrow might separate them, but now they

123

drew sustenance from each other, their revealed love the only light in a dark world.

She drew back reluctantly at last, and their eyes met in wonder at the unity they felt. He said solemnly, "I think I love you, Sophie."

Her lips trembled as she whispered, "And I love you, Marcus." The next kiss was the sealing of those vows.

Chapter 8

The village was larger than she'd imagined it. Marcus had described it carefully when he led her to the road in the darkness, but it looked frighteningly unfamiliar in reality. First she walked by the barns surrounding it and then past the houses scattered along the road in the growing dawn. Eventually she came to the stores and the square. If she remembered right, the meat market should be on the west side of it. People were busy in the streets even at this hour, and she didn't want to reveal any uncertainty, so her relief was great when she walked right up to it. There were patient women already standing inside, hoping to get some of the little available meat before it was gone. She joined them, fearful that they would hear her pounding heart. Would she remember the exact words? Would she say them too loudly? No one appeared to notice her in her nondescript clothes and the dark scarf that covered her brown hair, but she tried not to look into the eyes of the women around her. Finally she was at the counter, and the younger of the two women behind it asked, "Can I help you?"

"I'd like three Swiss steaks, please."

With no change of expression the girl responded, "Can you carry them?"

"No, I'd like them wrapped specially."

"I'm not sure we have any. I'll check and see." She disappeared through a green door behind the counter. When she returned she motioned to Sophie to join her and said, "You can see if there are any that will do," as she held the door open for her.

She walked into a kitchen where a dowdy, middle-aged woman stood. She stared piercingly at Sophie for a moment and then indicated she was to follow her. In the cluttered living room they entered sat a middle-aged man in a wheelchair, who looked at her with quiet kindness and held out a welcoming hand. With relief she grasped his hand.

"So, you want to get three people to Switzerland. It won't be easy, but I think we can help you. Where are the other two?"

"Hiding in the country. One needs help because he is ill. Do you have someone who could help carry him?"

The gentle man said reassuringly, "Yes. Will two men be enough to help? With your other friend's assistance, the three of them should be able to help the wounded man."

Sophie prayed that her face was blank. She had not mentioned any wound—she had only said "ill." Did this man know more than he should? The Germans knew, and she noticed for the first time the woman standing in the doorway so watchfully. Was this the right man? Had he turned traitor?

"I can't pay much but take this. It's almost all I have," she said as she squirreled in her pockets and handed him the results. Her voice faltered, and her trembling hand caused a few coins to fall on the floor. She dropped nervously to her knees to search for them, so she could have a good look at the crippled man's shoe soles. They were well worn! She didn't know what to do but she knew she must get away to think things out.

"Can you go get him tonight?" she asked.

"Yes, but you must tell me where they are." There was almost a hurt look in his eyes.

"I can't because I'm a stranger here, but I'm sure I can take you to them. I left some identifying things along the way."

"What were they?" he inquired casually.

"They were small things that would be hard to explain to you." She looked embarrassed. "Your men might not notice things like little piles of sticks or rocks set at funny angles."

"If you could draw me a little map, then you wouldn't have to walk all the way back there. How far would you say it was?"

She managed to slump a little as she said, "I wish I could tell you because I dread that long walk back." Thank God (and she did), he had been a little too knowledgeable. It might still be all right, but she was not going to reveal at this time that the grove was only about a mile from town.

His voice was more insistent now. "It's important we get to them soon, so you can get across the border at night."

"Let me rest a while." She shook her head as though to clear it. "It was such a long way, but maybe I can piece it together after some sleep and food."

He tried to hide his anger, but it showed in the impatient gesture that he made to the waiting woman who led her back into the kitchen. She silently set out thick slices of bread, pieces of beef, and a ripe pear. Sophie ate ravenously. It might be her last meal, and she'd enjoy it! She kept reminding herself to act frightened and simple and slightly confused. The first part wasn't hard at all.

She was afraid they'd not let her out of their sight, but when she asked hesitantly if there was a park where she might sleep in the warmth of the sun, the woman went back in the other room and after a whispered conversation, reluctantly told her of one just down the road that she'd come in on. "Do you think it wise to go outside?"

"No one knows me, and I don't want to take the chance of getting you in trouble," she said as she walked to the green door and then out into the market. She was headed toward the outer door when the young woman who worked behind the counter called to her.

"Your meat, Madam!"

Not wanting to attract any attention to herself, Sophie turned back to the counter. She started to protest, but something in the girl's face stopped her. She paid for the small package with a word of thanks and went out into the sunshine.

The park was a pleasant place, still quite deserted. She sat on a sunny bench, closed her eyes, and forced her mind to let go of its problems as she silently prayed for guidance.

She woke with a start and saw by the sun that it was almost midday. Hunger gnawed at her stomach as she opened the little meat package hopefully. How thoughtful of them to think of her! Perhaps they were all right after all. There were some thin slices of hard sausage, and she ate them with gratitude. She felt something in her teeth, and when she picked the object from her mouth, found it was a small piece of paper that had apparently been sandwiched between the meat slices. When she saw the tiny writing on it, she casually looked around to see if anyone was in sight. There was only a weary-looking worker in a soiled blue uniform sweeping the brick walk. She didn't want to take any chances, though, so she smoothed the meat papers on her knee with the small paper unobtrusively on the top.

"You're being followed. It's a trap. Try to get away and come to the last house on the left on the north side of the village after dark. Go to the back door. Destroy this!"

Sophie hoped her face had betrayed nothing. The Lord had answered her prayer in a sandwich. She silently thanked Him as she ate the small paper. Now she must do her part. She rose, stretched, and strolled down the path, leading further into the park. She saw it was quite wild in the back, but how was she to get there unnoticed? She could hear the workman sweeping the bricks closer to her now. On her right was a privy, perched with its side to a ravine. She sauntered in, used the facilities, and slid under some loose boards on the side by the ravine. Immediately, she was surrounded by a tangle of undergrowth growing on the steep slope. Fortunately, it had rained so she made little noise slithering down the soft earth to the creek below. As she started wading up the stream, she heard someone pounding on the privy door and shouting. Crouching even lower, she hurried on. About three hundred yards up the stream, she crawled up the side of the ravine and hid beneath some dense berry bushes that tore her hair and pulled at her clothes but gave her a feeling of security. After about a half hour, she heard people crashing among the bushes to her left, but they never came down the stream as far as she was hidden. She did glimpse one soldier in the distance, but he called back to his comrades and assured them it was a lost cause as he turned around to join them. She was now a real believer in the sandwich note.

By the time darkness fell, she had planned her route, and she crept up the far side of the ravine. She followed it carefully until she reached the road. Turning north but keeping close to trees and away from any houses, she reached the edge of town. There on the left was a small house, dim in the darkness. No lights showed in the windows, but she followed what appeared to be a little path to the back where a small porch announced a doorway. Heart pounding, she knocked quietly. She saw an even denser blackness and realized that the door had opened silently. Terrified, she stepped inside.

Someone struck a match and lit a small lantern. In the dim light, Sophie saw the serious faces of three middle-aged men and the woman from the meat shop. "What risks they take!" she thought and smiled at them gratefully.

Chapter 9

They took turns carrying Bill on their backs even though he tried to protest. That left Marcus and Sophie to bring up the rear. He held her hand as she told him quietly what had happened during the day.

"You're wonderful, my love! How clever to look at his shoes. I was worried sick for you all day, but I can see I wasted my time now that I know what a super spy you are." He grinned.

She glowed at his praise but said, "I have to thank the Lord. He was watching over me."

His voice was different as he pulled her to a stop. "While we can still speak privately, there are so many things I want to tell you and ask you. We know so little about each other, but I look forward to spending years with you, learning all about you, and loving you forever." He drew her to him as he whispered, "I do love you, dear Sophie!"

Their kiss seemed to light the night.

"Will we get through, Marcus? I can't bear the thought of being without you! The marriage can be annulled I'm sure, and perhaps we could live in Switzerland or England until the war is over and we can go home again."

"We'll find someplace, and wherever we are, it will be home as long as we're together. I'm a hard worker and know a bit about building and farming and . . ." They heard a low whistle. "We have to catch up to the others and go into our future," he said as he gave her a quick kiss before they hurried forward.

The little group threaded their way beside fence rows, through woodlands, and along streams. It was surprising how much cover there was for those who knew the area. Slowed down by the wounded man and the need for concealment, though, the tension mounted as the night wore on. Birds were starting to sing sleepily when the leader motioned them to stop.

"We are almost at the buffer zone between Austria and Switzerland. This is the most isolated section of it, but it is still carefully patrolled by soldiers. It was cleared of trees for a one-hundred-yard strip and heavily mined. Some of us were pressed into service and managed to keep a path clear of explosives. It's marked by a fine wire tied to a tree on this side and one on the Swiss side. I'll take you to the tree and give you the wire to guide you so you can find your way. I need not stress the importance of quiet," and he looked up at the faintly lightening sky, "and speed. You'll have to crawl a large part of the way because undergrowth has reappeared, but it isn't as thick as we'd like it. Fortunately, they can't mow it because they'd detonate their mines." Under his breath he muttered, "I wish they'd try!"

Like shadows, they flitted from tree to tree until they stood at the edge of the shorn buffer strip. Soundlessly, the guide attached a strand to the invisible guide wire, handed the end to Marcus, made the sign of the cross, and evaporated into the woods with the two other men.

As they stood trying to get their bearings, they heard someone coming through the woods behind them. Instantly dropping to the ground, they heard "Auf Wiedersehen" whistled windily by the German on patrol. Fortunately, Bill was lucid at the time, so the silence was unanimous. As soon as the footsteps were no longer audible, Marcus reached out and put Bill's hands into loops on his backpack so he could pull and carry him. He touched Sophie's cheek and motioned her to follow as he started along their lifeline.

Once they were about fifteen feet into the buffer strip, there appeared to be a faint path so they could move without having to gently release each branch and stem so no noise would betray them. Sophie kept as close as possible to the other two, her hands often touching Bill's shoes. Suddenly she realized with horror that she could *see* them. Dawn was breaking! Marcus must have noticed, too, because the feet were moving away from her more quickly. She hurried, too.

They went almost three quarters of the way across without incident. Then her backpack caught on the branch of a small tree with persistent thorns. She dared not reach up to free it and in desperation she gave a sharp tug that released it. Trembling, she lay quietly while the tree stopped vibrating before starting to crawl forward. She'd almost caught up with the others when there was a loud crack and she felt a sting on her upper right arm. Confused, she flattened herself to the ground. Behind her she could hear the German shouting for help, and there were more sounds that she knew now were rifle shots.

Suddenly Marcus' face was close to hers. "Get your pack off!" he whispered desperately, and he almost tore it off her back. When it lay on the ground beside her, she was appalled to see a crimson portion of her wedding dress protruding like a red flag from the top. Her face was ashen. "It must have caught on the tree branch," she stammered.

The shooting had stopped shortly, but the soldier continued to shout his alarm, and now there was an answering voice. She glanced at her burning arm and saw that it was red, too. She looked at it uncomprehendingly. Marcus saw it, and his eyes seemed to turn to black stones as he whispered, "I'll always love you, Sophie!" before he pressed the guide wire into her hand, snatched up her pack, and moved past her with his quick, fluid grace to go back the way they had come. She wanted to cry out after him but seemed to be struck dumb. Her arm was throbbing, and when she touched it, her fingers came away covered with blood. She must have been shot!

The firing started again, but it sounded further away. The Germans were shouting and one yelled, "I see you. You'd better give yourself up." She lifted her head in time to see Marcus raise part way from the ground with his hands in the air, wearing her pack with its bright marker. The moment seemed frozen in time until it was shattered by the sound of two rifles, and she saw his body almost lifted from the ground by the force of the bullets as they ripped into his flesh. And the noise went on and on as they showered bullets where he had fallen.

They'd killed Marcus! Her eyes had seen it, but her mind wouldn't accept it. It couldn't be true! She lay back, stunned, and tried to think.

"I've got to get Bill out of here. That's what Marcus wanted to do, and I'll have to make it happen." She dragged herself forward, almost mechanically but her arm wasn't working very well. It had become all red and slippery. "Silly arm," she said and pulled herself forward with her left one. There were Bill's shoes. She slithered past him, her whole attention on the wire. His eyes were filled with questions but neither said a word.

Slipping into the straps of Marcus' deserted pack, she inched forward. At first Bill crawled with her, but gradually she knew the weight of pulling his body besides her own. Time seemed to have stopped, and her world was made up of small rocks and little twigs that were the milestones of her tedious journey. She was very hot, and when she turned her head, she saw a bright light above her. How did the sun get so high? Where was she going? Why did her body feel so heavy? Her arm hurt, but it didn't matter because she was too tired to care anyway. She couldn't remember why, but she knew she wasn't supposed to rest yet. Marcus wanted her to do something, and she would because she loved him. Maybe he was waiting ahead. She inched forward again.

The men at the tree had almost given up when they were amazed to see a woman's face emerging from the weeds under the wire. They crawled out to help her and pulled in two fish instead of one. The man she was dragging was unconscious. They propped her up against a Swiss tree and asked her, "Where is the American?" She pointed at Bill. "I must tell Marcus we made it," she whispered, and then darkness swallowed her.

Chapter 10

She throbbed slowly into consciousness, wondering what world she was entering. For the moment, she had no past and no future, just a noisy, vibrating present. In front of her was a rounded, compartmentalized wall, but when she tried to look to the side, it was difficult to turn her head. Gradually she became aware that she was lying on her back and looking at a ceiling. She turned her head with difficulty and saw she was inside the open body of a large plane! When she tried to raise her arms, only the left one appeared. Had her arm been amputated? Perhaps it was the so-called "phantom pain" that seemed to radiate from that area. In alarm she raised her head and saw that her right arm was bandaged and bound to her side. Cautiously, like a tongue investigating a sore tooth, she sought in her memory for the cause of her injury. A gun shot? Something terrible was back there, too painful to remember, and she left that thought and watched the shadows highlight the angles of the ceiling and then she merged gratefully with the engine sounds into nothingness.

"Are you awake, Ma'am?' came a slow voice from nearby. Startled, she looked with puzzlement at a young, concerned face bending over her. "Can . . . you . . . understand . . . me?" he asked. She wondered if perhaps he didn't speak much English, but she could make no answer because no words could get through her parched throat. She tried to shake her head in affirmation, but the pillow hampered that movement. The person said, "Poor thing."

"Wa . . . ter," she whispered. His visage brightened. After fetching a glass of liquid, he gently raised her head as she greedily gulped it down—and then was sick. He carefully cleaned her face and helped her again with the water, but this time she was wiser and sipped a little at a time.

"Do you speak English?" he asked.

"Yes."

Relief flooded his face. "I'm Corporal Earl Jones, and I'm a medic with the 16th Airborne. I helped take the bullet from your arm after we left the ground. This is a temporary hospital plane. They're still working on your husband in the operating room."

"My husband?" she puzzled.

"Oh, don't worry. He's in good hands, though he did look terrible when they carried him on the plane. He was conscious, though, and he raised an amazing row when we told him we had no orders to take you, too. Sick as he was, he said he wouldn't go unless we took you. We'd arranged medical care for you in Switzerland, but he was in such a state that we just loaded you both and left. I hope they will understand when we land." He looked worried and then embarrassed. "It's good to have you on board, Ma'am, but I'd like to just follow my orders." Then he brightened. "How is it that you understand English? You do know what I'm saying, don't you?"

"My mother was an American, and she always tried to speak to me in English. It was a kind of game we played when we didn't want the neighbors to understand us." The thought of her mother brought a big lump to her throat.

Corporal Jones had moved on in their conversation. "You must have had some hard times getting out of there. You're lucky to have made it. I'm sorry about the guy who didn't but two out of three is better than none out of three."

Reality hit her like a sledge hammer. *Marcus was dead*! Had she shrieked it out loud? No, the corporal's expression hadn't changed. The pain of the memory filled her body like a heavy liquid, stifling her breathing, and she felt that her heart would surely stop. But it plodded on, and so, she realized with horror, must she. A world without Marcus? She didn't want it. He was her future, and now she had none.

"Are you all right, Ma'am?" He looked into her eyes and saw the despair that filled them and then overflowed in a steady stream that rolled down the sides of her face, trickled in and around her ears, and crept down her neck. Corporal Smith looked alarmed, said, "Ma'am?" and grabbed a towel. He soaked up some of the moisture and helped her blow her nose on his khaki handkerchief, but the stream continued to flow in its awful, soundless grief. He was kindness itself, only leaving her to get another handkerchief and another towel, which he put under her neck as a last resort.

She touched his hand and whispered, "Thank you."

Finally, he gave her a pill, and she drifted off into throbbing darkness. She woke gradually to her new reality. Life would go on without her home, her family, her country—or her heart. How could she face it? What could she make of it? Perhaps she had to give up her life and live for others now. She tried to pray and could only hope that God knew her intentions because she felt no faith, no hope, and no love.

When she finally turned her head, she saw that Bill was lying on a gurney to her left. He showed no sign of life, and she wondered numbly if he, too, were dead. Corporal Smith was hovering, and she looked at him questioningly.

"He isn't doing very well, I'm afraid. When we first picked you up, he was hanging on in a heroic effort to make sure you were going to get out with us. Once that was done, he let go and hasn't been conscious again. The doctor examined him and found him so malnourished besides an infected bullet wound in his chest that he was amazed he'd made it this far. The infection has spread, too. I don't know what all happened, but it hasn't left him much to fight with. I'm sorry to tell you this, but I think you'd best know the truth."

Again, tears wet her cheeks. Carefully, she raised her left hand and placed it on Bill's arm. "Don't die, Bill," she whispered. His arm felt cold through the sheet, and she kept her warm fingers on it until the heat transferred, and then she moved her hand a little higher. She rolled her head to the side and saw his eyelids flutter open. He tried to reach her hand, but his arm fell back on his chest.

"Sophie, are you there?

"Yes, I'm right beside you."

The corners of his mouth moved in an effort to smile, and his eyes closed again. She left her hand on his arm, and it felt warmer to her, but whether it was just the fever she didn't know. Somewhere she'd read that touch was important in crisis situations, and right now, that was all she had to offer—and prayer. If she couldn't pray for herself, at least she could for him.

The plane droned on and on, and Sophie's body seemed to be humming in tune with the vibration. She drifted in and out of sleep and dreams and consciousness but kept her hand touching Bill, her only contact with anything vaguely familiar. He was still alive when they landed on a military airstrip near Washington where they were whisked to Walter Reed Hospital in a flurry of medics and ambulances.

Chapter 11

Everyone was most kind to Sophie. They put her in a single room at the other end of the floor from Bill's room. Her arm was taken care of, and she was medicated, so she could rest completely. They knew she would be facing some hard emotional reactions and would need all her resources when that time came. The third day she woke to a room full of sunshine, and when the nurse came, she asked if she might have something to eat. Elated, the woman had a beginning meal sent up, and Sophie started to come back.

The next day she asked to see Bill and they brought a wheelchair and propelled her down to his room. He lay there, comatose, alive but unresponsive, and she sat beside his bed, held his hand, and talked to him sometimes in English and sometimes in her own language. His fever continued to heat his weary body and then send it into shaking chills. She studied his quiet face, so thin and pale. He would be quite handsome if he were healthy. She tried to imagine what he would look like and could not because she had never seen him in good health. Marcus had died for this man. She must do all she could to encourage him to come to life. If he died, nothing would make sense.

Apparently, the United States government was very concerned also because an intelligence officer was in and out of the room several times each day, checking to see if the patient had regained consciousness. They didn't intrude. They just kept watching, hoping he'd give them the information they so badly wanted. But all the locations and numbers were locked in his sleeping brain, and they could only wait and hope, too.

On the fifth day, he was thrashing around, muttering isolated words when suddenly he lay still. She squeezed his hand, his arm, his shoulder, desperately trying to pump life back into him. "Don't die, Bill!" she screamed. The nurse came running and thrust Sophie aside as she reached for her patient and felt his pulse. A look of relief crossed her face, like the sun coming out from a cloud, and she told the frantic Sophie, "His fever has broken. He's sleeping now," and put her arms around the weeping girl beside the bed.

The next morning, Sophie was allowed to walk down the hall, and she found the door to Bill's room closed with a soldier stationed outside. Apparently he'd been one of the "checkers" because he smiled into her frightened eyes and said, "He's fine, Mrs. Sedlecek. We're so glad he can finally give us all the information that he almost gave his life to gather. And I think he'll be happy to complete his mission. Do you want me to knock on your door when we're done?"

"Yes, thank you," Sophie answered as she turned to retrace her steps down the long corridor, thinking about her new name.

It was two o'clock when the knock came, and the soldier announced she could go down and see her husband. He looked concerned for a moment when he saw her untouched food tray and the way she sat so quietly with her hands folded lifelessly in her lap.

"Are you all right, Ma'am?"

"Yes, thank you."

Baffled, he wished her a good day and retreated.

She made her way back down the hall and saw Bill was peacefully asleep. Lowering herself into her familiar chair, she sat patiently until his eyes flickered open, and he reached for her hand. "I'm glad you're here."

"Were you able to tell them what they needed to know?" she asked.

"I hope so. I've tried so hard to remember things—locations, numbers, directions—and it's a relief to be able to pass them on and let them go at last. Now they can put them together and see if they can use any of it.

They hadn't told my parents that I was back in the States, but now they will. I expect my mom will come here to see me, but Dad probably won't be able to get away from work. You'll like them,

Sophie. They are both from Czechoslovakia, though they came here with their families when they were quite young. We lived in a Czech community so that was the language we used except for school. I think you'll feel right at home with them."

"Where do they live?"

"In a small city in the state of Iowa. I'll see if the nurse will bring me a map, and it will show you it's pretty much in the middle of the country. It's a great place to live. I'd like you to see it," he said wistfully.

Just then the nurse walked in.

"I thought you would be here, Mrs. Sedlecek. We are getting a new group of wounded in, and I'm afraid we'll need your room. Administration said that you can stay in the nurses' residence, which is very near the hospital. When I go off duty, I'll help you carry your things over."

"I don't have anything to carry except the hospital gown that I sleep in and the toothbrush they gave me. I wash my clothes each night," she explained.

"Well, we'll go down and check when we're ready to go. How are you feeling after all the talking you did this morning, Colonel?"

"Tired, but relaxed. Sophie will be okay in the nurses' quarters, won't she?"

"I'll keep an eye on her myself. But she needs to eat more, and I hope you'll talk to her about that . . . unless you like skinny wives."

At five o'clock she returned, and Sophie meekly followed her back to her room. After gathering the backless gown and toothbrush, the nurse checked the locker and commented, "This must be yours," as she held up a stained brown back pack with straps dangling from it.

Sophie's face went white as she reached for it and clutched it to her heart. "I guess it is mine—now," she whispered as she headed blindly toward the door.

She hardly said a word except, "Thank you," when the kindly woman wished her well as she left the small room Sophie was to occupy. The girl sat on the bed cradling Marcus's backpack as she rocked silently back and forth, mute with grief. Though she could never hold *him,* this was a thing he'd owned and worn and perhaps some essence of him was still in it. Finally she lay down, holding it close, and fell asleep.

A knock on the door ushered in the morning. When the nurse entered, she asked, "Would you like to go down to breakfast with me?"

Sophie shook her head from side to side.

"I wish you'd eat more! Well, if you don't want to eat, I'll stop by in about forty-five minutes on my way to work. Then you'll know the way and be able to go back and forth when you want. Today is Friday (at last), and I'll be gone for the weekend, so you'll be on your own. Oh, and by the way, my name is Virginia. Yours is Sophie, isn't it?"

The girl nodded disinterestedly. Virginia's smile faded. "I'll see you later," she said determinedly.

As soon as the door closed, Sophie threw the pillow aside to reveal the precious backpack. It was such a tenuous link to the man she loved that she hesitated to look inside for fear the meager memories she possessed might be disturbed.

When Virginia returned, Sophie inquired, "Is there a key for this room?"

Mystified, the nurse looked around the bare cell but explained that the key was in the lock on the inside of the room. Solemnly, Sophie took it, locked the door as they exited, and slipped it in her pocket. Their walk to the hospital was completed in silence.

It turned out to be a difficult day. There had been no need to talk when Bill was unconscious so much of the time, but now he was eager to communicate and to piece together the fragments of memories that had been interrupted by his illness. Since they were the same ones that were so precious and painful to Sophie, he found many of the answers he sought were, "Yes," and "No."

Finally he said gently, "You loved him very much, didn't you?" and she nodded mutely, her eyes dark with despair.

"I have no right to say this, but I want to try. Forgive me if it hurts you. He's dead, Sophie, and you are alive. You only knew him for two weeks, and it was in a desperate time. Would you have loved him if he'd lived down the street? If you'd met him at a dance in your village? You'll never know that, but think about it. You are young and beautiful, and I hope you have a long, happy life ahead.

Don't just give up. I want you to know that I'm your friend, Sophie. And I guess I can't say too much about the improbability of falling in love in two weeks because it happened to me, too."

She made absolutely no response.

He sighed. "It doesn't matter to you now, but I hope and pray that it will someday in the future."

After that, he tried to draw her out about her room, the hospital, and what she'd been doing since they arrived in the States. She could talk about those things, and the morning passed.

It was two in the afternoon when a plump, anxious, grey-haired woman hesitantly walked in the door. Sophie saw the woman's face dissolve into tears as she caught sight of Bill.

"Oh, Billy!" she cried and ran to the bed to throw her arms around him. There were many endearments, some in English and some in Czech. Finally he interrupted her long enough to say, "Mother, I want you to meet Sophie, the young lady who saved my life."

Libbie Sedlecek saw for the first time the girl seated in the corner—and immediately went to her and enveloped her in a grateful hug. Sophie's eyes filled with tears. She thought of her own mother with longing.

"Tell me what happened and why you're here, Billy. The army called us yesterday, and I came as quickly as I could. Your dad had to work." She looked expectantly at her son and patted his hand.

Sophie didn't know what had happened before she knew him, and it was a new story to her, too. He didn't say exactly what the army wanted him to find, but she heard where he'd been and how he was betrayed. He passed lightly over his prison experience, but his face belied his attempt at casualness.

"It must have been terrible, Son!"

"I don't even want to think about it—but I was determined to escape. And I did! Not everyone was that lucky." A shadow crossed his face.

When he told her about the wedding ceremony, she looked at Sophie with admiration, but the glance held an unspoken question. All she said was, "I remember those weddings from when I was little. The whole village celebrated. How I looked forward to seeing those beautiful brides and dreamed of being one myself."

To Sophie, it seemed like a story about someone else. Bill told what he knew of Marcus and their escape, and she listened but wouldn't allow herself to acknowledge that any of it concerned her. When Bill finished, Libbie hugged her again and pressed the girl's head against her ample bosom. "You poor dear! You've gone through so much, but you're safe now, and we'll be your American family. I hope this awful war is over soon!"

Bill began asking about the news from home, and soon he and his mother were deep in local happenings. Sophie was so silent that they quite forgot her until she said, "I think I'll go back to my room now. I'm so glad you've come, Mrs. Sedlecek."

"Please excuse us, dear. We shouldn't have started talking about things at home, which would have no interest for you."

"Oh, don't worry. I'm just tired, and I know Bill's in good hands, so I'll go take a nap. And you two have lots to catch up on."

Bill looked anxious. "Do you have to go, Sophie?"

"It's almost 4:30, and dinner will be coming soon."

His mother rose, too, and hugged the girl again. "I meant it when I said we'd be your family here. Please count on that. And thank you from the bottom of my heart for all you've done for Bill—and for us."

Chapter 12

Virginia found her sitting in the lounge staring dully at the wall as she walked past at 5:00. Sympathetically she sat down next to Sophie on the couch.

"Are you alright?"

"Yes, thank you," the girl answered politely.

"Do you like Bill's mother?"

"Yes," she said with more warmth than she'd shown at any other time. "But there is no need for me to be here anymore now that she's here."

Much to Virginia's surprise, she heard herself say, "I think you need to get away from here for a little while. Why don't you come with me to the Jersey shore this weekend? My parents have a cottage there, and I am going to go there as soon as I get off duty. Now that it's getting cooler, there aren't many people around. You can sit in the sun, walk on the beach, read, and sleep in. Have you ever seen the ocean?"

Sophie's eyes filled with tears. "How kind of you!"

Her own eyes smarted as Virginia said briskly, "It's settled then. The colonel's mother is here to keep him company, so I'll tell them where you're going while you pack up your nightgown and tooth-brush in your backpack. I'll pick you up out in front in twenty minutes, we'll grab a bite on the way, and we'll be off to the Atlantic!"

Sophie looked startled at the speed of the decision, but the older woman gave her no time to change her mind. Squeezing the girl's hand she moved rapidly down the hall, blowing her nose. For a moment Sophie sat there, then got to her feet obediently and did as she was told.

Dinner and the trip was quite silent after Virginia found her attempts at conversation met polite mono-syllabic responses. *"What have I done?"* she wondered.

Both women were tired when they arrived at the cottage. Since a strict blackout was maintained on the coast, it seemed easier to go to bed than to get all the curtains sealed off in the darkness.

Daylight brought Sophie her first view of the gray, endless, rolling waves so different from the lakes she'd known—and it brought a phone call for Virginia, asking her to go back to work in place of a nurse whose husband had one day of unexpected leave. Kind by nature and lonely for her own husband, she agreed.

It was with mingled regret and relief that she explained the situation to her reticent guest. It would have been a long, silent weekend, she feared.

As she was starting to pack up the contents of the freshly stocked refrigerator, a thought struck her. "Would you like to stay here, Sophie? There's no one around to bother you, and you might enjoy some time by yourself." The look on the girl's face was all the answer she needed. "I'll probably be back and pick you up tomorrow night. There's plenty of food, so you shouldn't go hungry." She smiled at this because all the nurses were aware that Sophie rarely ate, which was also obvious by the way her colorless clothes hung on her frame. And so it was settled.

Sophie just stared at the ceiling most of the first night, but after Virginia left that morning, instead of returning to the bedroom, she roused herself to see what the beach was like. There was no one on it as it was a relatively isolated stretch of shore, so she wandered along it, alone under the grey, overcast sky. The waves fascinated her as they advanced, broke, foamed, and retreated to their gray incoming sisters. The futile rushing and falling back, the endless vista, and the dark day mirrored her own situation.

It was some time before she became aware that the sky was getting even darker, and she realized with a surge of panic that it would soon be night. She turned and fairly ran down the beach, knowing she would not be able to find the house in the dark. Fortunately, the old green chair by the porch was still visible in the deep twilight, and she fled into the cottage. With a mixture of relief and exhaustion, she lay down on the couch for a few minutes but fell into a deep sleep.

At 2:30 a.m., she was startled awake as she dreamed she saw Marcus' body being riddled with bullets again, and she lay shaking and drenched with sweat. It was too awful, too real, too sad, and she started to cry. Once started, it was as though a dam had burst, and she couldn't stop. No one heard the sounds of her agony of spirit. It was not gentle crying but sobs and moans that seemed to be ripped from her soul. Even when she was too exhausted to make a noise, the tears still flowed on.

When morning dawned, she was drained of all energy and felt completely empty but oddly alive. Suddenly, she felt ravenously hungry, and she got up and rummaged through the previously ignored food supply. The smell of eggs and bacon frying was almost exquisitely painful, and she wolfed them down while they were so hot they burned her tongue. Milk tasted better than she could remember, and she drank it greedily.

Sitting at the little table, looking out over the rolling waves, she only allowed herself to examine the present. She was drawn to the beach again, but today she made a lunch and set out purposefully. This time, she really experienced it; hearing the waves crash, feeling the wind comb her hair, knowing the roughness of the sand on the soles of her feet, and seeing the gulls wheeling and riding the wind above her. She was alive! That *was* something to celebrate, even with the losses it involved. And her sandwich and fruit tasted wonderful.

The sun came out that afternoon, drenching her with warmth and light. She thanked God, actually kneeling on the sand. How often she'd wanted to scream at Him about the unfairness of finding and then losing so quickly and forever the love of her life. And her family and friends were gone from her, too. Now, on her knees in the warm sand, she felt His love and wished for the old simple faith she'd always known.

She was ruddy with sunshine when she returned that evening, famished. The phone was ringing as she came in, and she remembered that Virginia should be arriving soon. When she answered it, she found that her hostess would not be coming until the following

Sunday. Virginia was very apologetic, but there was nothing she could do since there had been an influx of seriously injured patients and everyone was working double shifts. She wondered if Sophie would be all right, and the girl was quick to reassure her. Her voice must have sounded different because Virginia asked again, "Are you sure you're all right, Sophie?"

"Yes, I think I need this time alone, and I'm grateful to you."

The older woman sounded more puzzled than ever, but there was nothing she could do, so she repeated that she'd return in a week.

After concocting a huge sandwich of meat, tomatoes, lettuce, bacon, and cheese following a bowl of steaming soup, she went in search of a book. Beside the fireplace was a bookcase stuffed full of what she assumed must be the owners' favorites. She reached forward to pull out a slim volume that had slipped to the back because of its size. She frowned at the title, *The Will of God* by Leslie Weatherhead. Who dared to think they knew the will of God, she thought bitterly. Curiosity got the better of her, though, and, once started, she read it to the end and then read it through again. The author stated his belief that God wants good for us, but due to man's free will, God's intentions for us are thwarted. Sophie thought of all the lives destroyed and the anguish brought about by the Nazis and the war and had to agree that man did cause so much grief. So what hope is there? But Mr. Weatherhead wasn't finished. The next chapter stated his belief that God still worked to bring about his good, even in the wreckage made by man, and He would not be deterred.

Her fresh-aired day caught up with her in the midst of the third reading, and she reluctantly put the book down and slipped wearily between the sheets of her bed. That night, she dreamed that she and Marcus were walking hand-in-hand on the beach, talking and laughing. She was so happy, but all of a sudden, a great black cloud came racing toward them. As they started to run, she let go of his hand, and when she looked back for him, he was nowhere to be seen. It started to rain, and she was drenched and cold and kept calling his name.

She woke up with a start and found she was cold and wet. The covers had fallen to the floor during the violence of her dream, and her pillow was soaked with tears. She turned the pillow over, pulled the covers around her, and waited for the night to pass.

Much to her surprise, the sun was shining on her face when she opened her eyes again. She was tired but not exhausted and determined she would get further down the beach, so she could walk around an old lighthouse she'd seen in the distance. She tried to scrub off the dream of the darkness as she showered and actually put on some lipstick that she'd found in the bathroom. Fortified by a huge breakfast and armed with a large lunch, she set out.

It was another sunny day and she was glad she'd thought to grab the old hat hanging by the door. She walked with more energy, and she reached the lighthouse well in time to sit down by it and have her lunch. She even went further up the beach, but hunger made her turn around, and she watched her shadow move swiftly over the sand as she hurried back to the cottage.

She ate very well that night, too. Again she searched for a book. There were many well-worn ones to choose from, and this time she reached for *Collected Poems* by Edna St. Vincent Millay. She'd always liked poetry, and she curled up in an old easy chair that had cradled many a reader. She sat upright as she finished the first poem, "Renascence," about someone buried by grief:

> And the big rain in one black wave
> Fell from the sky and struck my grave.
>
> I know not how such things can be;
> I only know there came to me
> A fragrance such as never clings
> To aught save happy living things;
> A sound as of some joyous elf
> Singing sweet songs to please himself,
> And, through and over everything,
> A sense of glad awakening.
> The grass, a-tiptoe at my ear,
> Whispering to me I could hear;
> I felt the rain's cool finger-tips
> Brushed tenderly across my lips,
> Laid gently on my sealed sight,
> And all at once the heavy night

Fell from my eyes and I could see!—
A drenched and dripping apple-tree,
A last long line of silver rain,
A sky grown clear and blue again.
And as I looked a quickening gust
Of wind blew up to me and thrust
Into my face a miracle
Of orchard-breath, and with the smell,—
I know not how such things can be!—
I breathed my soul back into me.

Ah! Up then from the ground sprang I
And hailed the earth with such a cry
As is not heard save from a man
Who has been dead, and lives again.
About the trees my arms I wound;
Like one gone mad I hugged the ground;
I raised my quivering arms on high;
I laughed and laughed into the sky;
Till at my throat a strangling sob
Caught fiercely, and a great heart-throb
Sent instant tears into my eyes:
O God, I cried, no dark disguise
Can e'er hereafter hide from me
Thy radiant identity!
Thou canst not move across the grass
But my quick eyes will see Thee pass,
Nor speak, however silently,
But my hushed voice will answer Thee.
I know the path that tells Thy way
Through the cool eve of every day;
God, I can push the grass apart
And lay my finger on Thy heart!"

Tears streamed down her face as she read it again and again,
but these were the gentle waters of healing instead of the bitter ones
of grief. She realized that her own "big rain" had been her night of

weeping. It had washed her from her grave of grief. She thanked God for the gift of those tears.

She didn't know what lay ahead, but for the moment being alive was enough. How would she learn to live in a world without Marcus? She mustn't think of that now but only concentrate on each day and find the things within it to treasure.

The next three days were spent on the beach. Thursday night, she built a cozy fire in the fireplace and ate her dinner of two ham sandwiches, a bowl of onion soup with melted cheese on it, a large Jonathan apple, and four cookies, washed down by iced tea since she'd consumed all the milk.

She knew she had to face the past and forced herself to go into the bedroom and gently extract the backpack from under her pillow. Holding it close to her, she sat on the floor by the fire, afraid to go any further. It was fifteen minutes before she could bring herself to reach inside it. The first thing she drew out was a pair of grey socks, neatly rolled into a ball. Carefully she unrolled them and exposed their tidily mended heels and toes. They must be his, but who had mended them? Someone who loved him must have done that tedious work. She tried to picture his mother doing the little things she could to make his life easier. She turned the pack upside down and emptied the contents on the floor in the circle of light. They lay there Pathetically, a shirt and a pair of underwear, clean but worn and grey. She felt embarrassed in the midst of her enormous disappointment at the meagerness of his possessions. She looked in the shirt pocket but it was empty, and there was no name or label anywhere.

Suddenly she was filled with rage! The pack which she'd hoped would hold something personal, a material memory of her love, had proved to be filled with dust and ashes for her. She was cheated even out of that. She threw herself on the floor and beat on it with her fists while she shook with sobs. Desperately, she tried to picture Marcus and was terrified by the knowledge she had no material part of him left to her. She cried herself to exhaustion before woodenly placing the socks and underwear in the fireplace where they smoldered instead of burning cleanly. She put the shirt on and tried to feel his arms around her. The betraying backpack sat limply at her feet. She grabbed it and frantically turned it inside out. Perhaps there was something pinned to the inside! Nothing!

In spite of the disappointment, she began to see why she could find nothing. This was all Marcus had had except for the clothes he wore and his coat. If the Germans had stopped him, they would have found nothing, and there would have been no identification to trace him back to his family or anyone in the underground. Why had she expected more?

She pushed the bottom of the pack inside to right it, but there was a stiff place in the center that caught. Her fingers moved to loosen it and slipped inside one of the seams and she felt a smooth, hard surface. Her heart was pounding as she gently loosened the object and drew out a small, flat, leather-covered notebook. With shaking fingers she opened it. The page was completely covered with tiny writing and even the edges of the page had a border of the same small letters. She tried to read it, but it seemed to be in some kind of code. Each page was covered with the small neat letters except for the last two. Was it his writing? She hoped so because then she would have something of his.

She dreamed of him again that night. He was leaning against a fence by a meadow and writing carefully in a little book. She tried to look over his shoulder, but a cloud came over the sun, so it was in deep shadow. Then he put it in his backpack, turned to her with a loving smile, and drew her into his arms. She nestled against him blissfully and woke with a happy feeling that lingered through breakfast.

The sunshine on the table lit the pages of the little book she held in her hands as she studied each page. On the last page of writing, she felt there were possible references to places and distances and finally concluded it was a record of the route they took, perhaps for future use. Her eyes happened to dwell on the border, and they widened as she read over and over again, "I love Sophie." She turned the book around and around and each border read the same. It must have been the only paper he could write on, and he had to declare his love and see her name. She had not been cheated after all! She had been affirmed, and any time she doubted his love, she need only open that little book and know it had been real. She had something to hold on to for the rest of her life!

Chapter 13

Startled best described Virginia's reaction when she pulled up to the cottage six days later and was embraced by a beautiful, sun-tanned, calm-eyed young woman, dressed in some of her hostess's ancient beach clothes. It took her a minute to find any remnant of the gray, listless girl of a week and a half ago. The features were the same, but this girl looked healthy, sun-washed and *alive*.

"What happened to you?" she blurted.

"It's a long story," Sophie answered. "Come inside, and I'll try to tell it if you want to take the time to listen. Did you bring any food? How's Bill?"

"Of course I want to listen. I'm absolutely dying of curiosity! Yes, I brought some food. You can't have run out because I brought enough for both of us." She paused at Sophie's expression. "Didn't I? And Bill is all right but instead of improving, he seems to have regressed a little. We aren't worried, but we are concerned."

By this time she had reached the refrigerator and her mys-tification increased when she looked inside and saw that the sole inhabitant was a small bowl of radishes. They were obviously the last resort before starvation.

"Did anyone stop by?" she asked over her shoulder.

"No, I was the only one here."

"Well, whatever happened to you seems to have affected your appetite. You've been eating like a horse!"

Her guest grinned sheepishly.

After the further feeding of Sophie, the two women each curled up in a corner of the couch cradling mugs of steaming marshmallow-capped cocoa and sat for a moment in companionable silence watching the leaping flames in the fireplace. The dancing shadows played games with the expressions on their faces as Virginia ordered Sophie to "Tell me what happened!"

The fire burned low, forgotten in the rush of words, as the girl finished her story. The nurse wiped her eyes and expelled a sigh.

"Thank you for listening. I never thought I'd begin to accept what happened to me, but in telling you, I realize I have in some small way. I'm going to have to learn to face the pain, live with it, and somehow go on. I'm not sure I'm brave enough to think *how* yet. Perhaps in figuring out how to make a living, I'll be able to keep busy and exist, and I don't have a clue how to do that. I'm in a foreign country, separated from my home and family by war, torn from the man I love by death, and I'm old at seventeen but have no job skills or money. I know hardly anyone but Bill and you," she smiled gratefully at Virginia. "Where do I start?"

Deep in thought, her hostess rose, replenished the fire, and returned to the couch. "I think you should start with what you *do* know. For one thing you know Czech, English, and German. Any French?"

"A fair amount. We spent one summer in Paris when I was ten, and I always found languages easily learned."

"So you have language skills. This war has shown us how provincial we are. There's a crying need for reliable interpreters to help us communicate with our allies. Through my husband, I know some officers in that area, and I'd like you to let me work on this. I don't want to raise your hopes too high, but I have the feeling they may be pleased as punch to have you."

"Pleased as punch?"

"Delighted. And as to your personal life," she paused, "I think knowing Bill may be an answer to that if you want it to be. I've seen his face light up when he sees you. He looks like a man in love, which seemed very natural since you *are* Mrs. Sedlecek."

Sophie looked doubtful. "In name only. I never noticed he was interested in me."

"What have you noticed since you got out of Austria? Do you care about him, or did you sit there day after day because you had nowhere else to go? I think you'll have to answer those questions eventually because since you've been gone, Bill's condition stopped improving. He watches the door, and the light in his eyes dims a little bit more every time the person who walks through it isn't you.

Sophie said humbly, "I didn't know. Of course I care about him, though I really know him so little, but my love died with Marcus. I don't have any left to give."

Virginia snorted. "I used to think that. The *great love* was the only love. Don't count on that! I fell in love with a married doctor when I was just out of nurses' training. He was handsome, funny, and romantic. He loved me, too, but after a while, I realized that he also loved his wife. I finally made him choose between us, and he stayed with her. I was sure life was over. I moved to a new town to end my lonely days—and I met George. He was balding, a little chunky, and a high school teacher. I started going out with him just to have someone to do things with, and he was comfortable. Gradually that comfort and that kind, good man became more and more important to me, and one day I knew I loved him. It wasn't the same kind of love I'd felt for Richard, but it was real and solid. I thank God daily that George loves me and had the patience to wait for me to find out I loved him, too. There are many kinds of love, Sophie, and don't close the doors of your heart when one of them is denied you by circumstances. You are alive and young and have much to give. I pray you won't let your love die in the dusty attic of the past!"

It was Sophie who wiped her eyes now. "Where is George stationed?"

"I don't know for sure because he can't tell me. I get letters from him almost daily, and I miss him dreadfully. He's so good, and I hate to think of him caught up in a war. I just hate it! But we're *all* caught up in it, and we can't get out until it's over. I hope you'll meet him someday. You probably won't be impressed, but it doesn't matter." She smiled fondly as her thoughts dwelt on George. "He would be one of the most handsome men alive if he looked on the outside like his wonderful inner self."

For a moment she was lost in thought, then she shook herself and said, "Time for bed, Sophie. We have to clear out of here fairly early, so it'll be up with the birds—or before them—to pack and be ready to go. And we'll need a little extra time because we are going to stop at a dress store on the way back and get you something different to wear. You've worn your escape suit long enough. It's time for the butterfly to come out."

Sophie looked puzzled at that statement, but Virginia just heaved herself to her feet, gave the girl a hand, and pulled her upright. Taking Sophie's face between her hands she smiled as she said seriously, "I wish you happiness and peace. You've already been through adventure and excitement and grief. May you find yourself and your way in life. You're so young, and you have much ahead of you. God bless you, dear girl!" and she kissed her on the forehead.

Sophie's eyes brimmed with tears. She hugged Virginia as she said, "I know I can truly feel thankful. I have a friend."

Chapter 14

The delight on Bill's face when Sophie walked through the door proved Virginia's theory. She was so touched that without thinking, she moved to his bed and kissed him on the cheek.

"I've really missed you, and I'm so glad you're back," he said earnestly.

His mother spoke from behind her. "I'm glad you're here, too, Sophie. Now I'm going back to the hotel and really relax. I know you're in good hands, Son." She kissed Bill's forehead, gave Sophie a hug, and walked out of the room, leaving husband and wife alone. The girl wondered how much she knew about their relationship.

"You look different." He struggled against his lethargy to focus on the change.

"I'm wearing a new dress," she said gaily and began to tell him about her holiday on the beach. He seemed to drift in and out of consciousness, and she found herself becoming increasingly worried about him. He was dozing when the doctor walked into the room. He looked concerned, too, and motioned her into the hall.

"What's gone wrong, Doctor? He looked much better a week ago."

"Nothing I can put my finger on. He was doing so well, but he's slipping backward now. He sleeps more and eats less. I'm hoping you can make a difference."

"How?"

Sophie sensed his disapproval. "He kept asking about you when you were gone, expecting that you'd be back sooner."

"I'm sure Virginia explained to him that she was called in and couldn't get back to the shore to bring me back."

"Well, now that you are back, if you can get him to talk, eat, and try to get well, it might get him back on the road to recovery. I think he may have just given up."

"How sick is he, Doctor? Will he be able to get well? Is it more than the bullet wound?"

"The infection was rampant when he got here, and he was generally so exhausted that we feared for his life. He must have had so little food and rest for a long time, and when the infection struck, it went wild. We were encouraged when we got that under control but now . . . it is as though he had so little stamina to fall back on that he's too weak to try. See what you can do. We've done about all we can."

She struggled to put on a confident air as she reentered the room. A look of pure relief crossed the patient's face when he saw her.

"I was afraid you'd gone again."

She made up her mind right then. "I'm not leaving you again, Bill. I had the time alone I needed to think and pray and begin to think ahead just a little. First you have to get well, and I'm staying right beside you until you're up and around and ready to move ahead, too."

"And then, Sophie?"

"We'll cross that bridge when we get there. Now, are you going to stay awake and hear about my trip to the Jersey shore? Or be rude and fall asleep again?"

"I'll try. You'll really stay with me?"

"I really will, Bill."

Two weeks later Bill, Sophie, and his mother were sitting on the lawn, relaxing in the weak winter sunshine when Dr. Ray approached them.

"You're a happy-looking group. I wish all my patients were coming along this well. Bill, I think you owe a lot to your cheerleaders here. You should be out of here in another week or so, but I doubt if intelligence will let you go too far."

It turned out he was right on both counts. Eleven days later, his orders to report to the Strategic Planning Committee at the Pentagon arrived, setting the date of January 20 to report. That only gave him a week and a half to find a place to live and be ready to go back to work.

When the older Mrs. Sedlecek left that evening Bill asked Sophie why she'd been so quiet. She'd hardly said a word for two hours.

"I know it's time for me to go off on my own, and I'm scared silly. Virginia is sure I can find a job doing translations, but I won't be able to stay on in the nurses' quarters. It should work out all right, but it feels really intimidating at this moment."

"Don't say no until you've heard all I have to say, Sophie. Washington is a difficult place to find housing anytime, but now that the war is on it's like looking for a needle in a haystack. I know because I lived here before I went to Europe. I shouldn't have any trouble because I have a high-priority job and every effort will be made to find me a place. I'll just tell them I need a two bedroom, two bath apartment, and you can stay there. Wait! Hear me out! You could do the cooking if you can't afford to help with the rent. It would be like having a roommate. I promise not to touch you. This will be convenient for you, and I won't have to live alone."

She looked distressed. "It's not fair to you, Bill. You will be tied down by a phony wife when you should be dating and having fun. No, I can't let you do it."

"I'll be too busy to be chasing girls. I'll be honest with you—I'm hoping that you'll like living with me enough that you'll want it permanently. Please give our marriage a chance. I won't push you into any arrangement that you don't want. I'll wait for you to come to me, and until that time, our relationship will be strictly platonic. You know you can trust me, don't you?"

"Let me think about it tonight, and I'll let you know in the morning. I do want you to know that I think it is dear of you to offer and, of course, I trust you. But I can make no promises, and I truly don't know how I feel about you other than as a beloved friend. Goodnight now. I'll see you in the morning." She kissed him on the cheek and left the room.

Chapter 15

Sophie did move into an apartment with Bill, and it was as he said. They were roommates and shared the duties and expenses in their own way. Sophie did get a job as an interpreter, and she was glad to be able to help with the rent. Bill had much more money, but Sophie contributed what she could and did all the cooking, laundry and cleaning. He would have been happy to hire someone for those chores, but she insisted, not wanting to be obligated to him. Also, wartime Washington was not an easy place to find domestic help.

Their jobs kept them busy all hours, and Sophie traveled quite often to various places in the United States and overseas where her interpretive skills were needed. When they both happened to be at the apartment, they were usually tired, but Sophie was aware that Bill desired a different relationship than the one they had.

In 1944, there was a lull for both of them, and they spent almost two weeks in each other's company. For the first time in a long while, Sophie really saw Bill. He was almost dangerously thin, his brown hair was liberally dusted with gray, and his face showed deep lines of pain.

"Are you well? You seem so thin. Is that old wound hurting you?"

"I think I'm just tired. As soon as I get a little rest, I'll be all right. I'm probably just getting old with aches and pains," he explained lamely.

She felt it was more than that. When she wrote to her mother-in-law in Iowa, she mentioned it and suggested that a visit would be most welcome. Libbie appeared two days later.

The kitchen became the favored room in the house. From it, emanated all sorts of wonderful odors, Czechoslovakian in nationality. The apartment became a real home, and evenings were spent in loving conversation and occasional plays and entertainments. Sophie cried when she took Bill's mother to the train station two weeks later.

She went back to a quiet apartment, made a simple meal, and as she and Bill ate it, she realized how empty their lives were. They both were missing the cheery, affectionate woman who had made their world brighter for a while.

Sophie woke up about three in the morning and on the way back from the bathroom, noticed that Bill's light was still on. Thinking that he'd fallen asleep, she knocked very quietly and opened the door, planning to turn off the light for him. He seemed to take up so little space in the big bed, and she felt a surge of pity for the kind, good, brave, dear person who had been her companion and support for over two years. He must be so lonely. Then she realized that his eyes were open, and he was just looking at her. She hadn't bothered to put on a bathrobe, and she became aware that her thin, cotton nightgown was quite revealing with the hall light on behind her. In her embarrassment she turned to go, when he said, "Sophie," very quietly. And then, "Please."

As she stood there with her hand on the doorknob, she thought about the dead Marcus, Bill's love and faithfulness, her own emptiness, and the future. Quietly she turned back into the room, walked over to the bedside table, and turned off the light. As she slid between the sheets, she felt his waiting arms and heard him breathe, "My love." And so Sophie began her married life.

Chapter 16

They moved to Cedar Rapids, Iowa, in April of 1945 when Bill was finally released from the army. When they got off the train, there was a Czech band and a crowd of people, led by Libbie and Emil Sedlecek. She met more old friends of Bill's than she thought she'd ever remember, and everyone was so pleasant. Apparently, her story was known because there seemed an outpouring of kindness, not just to Bill but to her as well.

The crowd escorted them to a small, white clapboard house with a porch in front, much like the houses on each side of it. The community and Bill's parents had made a large down payment on it in gratitude for the hero's service. It was sparsely but nicely furnished, and Sophie was overcome by such generosity.

The first week was spent visiting and entertaining. After that, they talked about what Bill might do now that he was home. His father had a furniture store near their home, and it was natural for Bill to go to work there, where he'd worked when he was younger. He walked to the store about 7:30, came home for lunch, and finished the working day at 6:00 when the store closed. It was a nice, quiet life that they shared.

Sophie found it difficult to get accustomed to America. As long as she stayed in "Czechtown," it felt familiar, but when she ventured out, everything seemed to go so fast and be so foreign, even though she could speak the language. She knew that several neighbor women only spoke Czech and that they never went outside the community without their husbands, and she understood their feelings. Since she had never driven, she took the bus when she

161

needed to go any distance, but she was able to walk to destinations around her home. She kept hoping that she might become pregnant but that didn't occur. Bill's parents would have been so pleased, too, but almost a year went by and still she waited.

It was the third week of 1948 when Bill came home early one day. He was pale and perspiring and immediately went to the couch. He assured his wife that he was all right but just a little tired. The next morning he didn't get out of bed. Sophie called Dr. Fiala who poked and prodded the sick man. Then he shook his head and called an ambulance.

The doctor at the hospital took Sophie and Bill's parents into his office after the results of many tests had come back.

"Has Bill always been this thin?"

His mother answered. "Ever since he was in the war but not before that."

"I believe that he has been pushing himself ever since, and his body is finally giving out. Apparently his injuries in the war permanently weakened him, and I'm not sure there's anything we can do about it. I think rest is the only possibility and good, nutritious food with as little stress as possible. Can that be arranged?"

It was. Someone else was hired at the store, and Sophie took care of him at home. Bill hated his uselessness, but they all assured him that it was temporary. He read a great deal, and for a while, he tried to write about his war experiences "for the children" that they hoped to have. But the children didn't come nor did his health. He grew weaker and weaker and died quietly one night in July. He had just seemed to fade from life.

He had a military funeral with honors, and as his casket was lowered into the ground, his wife knew that the living connection with her past was broken. She had loved him faithfully, with gentleness but not with passion, and he had appreciated all she could give and had not demanded more.

After the lunch at the church, Bill's parents asked if she would like to leave her house and live with them. They had loved her from the first and were so grateful for all she'd done for their son. She loved them, too, but yearned for solitude so that she could think what might lie ahead. Thanking them graciously, she promised to spend one night a week at their house, and then they walked her to her empty home.

Dry-eyed, she sat in the bedroom she'd shared with Bill, waiting for the terrible grief she remembered. Instead she felt a gentle sadness, and the tears began to fall for Bill's short, brave life and for his parent's loss and for the friend who had offered her his love and name. She wept silently for the children that had never come into being and for the unknown future she faced.

That night, alone for the first time, was spent tossing and turning, wondering where her life could go. She'd married so young, before she'd hardly known herself, been a wife as women she'd known were intended to be, and instead of caring for children, she had cared for Bill as his health failed. And now what would she do? She was terribly frightened and lonely. Then she remembered to pray.

"Oh, Lord, You have taken care of me all my life. Don't let me forget that. Please help me not to fear the future. Guide me, I pray, to be who You want me to be and then to do what You want me to do. I will *try* to place my future in Your loving hands. Thank You, Father. Amen." And she slept.

She and Bill's parents were going over the bills from the funeral and the cemetery the following day when she had the first glimpse of what lay ahead. They had offered to pay the expenses when Sophie proudly showed them the ledger she'd kept of Bill's money, and she told them there was enough money to pay for everything. Mr. Sedlecek's eyes widened when he saw the neat, accurate columns of numbers.

"Were you a bookkeeper, Sophie?"

"No, Emil, but I liked working with numbers in school, and my father used to have me check the ledgers for the factory when he felt there was some problem. It's just the way my mind works, I guess."

"This may not be the right time to bring this up, but I have been wondering how the store will run without Bill. I'd like to ask Leo Koza to work out in the salesroom, but that would leave us without a bookkeeper. Would you be willing to give it a try? I don't want to offend you by speaking of the business so soon, but it does provide for us. I would pay you, of course."

She started to cry.

"I'm sorry, Sophie," he said contritely.

"Oh, dear Emil, I'm crying with relief. Last night, I wondered how I would ever make a living. I prayed for an answer, and I think you just gave it to me. I'm sure Bill would be so grateful to you, and I assure you I'll do my best. I hope it will be good enough."

That was how Sophie began a life of her own.

She enjoyed working in the store. Primarily, she was the book-keeper, but since it was a family business she filled in wherever she was needed. She began to feel at home among the people she met. Many of them had left their pasts in another land, and she felt a kin-ship to them. She bought a small car, took driving lessons, attended community events, and was becoming recognized for herself rather than her deceased husband's family.

Almost five years later, Emil gathered the employees together after work one day and told them he was seriously thinking of selling the business. He wanted to talk to them first, but he felt sure that the time had come for him to retire and spend more time with Libbie. This brought smiles to the faces gathered round him. They knew that Libbie spent every day at the store, so he could hardly spend *more* time with her, but they understood what he meant. He wanted time with her to do some of the things they'd dreamed of doing when they grew older.

Chapter 17

Sophie remembered what the Lord had done for her earlier, and she knew she must trust Him again. Two days later, she answered the phone to hear, "This is Edward Benesh. Is it true that Emil is going to sell the furniture store?" She had occasionally seen Mr. Benesh, the hands-on president of the Czech National Bank, since she'd taken over the bookkeeping duties at the store, but she really didn't know him personally.

"He hopes to be able to do that so he and Libbie can follow their dreams a bit. He got a good offer. They haven't been the same since Bill died. I pray this will bring some new beginnings and adventures into their lives and heal some of their grief."

"They deserve to retire. They've worked long and hard in this community. But that's not the reason for my call. I wonder if you could come down to the bank tomorrow afternoon at 4:00. Will you be able to leave the store a little early?"

Puzzled, she responded, "I suppose I could. Is there any trouble with the account?"

"No, I just wanted to visit with you about something. I'll explain when I see you."

Ed beckoned her into his office when he saw her enter the bank.

"Hello, Mrs. Sedlecek," the older man said. "And how are you doing?"

"I don't know yet, Mr. Benesh. Emil just told us at the beginning of the week."

She felt herself relaxing but sat up straight at his next sentence.

"What will you do, Sophie?"

She was surprised that he knew her name since they hadn't ever conversed before.

"I don't know, Mr. Benesh. I'm praying about it."

He laughed awkwardly. "Maybe the bank can be part of the answer to that prayer. I've talked to Emil and a few others, and they all agree that you are a first rate bookkeeper. I wonder if you'd like to come to work here at the bank. I've noticed that you are very good with numbers, and I need a person who can speak good Czech to my customers who don't speak English. Many of my tellers are younger, and they were born in this country with little interest in learning the Czech language. I'd like to offer you a job at the bank as a teller. It will be a bit different from what you've been doing, but we'll train you, and it's still working with numbers. Will you consider it?"

"I don't think I need to." Her voice broke as she answered, "I'd be honored." She smiled shyly. "I have lots to learn, but I like to do that."

She'd been afraid that he'd offered the job out of pity but the look of pleasure on his face belied that.

"I think I'll have a top-notch employee. Thank you, Sophie. When would you like to start?"

"I want to talk it over with Bill's parents, and if it's all right with them, I could start next week. Would that be satisfactory?"

The following week began a new phase of Sophie's life. With the Sedleceks' blessing, she went to work on Monday morning and started her training. Much to her surprise, she found it easier than she'd anticipated. She discovered that learning one thing at a time suited her mind, and Mr. Benesh went at her pace. First she was an assistant to a teller, and the following month became one herself. The customers were able to converse with her in Czech or English, so she was popular with all ages. She began to suspect that some of the little old ladies used a small deposit as an excuse to visit with her, and a few teen age girls came in every other day to report on their love lives (or lack of them). She really enjoyed the customers, and they became almost family to her.

It was a little over a year later that Mr. B. called her into his office. She wondered if she'd been too friendly or if there'd been a complaint. It was with some trepidation that she knocked on his door.

"Come in, Sophie."

He rose from behind his desk and asked her to be seated. He looked so serious that she wondered if she'd be fired on the spot.

"Do you like working here, Sophie?"

"Very much!"

"Is your teller job satisfactory?"

"Yes. I really enjoy the customers. If I've talked to them too long or if I'm not fast enough, I can improve, I'm sure. Some of the little old ladies are so lonely for someone to talk to, and I enjoy hearing about when they were younger. I do try to only really converse when there's no one waiting. Has someone complained?"

He smiled. "No, Sophie, no one has complained. Quite the opposite. I've watched you dealing with a variety of customers, and from the businessman to the elderly woman who is lonely, you treat each with interest, kindness, and efficiency. I hear so many comments about that nice young Mrs. Sedlecek. I wondered if you'd like to try another part of the banking business. I think you'd be very good at it. I've been thinking of trying something new. Ever since I took over the bank from my father three years ago, I have wanted to explore some new possibilities. One of them is to have a woman loan officer. You may not be aware that there are no women in that position in any bank in the city. I think 1949 is the year that should be changed. Will you be game to give it a try? We'll train you, so you'll be comfortable in the position." He looked at her hopefully.

"I'm finding that I enjoy a challenge. It's funny; I never saw myself as anything but an accessory and it's exciting to find that there is more to me than that. I appreciate your confidence in me, and I'll try to live up to it."

He rose, and they shook hands on it.

Sophie's world outside the bank was beginning to blossom gradually, too. She helped teach the Czech language in late afternoon to young people who were interested in learning their grandparent's language—or their grandparents were interested in having them learn it. Then she started teaching classes about Czechoslovakia— its history and culture—and found that many adults were joining the children in class, which led her to start a night class for adults.

That turned out to be a lovely experience because many of the older people had stories to tell of their own experiences, and she learned more than they did. Unnoticed, she became a valued member of the community. Walking down the street where all the stores were situated, many people greeted her, and it wasn't "Mrs. Sedlecek" anymore. It was "Hi, Sophie!" Bill's parents were so proud of her. She overheard them say, "She's our Bill's wife."

One night in the Czech culture class, someone raised their hand and asked, "Why did you come to Cedar Rapids?"

"Let's have a potluck at my house next week instead of class, and we can sit around and tell our stories. Mine's pretty long, but there'll be room for more." And there was! When they left their heads were full of stories from people they'd known for a long time but had never really heard how they ended up in Cedar Rapids, Iowa. It was an exciting evening.

As Sophie was climbing into bed, she thought about those stories and in particular, one that was told by a dear, white-haired lady named Blanche Seville who worked in one of the county offices.

Her father had come to the United States to make a better life for his wife and four girls. He worked on a farm near Cedar Rapids and saved his money to bring his family over. The year before they were to come, he managed to make a trip back to Czechoslovakia and talk to them about the trip and what kind of place they were coming to. In his homecoming, a little child was conceived and nine months later a son was born.

By this time her father had saved enough money to bring his family to the United States. Blanche's mother made all the preparations to bring her four girls and new son to be with him. Blanche was one of the little girls. Her uncle sailed with them to help her mother and the children. Blanche didn't describe the voyage except to say that the baby boy died during the crossing, and she didn't know what was done with his little body.

When they arrived at Ellis Island, her uncle was sent back to his homeland because he had no sponsorship and they never saw him again.

Blanche's oldest sister had had polio a few years before and was crippled. They were not allowed to leave the island for three weeks while her father desperately sought proof that she didn't have a communicable disease. Blanche didn't say what it was like to live on Ellis Island, but we all could imagine her mother's grief over her son's death and fear in a strange country whose language she didn't understand, living in dread that she would be sent back to her homeland.

Three weeks later, they were put on a train with notes pinned to their clothes, telling their destination with the hope that someone would help them off at the right stop. And that's how Blanche came to Cedar Rapids. There were more stories that sometimes brought tears and sometimes laughter.

Chapter 18

It was only a year and a half later when Mr. Benesh called her into his office for another serious discussion.

"Sophie, you've been a real success as a loan officer, and now I notice other banks are hiring women for their loan officers. You proved it was a great idea. I've liked the way you meet a challenge with enthusiasm and eagerness. Now I have a new project I'd like to try, and I think you're just the one to start it. I know you've been working with young and old people in this community."

She looked surprised. "How do you know that?"

"I'm part of this village, too, and there's not much I don't know that goes on here. Besides, so many people praise you that it would be hard not to hear about 'that wonderful Sophie!'

"I want to have a community relations department, and I'd like you to be in charge of it. In a sense, you'll invent your own job, but I'll work with you and the vice presidents to brainstorm some ideas and try to get a picture of the department's possibilities. One of the advantages of being a private bank is that we can try some things that larger banks might overlook."

It turned out to be a most interesting change for Sophie. She was encouraged to be a personal banker but also to see the needs of the community and how the bank might help meet those needs. The days when she'd been overwhelmed by the bus rides in the city seemed far behind her. She bought some professional clothes, a rather sporty used car, and never looked back (except in her rearview mirror). Bill's parents were so proud of her, and on the night each week that she spent with them, they always wanted to hear what she'd been doing. They'd aged a good deal since their son's death, and since Mr. Sedlecek had sold the business and retired, they had quietly grown old. He looked to her for advice now and she was so glad to be able to be of service to the two fine people who had loved her so generously.

Part of her job was instituting community projects, and she had great joy in drawing on the talents of some of the lesser-known members of the community as she promoted the Czech heritage for the whole city to enjoy. The bank started to develop a reputation for civic betterment, and some of the local businesses that had used the larger city banks changed their accounts to the Czech National Bank. Mr. Benesh was very pleased with the job she was doing.

It was almost two years later that he asked her very seriously to join him again in his office. By that time she had lost her previous fear of that inner sanctum. She was a bit surprised, though, to find four of the local, established businessmen already seated around the conference table. Ed pulled out a chair for her, and she was greeted with enthusiasm—and respect.

"Sophie, here's what we are thinking about," he began. "You know that Czechoslovakia was well known for its glass production, and now there is very little being made since the war and the occupation. We are considering the possibility of starting a glass factory here."

She must have shown her surprise.

"We are only investigating it right now, and we want you to help us do that. You know many of the older people in the community. Do you know of any that were involved in the production of glass? Will you find out what supplies are needed, and how expensive a startup would be?"

"Did you know that my father owned a glass factory in Czechoslovakia?'

The men all looked surprised.

"Then I guess you *are* the right one to take on this project, Sophie," Edward Benesh said. "I knew you'd do a thorough job for us, but I didn't know the background you had for the project. Let us know what you need, and let's meet in two weeks to see what you've found."

When they met again, Sophie had the projected expense figures for three different-sized new factories, figures on the cost of four existing buildings in the community that could be refitted for the proposed new use, the cost of basic start-up equipment, and a list of the local people who had been involved in glass production in their native country at one time. After the group looked over her report, they asked her to give them her impression of the feasibility of the idea.

"I think it has real potential with two possible liabilities. It would need to be well capitalized because getting a standardized production would not only require considerable effort, but if it is to produce art glass of high quality, it will take artisans time to perfect their techniques, and it is well known that art doesn't occur on demand but on inspiration. Thus there would be no profit for some time, if ever, if production could not be achieved. From my research, there's a good market for art glass, and there is a container market that we could compete for. The cost of supplying the raw materials, which do not occur naturally here, could be offset by quantity purchases from the suppliers." She paused.

"You mentioned two possible problems. Capitalization and ...?"

"Labor. There were at least twelve people in the community who had worked in glass production but none were glass blowers. They would be useful in the production end but not in the creative part. I enquired about the cost of hiring some established blowers, but it would take big bucks to lure them and their families away from their current locations. And two or three major payroll expenses could threaten the whole project."

"So what is your bottom-line appraisal? Do you think those problems could be overcome, or are they insurmountable?"

"Only you can decide what you five want to invest in this idea. It seems like a natural, considering the ethnic reputation already established and would add to the employment in the area. I do have a suggestion for the problem of the need for skilled personnel that you might consider. Do you know anyone behind the Iron Curtain who could get some of those old glass blowers and their families' permission to leave the country? As I understand it, the glass factories were converted to wartime use and have never been converted back. I assume some of those fine artists are working at other jobs and might be glad to have the chance to pursue their craft again. I'm not sure how the current government would look at letting them go, but if we didn't make an issue of their value, it might be possible."

"Good job, Sophie!" her boss said. "You've given us a lot to think about, and when we've looked over the projections you've given us, we'll meet again."

It was only three days later that Sophie was asked to step into the bank president's office. All five men were there.

"We've thought it over and think it's something we should pursue. We aren't to the point of buying a building yet, but we are willing to finance a trip to Czechoslovakia. We have decided that you are the natural one to go—if you are willing. We've given some thought to this. You're familiar with the industry and probably already know glass workers that you could talk to. You speak the language and you don't look too official. This trip would just be to sound things out. We aren't asking you to smuggle any families out in your suitcase. We'd have to go through official channels to get people through the Curtain. Would you be willing to be our scout?"

"If it's all right with Bill's parents, I'd like very much to do it. I just can't leave them if they feel they need me. If they'd been my parents, they couldn't have been more loving and supportive. I'll ask them and let you know tomorrow."

As it turned out, they were so proud of Sophie's success that they wouldn't hear of her turning down the trip.

Just then, the lights went on in the airplane and Sophie came back to the present. Her seatmate had apparently been lulled to sleep by the younger woman's exciting story. Sophie didn't mind a bit. It had given her a chance to relive her past just as she was about to reenter it.

Chapter 19

Prague looked grey and depressing as Sophie was driven through the streets in a dilapidated taxi. She had not been there since she was twelve years old, but she still remembered the beautiful buildings and the colorful displays in the windows of the shops. There had been a parade that day and ever since, she'd thought of Prague as bright and wonderful. She could hardly believe the change.

The people had been so gay and friendly then, and now no one smiled. Everyone seemed to be hurrying somewhere without looking up from the pavement. She'd noticed the feeling of tension immediately at the airport. Most of the immigration inspectors were Russians, and everyone was being questioned and all luggage searched. Even though she had nothing to hide, she felt nervous. The woman going through the things in her suitcase wanted to know why she had come to Czechoslovakia.

"I plan to return to the town I lived in as a child and to visit relatives if I can locate them."

"When did you leave this country?"

"I left in June of 1942."

"Why did you go?"

"My parents were afraid that one of the Nazis was going to take me away. I was only seventeen, and they could have done nothing to protect me."

"How did you leave the country?"

"The underground smuggled me out."

"Where have you lived since then? I see that you have a United States passport now."

"I went directly to the United States when I left here, married an American, and have lived there ever since."

"Have you been in contact with anyone in this country?"

"No. I have tried, but mail doesn't seem to go through. Someone from our town contacted me after the war to tell me that my parents had died when a bomb hit their house, and I had no brothers or sisters, but I hope to find some of my cousins and perhaps some neighbors.

Grandmere Hersh saw her tears when she returned that evening.

"Come and sit with me, Child, and we'll have some tea together. I even made your favorite kolaches, the ones with apricots from our tree. You see, not everything is changed. It must seem to you that all of your past is gone, but that is not so. Your past lives on in your memories and is never gone. It is the present, here, that is gone for you. Your life has gone on in a new way, and it must be hard to come back and know that the people you loved are no longer here and familiar places have been destroyed. But you couldn't have gone back to the life you had here because you are not the same person anymore. It may seem sad to you, but it is really the moving of time, which only goes forward."

She had the table set with her best china cups and the blue teapot with the kitten looking through the flowers that Sophie remembered from the special times when she'd seen it as a little girl. They sat down in the little wooden chairs, and the older woman poured the tea with a hand that was not quite steady. They took their first sips in silence.

"Oh, Grandmere, I miss them so! I think of my dear mother and how sad she looked when I left that day. It was the last time I ever saw her. And father cried! I had never seen him cry before. I wonder if I should have stayed with them. Wasn't I wrong to leave them? I should have stayed and died with them!"

Her teacup clattered into its saucer, and she burst into tears, sobbing uncontrollably. Her grandmother handed her a handkerchief and let her cry as she gently patted her shoulder. When Sophie paused to take a breath, the wise old woman spoke again.

"Think back, Sophie, to when you left. Do you think you would have still been here when the bombs came? Do you think that your parents would have been able to protect you from that German left-enent? What would have happened to them if they'd tried to do that? Do you think their grief would have been less if he had taken you away? At least this way, they knew you had a chance to live. Think what that meant to them! Word got back to them that you were on your way to America, and they were so happy for that. And they were sad, too, but they had hope that they'd see you again. And, as a Christian, you have that hope, too.

"I assume that I am closer to death than you are, though God only knows. I've seen so many people die." She paused here, and Sophie could see her reviewing the departed faces from the past. She looked so sad. Then she brightened as she continued. "Death has become a friend in many ways. So many of my loved ones have walked through that door, and someday I will, too. It is the moving of time. I thank God for the hope that my faith brings me, hope that I will be reunited with my loved ones again and will be with my dear Emil and see your sweet mother's face and greet my beloved son. Oh, what a day that will be! And I'm not sure that the length of someone's life matters. If we are all to be reunited, then it is only a matter of waiting until we see each other again. What joy is in that thought!"

There were a few others that Grandmere told her about and among them were her dear friend Sylvia's parents. She went to see them later and found out that Sylvia had married and lived in Milan, Italy. She got her phone number and called her the next day. Her old friend was so glad to hear from her, and they made plans for Sophie to fly to Milan when she left Czechoslovakia.

In the meantime Sophie pursued information about glass blowing and glass blowers. She even talked with some that she had known that worked for her father. They were old, but some were interested in getting back into the trade.

Chapter 20

Sylvia met her at the plane, and it was a wonderful reunion. She looked even prettier and was very well dressed and happy. She loved her husband, and they had three children who were in their teens. When she took Sophie to her home, it was a lovely apartment with plenty of room for a guest.

"I'd like to show you a little of Italy, Sophie. Rolf will be working in the city, so he can keep track of the children, and we won't be gone long." They left the next day and had a marvelous time and saw wonderful sights, not even noticing how long they'd been gone. When they reached Florence, they suddenly realized it had been more than two weeks, so they decided they would go no further south.

The second morning they were there, Sophie woke to darkness. She tried to will herself back to sleep but finally gave up and laid quietly thinking of all the history and art and beauty surrounding her. She walked in her memory through the city and treasured it all again. She had reached Michelangelo's Plaza on her mental stroll when she sat straight up in bed, energized by the idea of actually being there when the sun rose over Florence. She held her watch to the light filtering in through the window from the street lamp outside and saw it would soon be dawn. Galvanized into action, she dressed quickly, did the minimum on her face and hair, scribbled a brief note for Sylvia, grabbed her camera, and let herself quietly from the room. The lobby, though brightly lit, was empty, and she paused, wondering for the first time if this was a good idea to go by herself into the dark morning streets. Then the desire to see the city "born anew" overcame any misgivings, and she pushed out the door into the night/morning.

She was glad for her wool slacks and warm blue sweater, and she stepped out quickly to get her blood moving. The street lights shone golden on the old worn pavement and the rough stone bases of the buildings. When she looked down at the water of the Arno as she walked across the Pont de Vecchio, only a few stars were reflected there. Her speed increased in her race with the dawn. Passing the row of large buildings beside the river, she entered the maze of small streets beyond them.

Sophie hadn't brought a map, but she knew the direction of the plaza, so she just aimed uphill and urged herself on. She hadn't realized there were so many twisting, upward streets, and once she almost turned back after a lane turned into a cul-de-sec, but her dream of dawn over Florence drove her on with increased determination. No one was about of whom she could ask her way, so she just pressed upward. When she stopped to decide on her course at an intersection, she became aware of the silence. It was as though for one magic moment she had the whole city to herself—and then a rooster crowed, and she dashed on.

The sky was lightening when she saw the balustrade ahead, and she hurried up the incline before almost strolling on the blessedly level plaza. Stopping at the southern corner, she was awed by the beauty of the twinkling lights below, reflected in the dark twisting ribbon of the Arno. Bramonte's dome on the cathedral was only faintly visible as was Giotto's bell tower. Gratefully, she sank onto the railing and drank in the beauty. She took her camera from its case, uncertain when a moment might come that could be captured on film but was quite prepared to find this experience too subtle to be recorded except in memory.

Imperceptibly, the light increased, and as she glanced around the plaza, she noted a figure at the opposite end of the balustrade. She hadn't noticed anyone when she entered the plaza, but in the dim light it would have been difficult to see anything. The other person, also apparently enchanted by the dawn, seemed unaware of her presence, and she redirected her gaze to the growing pink glow that began to wake the sleeping city. She was reminded of

Freddie Gofre's "Sunrise" from the Grand Canyon Suite as the light strengthened. There should be music to accompany this miraculous rebirth of the day! Her camera forgotten, she watched the first rays of the sun touch the dome, move on to the bell tower, and then drench the city with its warmth. She suddenly realized that she, too, was bathed in light.

Then the spell was broken by a paroxysm of coughing from her fellow observer. She looked over with irritation at the cause of the interruption of the magical moment, but her emotion changed to one of concern as the coughing continued, unrelieved. Suddenly the figure leaned straight forward from the waist with head hanging down and grasped the railing. Gradually the quiet resumed.

In an instant she was back in the barn, frozen with fear as Marcus leaned over with his upper body perpendicular to the ground, his head hanging down and his body shaking with muffled coughs.

She heard a voice cry, "Marcus!" She knew it was hers, but was it during the war or in the present? The sense of unreality continued when she heard, "Sophie?" Then she was running across the plaza toward the figure now running toward her.

There was some disagreement among the tourists on the bus that had pulled unnoticed into the plaza on the "Florence at Daybreak" tour. Seven (all women) thought the couple embracing so frantically were the most romantic thing they'd ever seen. They justified their decision by assuring the rest that they could see tears running down the woman's face. The other thirty-two were not convinced since they suspected it was a cheap attempt on the part of the tour company (who knew the exact time the bus would be there) to shine up a mediocre tour called "Romantic Italy." By the time they went on to "Breakfast with Michelangelo's David," there was a sullen silence on the vehicle. But the seven were still watching the clinging figures as the bus roared around the corner and out of sight.

Chapter 21

She was afraid to step away from his warm embrace—afraid to look at his face and find him changed too much or not Marcus at all. She imagined he felt the same anxiety. Then he gently held her away from him, and they looked at each other, seeing the present person through the eyes of the past.

It truly was Marcus! His face a little thinner, his curls cropped and dusted with gray, and deep lines of pain combined with smile lines at the corners of his eyes, but those were the same gold-flecked dark brown eyes that she remembered so well. There was a difference that she couldn't quite capture though—and then she knew. The bitterness was gone, and she looked into a face at peace with life.

Stepping back from their proximity a little awkwardly, he appeared taller and thinner than she remembered, though with the same broad shoulders. He was dressed neatly in gray slacks and V-necked sweater over a pressed white shirt open at the neck. He was tanned and healthy looking as though he spent time in the sun or was on holiday.

From his expression, she felt she'd passed inspection, and it was confirmed when he drew her to him again. All he said was, "It's as though those years had never been, and we are young again."

They finally sat on the balustrade in the warm sunlight, and she spoke first. "I feel like a part of me is alive again now that I know you didn't die in that barrier zone. All these years I've suffered, thinking that I caused your death by my stupid clinging to that wedding dress. I've seen you running back in order to distract the Germans a million times—and the moment the bullets hit you and spun you around has been in my nightmares and waking dreams ever since. I tried to go to you once Bill was in the hands of the men in the trees, but I guess I fainted because of the blood loss and woke up on a plane flying to America."

He gently wiped away her tears and held her shaking hands.

"All those nightmares are past now. I am alive and well, and I can't tell you how I've longed for this moment. I never could find out what had happened to you and Bill. It was as though you'd never been."

"Apparently getting us out was not really legal in a neutral nation, so they probably made an effort to forget it. And I didn't come back and look for you because I was so sure you were dead. When you fell . . ." She covered her face with her hands for a moment, and when she looked at him again, her eyes were swimming with tears. "I finally did try to look for you, though, because I went back to that Swiss border last month, before I returned to Czechoslovakia, to put flowers on your grave and try to tell you goodbye, but there was no grave there."

Suddenly he stood up, threw an imaginary cape over his shoulder, bowed from the waist, and said in a very deep and sober pretend voice, "Miss Sophie, will you do me the honor of breakfasting with me this morning?"

It was so theatrical, and rising, she dropped him a deep curtsy as she answered in a very high, sugary voice, "Why, Mr. Marcus! I'd loooove to."

Taking his arm, they walked very straight and dignified to the edge of the plaza where they both burst into laughter and went running down the hill, hand in hand, like two joyful children.

Chapter 22

B reakfast was punctuated by casual questions and unbelieving glances. She lived in America; he lived on Lake Maggori. She worked for a bank; he worked for a communication firm. She'd been back to Czechoslovakia and had found Sylvia's whereabouts; he'd gone back but found no one. His parents had been killed in a bombing raid that destroyed his whole town.

"There was one good thing that was found, though. Actually two good things. A few years after the war, I managed to track down my brother's children, Emil and Libbie. They have been adopted by a very nice German family who permit them to spend time with me during school holidays. It allowed me to get to know them and to be able to tell them about their father and grandparents. So many people in Germany were desperately poor after the war, and I was able to help the family financially. That dear family helped me to forgive their county for what it had done to my life. I learned that there are good people everywhere, but they aren't usually the ones seeking power in the government.

The children are almost grown up now, and I think their father would be proud of them. Greta died in one of the Allied bombing raids, and they grieved for her, but from what they've said, she had become a frightened, guilt-ridden woman before she died."

Sadness descended on them both, but it was a shared grief and more bearable. Then a raucous horn on the nearby street brought them back to Florence and their good fortune in finding each other well and whole, and when he reached over to clasp her hand, she could smile through her tears.

Then they got down to the other questions, now that the initial shock had worn off.

"Did Bill make it?"

"Yes, and he told Intelligence all the locations. It was nip and tuck because he was really in bad shape. But he managed to recover and spent the rest of the war in Washington, DC."

"And you?"

"I had nowhere to go so I stayed there, too, and was an interpreter until the conflict ended."

"Where did you stay?"

"I stayed with Bill, as a roommate, and then as his wife." She was horrified to find herself blushing. "I had no one to come back to here, and he loved me and was so good to me and I was his legal wife." She wondered if he felt any emotion at that news.

"What happened after the war?"

"We went back to his hometown in Iowa. He worked at his father's store, and I kept house. There was a large Czech population there, so I fit in quite well, and I found some jobs in the community

"Do you and Bill have any children yet?'

"No, we had no children. Bill died three years later. Apparently, he could never really recover from what the Germans had done, and he gradually weakened until he was gone."

"I'm sorry. He was a good man. What did you do after that?"

"I worried about that because I had so little education, but Bill's father offered me the job of bookkeeper in the furniture store he owned, and when it closed four years later, the man who was president of the local bank suggested I work there. I found I really liked it and apparently did well."

Did she only imagine that he hesitated on the next question?

"And have you remarried?" He smiled. "Are you the banker's wife?"

"The banker already has a wife, and she's a dear friend of mine. No, I never remarried. And what about you? Do you have a family? Children?" The question had been bursting to come out but once it was out, she was terrified. He looked happy. He looked married. Unfortunately, the waiter arrived at this time to inquire if they need anything more.

Post waiter he answered, "No." He smiled gently. "I just never found a woman like you."

Uncertain how seriously to take his response, she blurted, "But there are girls like me on every street corner." When she heard what she'd said, all the resolve in the world could not hold back the tide of rose that suffused her cheeks.

He smiled, then chuckled, and then dissolved into gales of laughter. Some of the other diners tittered, then joined him, not knowing the cause but finding his merriment contagious. She tried not to laugh but soon was rocking in her chair and gasping for breath.

He wiped his eyes and managed to get out, "I think I've seen a few of those girls, but they didn't remind me of you," and then he was laughing again.

It was the nine chimes from Giotto's bell tower that caused Sophie to leap to her feet.

"Oh, Marcus, I forgot about Sylvia in the excitement of seeing you! She'll think I'm dead! And I was supposed to check on the bus tour to Assisi when I went past the desk. They didn't know if there were enough people signed up to warrant the trip. My thoughtlessness may have caused us to miss it, but I wouldn't have traded seeing you again for *anything*."

She looked ready to flee so he quickly said, "I've rented a car for today because mine is being repaired, and I would very much like to go to Assisi, a place I have looked forward to seeing. Would you allow me to take you and Sylvia to that lovely hill town?"

She looked thrilled, relieved, and embarrassed all at once.

"I'll talk to her and be back down in a few minutes," she promised.

Sylvia looked a little dazed as she met Marcus in the promised time. Sophie had burst into the room babbling about Marcus and Assisi while pulling her out the door. They were in the car and on their way before she began to make sense of the situation.

"So you are really alive and did not die on the Swiss border? What a wonderful relief for Sophie! And I imagine it was a relief for you, too." They all laughed, and the day progressed into one of great joy for the three travelers. They entered the beautiful city of Saint Francis with anticipation and voracious appetites. Marcus parked the car in the parking lot at the lower end of the city and arranged for a picnic from a small restaurant nearby. He carried the carefully wrapped sustenance as they strolled through the upward-twisting, quaint, cobbled streets, into the lovely open square, and then up and up until they reached the old fort brooding above the town. The landscape stretched out before them like the background of a Leonardo Da Vinci painting, and they drank in its beauty.

Marcus seemed to have thought of almost everything because he pulled out a waterproof red-and-white striped tablecloth and napkins to match, and spread their meal on it with a flourish. He uncorked a bottle of local wine and due to lack of cups (the one thing he'd forgotten) just passed the bottle around, so they all shared "the common cup," as he called it. It was a festive meal. Feeling satisfied and a little winey when they were done eating, there was a quiet time of peace when they all lay on their backs on the tablecloth and watched the clouds move majestically across the sky.

Sophie looked over at Marcus and suddenly she saw him as he'd been fifteen years earlier. The dark curls were back, and the closed expression on the angry face. As quickly as it had come, it was gone. She stared at him in the present, and saw the clipped dark hair edged with grey, the quiet amusement in his dark eyes, and the relaxed look his body had as he leaned on one arm on the tablecloth. She felt that she had looked at him with two different eyes, and then it all came together and she was seeing him as he was. Her binocular vision saw a youngish man, comfortable in himself, latent with energy, confident, and thoughtful.

That was the moment that she accepted the fact that he wasn't dead and that she need no longer blame herself for his death. Sophie felt lighter, as though the gray mantle of guilt that she'd worn all those years was lifting from her shoulders and was flying away with the scudding clouds above. The deep breath she inhaled made her feel that she might be able to fly, too. And then she started to cry.

Marcus must have been watching her because he was at her side immediately, pulling her into the safety of his arms. She sobbed and sobbed, shaken by the relief of knowing he was safe. Trying to speak, she could only gasp out words between sobs. "You're alive!

I didn't cause your death. I've carried the guilt so long. I'm *so* glad you're here!" And she held on to him for dear life.

Sylvia began to be anxious about her friend after about twenty minutes, but Marcus said to her quietly, "She's held those tears in for a long time. I hope she'll get them all out."

It was midafternoon when they entered the church at the lower part of the city with its famous frescos by Giotto. The quiet was a benediction on them, and when they wandered into the lower level, it continued with a mass being said and a choir of monks whose singing echoed through the stones of the ancient building.

On the way back to Florence, Marcus asked Sylvia about herself. When he found that her husband worked for EuroCom, he quickly asked her which office he was located in.

"He's in the Milan office. Why do you ask?"

"Because I work for EuroCom, too. I wonder if I've ever met him."

"His name is Rolf Laska, but I doubt if you'd know him. It's a huge company. But who knows? Maybe someday you will."

The conversation was easy, and occasionally they would lapse into Czech as they talked about their homes, now taken from them. Marcus was a skillful driver as Sophie knew he would be. He had an air of strength and competence about him that made him appear quite powerful. His quick smile put her at ease though, and she felt a relaxation that she hadn't felt since she was a child. She felt safe.

As they drew closer to Florence, she suddenly noticed that Sylvia was very quiet in the back seat. She looked at her friend and saw that she was quite pale.

"What's wrong, Sylvia?"

"I just got a migraine headache. Remember when we were growing up and I used to get them? They always go away in a couple of hours if I can just lie down for a while. When we get back to the hotel I think I'll go right to bed. Sorry, Marcus, because I'd like to get to know you better, but when I get one of these I'm not good for anything. It's been a wonderful day, and I wouldn't have missed it for anything. Thank you so much!"

186

Sophie was waiting comfortably in the lobby when he returned, grateful to him for seeing Sylvia back to the haven of their room. She smiled that gratitude at him, and the warmth in his eyes was the proper answer. They walked hand in hand to a nearby restaurant.

"What a wonderful, golden day!" she remarked as he seated her and then himself. "How can we ever thank you for making it unforgettable—the kind of memory one hugs about oneself on the difficult days. We, both Sylvia and I, will always treasure it"

"We can try to make a day pleasant, but it is only the good Lord who makes a day blessed."

At that moment, in the midst of her surprise, the food arrived—steaming and aromatic. When the plates were distributed, he continued.

"Let's thank God not only for this food but for this glorious day."

He took her hand, and they bowed in silence as their thanksgiving rose with the incense of the food.

He amazed her! She had not expected him to say grace in a public restaurant but instead of embarrassment, she felt delight like an iridescent bubble within her.

They ate hungrily in an easy silence. The food tasted wonderful, and she was aware that it was part of a larger joy, as though she and Marcus were wrapped in peace and communion.

When they laid their forks on their plates, she asked him when he'd found his faith. She hadn't felt it was a part of his life when she'd first known him, but those were such stressful times she might not have known.

"I found my faith the usual way—on my knees. The Swiss had to wait for nightfall to try and get my body out of the mined area. When they reached me, they found me unconscious but alive. I'd lost a lot of blood, and for a while they thought I was a goner. But you know how tough we Czechs are!" He smiled at her conspiratorially. "After they released me from the hospital and I began my work for the allies, I found I had no one to support me, no way to go home, no family, no friends, no money, and no country. The only one I could turn to was God, and He had been waiting for me all along. I had to repent from a load of bitterness and hatred, and once I gave that up I began to find the peace and support I needed so badly. Looking back, I think much good has come into my life because I was driven to my knees. And now He has given me this blessed day with you!"

Her eyes were misty as she said to him, "No wonder you seemed diffcrent. You are! I, too, turned to God on a beach in New Jersey, and He has sustained me ever since. He hasn't made life easy, but He's been beside me through the rough and the smooth and given me a joy in my heart that's unrelated to what happens. Aren't we fortunate to have such a wonderful Lord?"

They smiled in agreement and felt the presence of that God.

When things returned somewhat to normal, the subject was not resurrected. Instead, he said, "So I seem different from the Marcus you knew during the war."

She thought for a moment. "I really didn't know that Marcus in a normal way. We were in such a frightening, desperate position, and we never had time to talk of common things. Of life and death, yes, but not of friends and food, of school and growing up. Now I wonder why I felt I knew you so well."

"Shared dangers can bring people together quickly. I think you did know me well, but I think I may have grown up a little. Hardships have a tendency to mature one."

She studied him for a moment. "You seem more gentle to me, not as nervous or critical. And from the crinkles by your eyes and the laugh lines around your mouth, I think you've learned to laugh at the world without anger. You seem more at peace."

After a moment's reflective silence, he responded. "I believe you're right. How different it is to see one's own growth through another's eyes! We can only ask those who have walked beside us and then examine ourselves to see if it's true. I found life so difficult at times that I had to learn to laugh or go mad. It was a hard-won lesson but worth every painful stripe."

"And me?" she asked shyly. "Do you see any of the young Sophie in me now?"

"Yes. The way you look straight out at the world with courage and kindness and often affection. You still stand proudly, facing the world with interest and curiosity. I feel that you, too, are slower to judge." He paused. "But you were always ready to smile."

For a few minutes both were lost in memories. Then a cuckoo clock proclaimed the hour of eleven and she started.

"I must go back to the hotel. I hope Sylvia is feeling better." She rose to her feet.

Sophie gave him the money for the dinner as they walked the short blocks back to the hotel. "I must really insist on taking you to dinner after you provided us with that wonderful tour." He was reluctant but finally honored her intention. She wondered if he needed the money.

For the first time, the peace between them seemed to disappear and a strained silence resulted. It was as though they were in a cloud of unanswered questions about the future, and neither knew how to break through it.

Just before they turned the corner into the brightly lit square, he stopped her and gently drew her into his arms. She went to him as a child going home—confidently and willingly. He kissed her cheeks and then her mouth. It was almost in disbelief that they could actually be together at last. She would have stayed forever, but he stepped back and in the dimness she could see him studying her face as though memorizing every plane of it.

"This is goodbye," she thought, and felt again the pain of the years apart. Could she bear to lose him again? She assured herself that she'd had life without Marcus before and that she would again and looked straight into his beloved face, so she would never forget it.

"When do you and Sylvia leave tomorrow?" he asked as they stepped out into the square.

"We thought we could take our time getting packed, do a little more sightseeing, and then head north toward Venice. I've never been there, and I always dreamed of staying at the Danilli someday."

He opened his mouth to say something when the bellboy from the hotel came running toward them.

"There's an urgent call for you, sir. We've been looking for you."

"Do you know who the call is from?"

"I believe it's from your office in Rome. They said they'd stay on the line until we found you."

He handed the boy a handsome tip and said hurriedly to Sophie, "I'm sorry. I asked not to be disturbed unless it was something really important, and I think it's a situation that has been brewing and must have become a crisis. I'll see you later." He moved quickly toward the lobby.

She followed with a slightly startled look on her face, and when she entered the hotel, there was no sign of him by the telephones.

Sylvia had taken her headache to bed, so Sophie sat on one of the comfortable chairs in the sitting room and reviewed the day. It had all seemed so wonderful until the end of it, and she had a sinking feeling in her stomach. How had the bellboy known who he was? He wasn't staying at their hotel. Had he set it up with the young man beforehand? Was the signal his appearance in the square? She remembered that kiss in the darkness, but he had immediately propelled her into the square, and it was almost as though the bellboy had been waiting for his cue. If he had had that call, why wasn't he talking on the telephone when she came in a few seconds later? Had there been a phone call?

Her head was beginning to ache now, and she thought of going to bed, but she knew she would not sleep. What could have happened? The day had been such a happy one. They'd been together the whole day except for the time when he took Sylvia back to the hotel when her headache started. Had he hired the boy then? Perhaps he realized it was going to be awkward to say goodbye without making some kind of plan for the future, and he felt this was the easiest way.

The light hurt her eyes, and she turned it off. The darkness seemed to be full of questions, and she started to cry. She'd cried so much in the last day that she must be dehydrated. He said he'd see her later, but when she looked at the luminous dial on the clock she saw it said midnight. It had been over an hour since he'd left her, and if he planned to see her, he'd have knocked on the door before now. Reluctantly, she walked into the bedroom, shutting the door on her troubles and worries—or so she thought. Five hours later, they were still with her, and she felt a desperate compulsion to get out of Florence. What if they should see him on the street? She'd die of embarrassment, and he might, too.

She walked into her friend's room. "I'm sorry, Sylvia, but I want to leave right now. How is your head? I'll drive. I'll pack. I just have to get out of here."

Her friend looked at her groggily. "What happened?"

"I'll tell you about it on the way."

"Is it Marcus?"

Sophie nodded.

"But he seemed so nice and so fond of you."

"I think he just didn't want to have to hurt me," she said sadly. "He didn't know how to say goodbye."

Chapter 23

It was almost twilight when they finally reached Milan. It had been a very quiet trip from Venice. Sophie went over and over her questions on the way from the city of canals, but since no answers seemed to fit, she gradually sunk into silence. Sylvia wondered if she'd actually seen any of the city's wonders because when she suggested they leave early, Sophie had been quick to agree. Actually the older girl would have been delighted to get home early to her dear Rolf after the sad events of the last four days.

When they finally pulled into the parking garage under the expensive apartment building where she lived, she could hardly wait to get into her familiar home with her beloved husband. Her time with Sophie had been wonderful until Marcus, but the sadness in her friend's heart had begun to settle in her own.

Sophie was very tired, even though she'd done none of the driving on the way into Milan. She wondered idly if it could be the weight of her heavy heart that was the cause of the great weariness she felt through her whole body. She kept assuring herself that someday she would feel happy again, but her emotions failed to respond to reason, and the future stretched ahead endless and gray. She knew she'd been happy before her trip to Florence, but it was so hard to remember how it felt.

They unloaded the trunk of the car in silence, each in her own thoughts. Even her suitcase seemed elephantine to Sophie, and when she saw the "out of order" sign on the elevator, she just wanted to sit down and cry. Sylvia, with her homecoming in sight, began to take the stairs in stride. She was on the first landing as her friend started dragging herself and her leaden suitcase up the first stair. Sophie heard her cry of delight and hurried up to where Sylvia stood, looking at an exquisite arrangement of violets, lily of the valley, and tiny pink rose buds in an elegant crystal bowl.

"I wonder what lucky lady received this," she said. "I don't think Rolf would have done this because he wasn't sure I'd be home tonight," but she still sought the name on the card attached to the bowl. All she saw were the bold initials DID. Her mind grappled helplessly with them, and she could only look in confusion at Sophie.

Her friend of course knew no one in the building, so she asked, "What is the name of your apartment manager? Maybe he has this bouquet for all the ladies who have to walk up the stairs."

This absurd idea almost seemed a possibility when they reached the second-floor hallway and saw a tall vase overflowing with lilacs whose peculiar aroma brought spring to Milan in September. Sylvia reached curiously for the card attached to the bronze container and saw the initials YOU.

Both women were completely mystified. The weight of their suitcases was forgotten as they hurried to the next landing. There was not one arrangement, but two. The first card said THINK and the next one had only THAT I on it. The luggage landed with a thud, abandoned, as the two friends ran to the third floor hallway. Two more bouquets in the glowing procession awaited them there. Sylvia read the first which said "WOULD" as Sophie spied "EVER" on the second. If anyone had been watching they would have been astonished at the speed with which two weary travelers could conquer a flight of stairs.

The cards on the next two magnificent banks of flowers said "LET" and "YOU." Ahead they could see the door to Sylvia's apartment and the scent of the dozens of roses by it filled the stairway. There was only one card on these and written on it was "GO?"

Sophie turned and saw Marcus, resting casually on the first step of the next flight. The fragile spark of hope that had come to life in her heart was burning with such intense joy that she thought she might set the building on fire. Then she was in his arms and home at last. They didn't even notice Sylvia eagerly entering her apartment.

Chapter 24

When the kisses slowed, they sat on the stairs with their arms around each other and answered some of the questions foremost in their minds.

"Why did you leave without seeing me?" he asked.

"I thought you didn't want to see me again, and when you dashed away into the hotel but were not at the phones and then you didn't come up to the hotel room later, I believed you'd tried to find a way out of saying goodbye."

"Oh, Sophie, how could you think I didn't want to see you? I thought I was so obvious that I might scare you."

"I knew what we felt before, but we are two different people now, and I didn't know how you felt about me as I am today. I was afraid to hope."

The conversation was interrupted by a long, reassuring kiss.

"To go back to the hotel," he said. "I had to keep in touch with my office, and I knew the situation I was talking about was getting tense, so when I took Sylvia back to the hotel, I told the bellboy an important call might be coming for me and when we expected to be back. I had left the manager's number because, like so many business deals, confidentiality was necessary, and it was in his office that I talked until after two, trying to get things straightened out. When I went to your room, I knocked quietly because I didn't want to disturb anyone, but when you didn't answer I thought you must have given up and gone to bed. I was sure I'd see you in the morning, so I didn't worry."

"Oh, my! I didn't sleep. It was during that long night that I put two and two together and came out with seven. I sat in the dark a long time and then went into my bedroom and shut the door, so my tears wouldn't wake Sylvia. At five, I woke the poor girl up and insisted we leave, terrified that we might run into you, and I'd cry and you'd be embarrassed. We left about five-thirty."

"Yes, I found that out—but much later. I pulled up a chair in the hall outside your door at six-thirty, so I wouldn't miss you. By eight, I was getting concerned, so I went down to the desk to ask if the clerk if he'd seen you, but he said he hadn't. Back to my chair I went. At nine the maid came to clean. She'd looked at the checkout list, so she knew you were gone. I found out later that the desk clerk had come on duty at 6:30, so he wouldn't have seen you. If I hadn't remembered Rolf's name and assumed I could find his address, I think I'd have lost my mind. We had never mentioned where we lived because I felt we had such a long future ahead for us, and it seemed unimportant."

(Time here for another kiss.)

"I remembered you mentioning you were going to go to Venice and stay at the Danilli, so I felt sure I had time to catch you here in Milan. I must admit I did drive very fast to get here, though," he said ruefully. "And I did call and make sure you checked in at the Danilli. But when I went there the next morning to catch you, they told me you'd checked out the afternoon before."

It was at this point that a weary woman rounded the corner on her way to the fourth floor. Marcus looked at Sophie in horror.

"I forgot to take down the 'out of order' sign!" He moved swiftly to the elevator, pushed the button, and gave her a grimace as he stepped into it.

When the elevator door opened upon its return to the third floor, Marcus found Sophie waiting with her arms open wide and joy and love shining in her face. His eyes misted with tears as he stepped forward to claim her.

"I don't believe I could ever be any happier than I am now. What absolute joy to have a door open and find you waiting for me!" He took her by the shoulders and held her gently away from him.

"Sophie, I have never asked this question before. Will you do me the honor of becoming my wife?"

She looked at him steadily and lovingly, as though etching this moment in her memory. He began to feel anxious until she said simply, "Yes, Marcus." He was hugging and kissing her when the elevator door opened unnoticed beside them. They heard a gasp and looked up to see Rolf's astonished face disappearing behind the closing door. He'd apparently been so astonished that he forgot to get out on the third floor.

"Does Rolf have a sense of humor?" he asked.

"Yes, I understand he loves a good joke."

"Before he collects himself and gets back up here, let's go in the apartment, and I'll go in the bathroom and you act as though nothing has happened." There was a twinkle in his eye that she just couldn't resist.

They swooped into the apartment, quickly letting Sylvia in on the joke while they giggled like children when they recalled the absolute astonishment on her husband's face.

All was in place when they heard Rolf's key turn in the lock. Sylvia greeted him with all the enthusiasm that she felt after being separated for two weeks. She noticed a strange expression on his face as he asked immediately if Sophie was there.

"Yes," she answered, "but aren't you glad to see *me?*"

He must have realized how he'd sounded because he gave her the welcome for which she'd been waiting.

"Sophie!" she called and her friend came innocently into the entryway.

"Rolf, you're home!" She shook his hand warmly. He just stared at her.

"Were you just out in the hallway?" he asked.

"That's how I entered the apartment," she answered innocently

He looked totally bewildered. "I know this will sound completely crazy." He took a deep breath. "I thought I just saw you out in the hall in the arms of the head of the EuroCom Company."

Now it was their turn to look astonished. "What's his name?" Sylvia demanded.

"Frederick Sedlecek."

At that point Marcus sauntered into the room. "Did someone call me?" he asked innocently.

"Mr. Sedlecek?!" said Rolf at the same instant Sophie exclaimed, "Marcus!"

"One and the same. Rolf, I feel like I know you quite well after hearing these two ladies talk about all your virtues on our excursion day. I believe we only met once, and you are kind to remember me." The two men shook hands before he turned to the puzzled women. "I never really had a chance to introduce myself properly. My middle name is Marcus, and it was the only one I used when I was working for the resistance for fear my family would suffer if my real identity became known. I realized when you were gone from Florence that I didn't know your last name, either, Sophie, because I only knew your husband as Bill. That almost threw me into a panic."

Rolf spoke up now. "Will someone please tell me what is happening? I let you two girls go south for two weeks, and obviously all sorts of things have happened — quickly!"

Marcus answered smoothly for them. "Sophie and I were old friends from the war and we ran into each other in Florence on Michelangelo's Plaza at sunrise. Doesn't that sound romantic?" He looked over at Sophie, and the smile he gave her was warm. "And it was. Through a misunderstanding we got separated, and I had to track these ladies down here at your apartment. I didn't want to lose this woman again!" He reached for Sophie's hand.

Now it was her turn. "What did Rolf mean when he said you were the head of EuroCom? You said you had a job with them."

"I do. It's a big job to head a company of this size. I started out when the war was over. I didn't have much money except for what various allied armies had paid me, but I had done a lot of work in communications for them, and the destruction was so great across all of Europe that I started locally to rebuild telephone service. One thing lead to another, and it became quite large."

"Quite large!" Rolf snorted.

"I guess I was in the right place at the right time. And there were good, experienced men and women looking for jobs and a new way of life. The war changed people so much. They were in new places being asked to do things they'd never done. Many just couldn't go back to what they'd been. I gathered a really talented group of people, and together we built the company."

Rolf spoke up. "I'm glad to hear about how you began, but I already knew about your philosophy. I was one of the people you picked up, though, at a local level. The pay is great, we're treated with respect, and we feel that what we think is important to the company. I've never worked in a situation where my boss wanted to know my opinion on things and would really consider any suggestions I made. I believe, in a sense, that EuroCom is my company, too.

Marcus put his hand on Rolf's shoulder. "You are absolutely right. It isn't *my* company. I could never run it by myself. It's a group project, and that's why it's succeeded. Whenever you get the talents of a number of people working together, it multiplies your possibilities of doing well."

He looked at Sophie and Sylvia. "Sorry. I didn't mean to get going on the company philosophy, but I think you can see that it's really a big part of me. I had no wife, no children, no living relatives, and the company became my family, my life." He looked at Sophie with love shining in his eyes and said, "I think that's going to change now," and he took her in his arms and gently kissed her.

She looked like a different person than the drooping, grieving woman who had entered the building earlier. She glowed with happiness. She could hardly believe what a difference a half hour had made.

It was Sylvia who brought them back to the practicalities of life. "I'm hungry! We haven't eaten since breakfast, and it's almost time for dinner. Does anyone want a sandwich or some fruit or a cup of coffee? I can't offer dinner because, knowing my dear husband, Rolf has probable eaten everything in the apartment except the wood-work." She smiled at him fondly.

Marcus responded. "I'll take you up on that sandwich, Sylvia, and then offer to take us all out to dinner at the fanciest restaurant in Milan. We have so much to celebrate!"

It was Rolf who spoke next. Sophie was still trying to assimilate all that had transpired since she got out of the car.

"I'm for the sandwich, but would you mind skipping the fanciest place and changing that to the best local restaurant? We have a great one a few blocks away, and I think you'd enjoy it without having to dress up for the fanciest."

"Sounds great to me! I would like to go home and put on fresh clothes, though, because I've been sitting (on the stairway) in these for a long time." He grinned at his lady love.

They gobbled down sandwiches, after Rolf had made a run to the store. Sophie found that she was suddenly famished and ate her share wholeheartedly. Conversation was punctuated with laughter and someone looking in on the scene would have thought they'd all been drinking.

Belatedly, Marcus said, "Would you mind if I returned thanks for what we *have* eaten, not for what we are *about* to eat?"

Sylvia laughed as she said, "If you can truly be thankful for these hasty sandwiches."

He took Sophie's hand, under the table. "Dear Lord, we thank You for these hasty sandwiches." A few giggles were heard. "They feed our bodies, just as You feed our souls. But mostly, I thank You for a lost love found out of the whole world. It could only have been Your loving hand that brought us back together again. How can I possibly thank You for that amazing blessing? Thank You for this home and these new friends who make me welcome and feel like family already. My heart is full to overflowing with gratitude to You who have seen me through so many things. May I be of service to You and never forget to thank You. In Your Son's name, Amen."

Sophie wiped her eyes and blew her nose. The look she gave Marcus was one of wonder and love and joy, and he felt that the sun was shining on him.

When he rose from the table, he turned to her and asked, "Will you ride along with me? I'd like you to see where I live, and," he paused, "I don't want to let you out of my sight."

"I'm afraid you will have a hard time getting rid of me now. I was going to ask you if I could go with you."

As he helped her into his sleek Lamborgini, she looked a little overwhelmed. "One of the perks of my job, Darling. I'll sell it and get a used sedan if you would feel more comfortable."

"Oh, no. It's lovely. I've just never been in a car remotely like this one." She grinned. "I suppose I could get used to it if I forced myself."

The powerful car moved them swiftly through the beautiful countryside once they escaped Milan's busy streets. Again, she was aware of how safe she felt with him. She relaxed against the leather seat and surreptitiously studied the profile of the man she loved so deeply. It was as though the years had fallen away. How they would have loved to have a car that could have carried them so swiftly to the border! She fantasized for a moment. They probably could have driven right into Switzerland in such a splendid vehicle.

Then Marcus was gently shaking her shoulder. They had stopped at a beautiful wrought iron gate. "I'm sorry," she said contritely. "I must have fallen asleep. I was so happy and relaxed and off I went."

"We're home," he said quietly.

They proceeded up the semicircular drive and stopped in front of a building so large that the word "edifice" sprung up in Sophie's mind. It was enormous! She started to laugh.

"What makes you laugh?"

"When I paid you for the dinner the other night, I thought you needed the money. I see how wrong I was."

He smiled at her. "I was afraid I would injure your pride if I didn't take it. I have made lots of money. I didn't have any other life than the company. The funny part about this big house is that I live in three rooms—a kitchen, a bedroom, and a study. Oh, I do have a bathroom, too. This house was purchased to entertain clients and employees. We often have big, catered affairs. And I continue to live in my three rooms."

She squeezed his hand. "When I look at you, I remember the bitter man I loved with all my heart, and now I see you successful in your work and lonely but somehow happy still."

"The Lord has given me hope and an inner joy that I can't explain. It puzzles me, too. And I wonder about the fact that I never found a woman to love. I think I had faith somehow that I'd find you. Or maybe, once given, my heart wasn't there to give anymore."

He squeezed her hand.

"Now, how would you like to see my three rooms? I'd take you on a tour but we have to leave very shortly if we're to meet Sylvia and Rolf on time. I'll just take a quick shower and change into clean clothes, and we'll be on our way." That said, he got out of the car and helped Sophie out.

They walked up the cascade of marble steps, across the marble veranda, and into the house. Sophie could hardly take it all in. From the entry, she looked into a large, marbled room surrounded by columns that held up three balconies. It was the grandest room she'd ever seen. It was Marcus's hand under her elbow that propelled her down a hall to the right, or she'd just have stood and gawked. They went down several more halls until they came to a plain door.

"Don't leave me," she pleaded. "I'd never find my way out again."

"We're back in the servants' quarters now. This is the part that could be modernized, so it will look quite different."

He was right. When the door opened, it revealed a modern room that could have been in an elegant apartment building. The room they entered was paneled in walnut with a thick, dark green carpet and had comfortable-looking chairs, a large modern desk, and a sleek television. It looked almost impersonal. There seemed to be no evidence of the owner.

"Where are your personal things?" she asked.

"I have very few, Sophie. I've traveled light since I knew you. I learned it then, and there's never been a reason to change."

"Oh, Marcus! That reminds me. I have something of yours that I think I should return to you."

He looked puzzled as she reached into her purse.

"I always carry it with me because it is the most precious possession I have."

She handed him the little notebook. It looked older than when she'd found it that night in Virginia's cottage but it had been cared for (and carried) lovingly.

He looked mystified, and then he looked at her in wonder as he recognized it. "Where did you find it?"

"The only thing I had left of you was your backpack that you gave me when you took mine. I held on to it tenaciously, but I was afraid to look inside. When I finally found my courage, there was nothing of you in it. Clean clothes were all I found. I thought I'd lost the last possible connection with you. As I was despairing I felt something in the bottom of the pack. Then I saw your handwriting for the first time, but there were only codes and directions. At least I had something you'd touched and a little part of you."

He asked quickly, "Did you see the edge of the pages?"

She smiled, as the sun comes out after rain. "Yes. I had just found my peace in the Lord, and I felt it was the most wonderful way He could bless me. That book has kept you with me ever since. But it's yours, and you should have it back at last."

"I do want to look at it later, but I'll return it to you if you want it. Now you can have me instead, though."

That led to an embrace that threatened to make them very late indeed.

He finally stepped back and said, "I'll give Rolf a call and tell them we'll be a bit late. I have something to give to you, and I think this is the right time."

He spoke briefly to her friend's husband and then held out his hand and led Sophie into the next room. It contained a large bed set on a white carpet in a room that was almost totally white. It was stunning after the rich colors of the preceding room. Marcus went to one of the sliding white panels in one wall and when he opened it, Sophie saw many suits hanging neatly inside. He pushed them aside and reached into the very end of the closet. She gasped at what he held up for her to see. It was her *kroje*!

"You still have it! How did you manage to keep it?"

"When they pulled me back into Switzerland, they didn't stop to take off your backpack, and since it was all I had, they kept it with me in the hospital. I know what you mean about your most precious material possession. When I had nothing and was moving through so many war zones, I always made sure your *kroje* was in the safest place I could find. And when I started EuroCom, it was the only thing besides underwear that I had in my suitcase. I still hide it at the back of my closet, out of sight from any prying eyes."

Her eyes were sad as she fingered the familiar garment. "I remember how innocent and happy I was when I did this embroidery and made the dress. How I dreamed of wearing it proudly when I married and how the village would celebrate with me, and I would always be happy with the man of my dreams, and we would live happily ever after. It seems a hundred years ago."

"Sophie, will you marry me in your "garment of splendor"? And then let's finally begin living the happily ever after!"

MOUNTAIN HIGH

Lightning seemed to be bursting on every side as Sue looked frantically for a place to hide. She'd noticed a semi-boarded-up mine entrance on the previous switchback and ran desperately back to it, scraping her leg as she dove through some rotten boards to get under cover within the cave-like entrance. She was hurrying down the tunnel to get away from the flashes of light and booming thunder when a man's voice shouted, "Stop!" She'd always wondered if she would scream if truly frightened and now found the answer. Her scream echoed back and forth within the mine, and even the thunder didn't drown it out.

She was so disoriented by the storm that she couldn't tell if the voice came from behind her or before her. "Who's there?" she quavered. From behind her came the voice again.

"A fellow hiker trying to avoid the lightening, like yourself. I just didn't want to see you fall down a shaft or a stope. If it weren't such a storm, I would never come into a mine. Why were you going further into the tunnel? Hasn't anyone told you about how dangerous these old mines are?"

She thought the question was asked by a critical voice and bristled but then realized perhaps she *had* been ignorant.

"I'm from Iowa," she stammered, "and I've never really hiked on a mountain before. I have an idea what shafts are, but what are stopes?"

"Shafts go straight down and stopes slope down diagonally. Often these old mines are just boarded up or abandoned, and there is no protection for unwary explorers without flashlights."

"I think I owe you a thank you for warning me, but why didn't you let me know you were here when I came in?"

"You must admit you entered rather quickly, and I was startled to see you, too. If I'd known you were coming, I'd have baked a cake, to borrow an expression from an old song."

"Sorry to be bad tempered, but you scared the socks off me."

"And I do apologize for that. Shall we start all over? Welcome to the Lightning Mine. I am the current resident, and my name is Tom Smith. I'm glad you could pop in."

"Thank you for your hospitality." She was beginning to recover her normal good humor. "I was in the neighborhood and thought I'd drop by. Are you serving any refreshments, or am I too late for that?"

"The kitchen is closed, but I can offer you one of our famous water cocktails. Would the lady be interested in that? Our well-known trail mix platter is the special for lunch served in a few minutes."

"My favorite entre! I'm certainly fortunate to be here on Tuesday. My chef sent me off with such a poor meal, and I'm afraid I had a few too many cocktails on my way up the mountain because my canteen is almost empty. I can see I have a lot to learn about hiking in the mountains," she said rather contritely.

"I believe that can be taken care of rather quickly. The Tom Smith School of Mountain Lore is housed right here in this facility, and a new class was just starting."

"I definitely should sign up for that," she responded enthusiastically.

"To register for the class you must give your name."

"Oh, I'm sorry! I'm Sue Smith, probably a close relative. Did you have an Uncle Herbert or an Aunt Ruby?"

"I can't say that I have. Does the name Citirus ring a family bell?"

"No. Is that a real name?" she asked suspiciously.

"If not, my grandfather was nameless. He carried it all his life and even had to live with the nickname 'Tight.'"

"Well, I won't feel so sorry for Herbert and Ruby anymore."

As her eyes became more accustomed to the darkness and by the stabbing light of the lightning flashes, she could see a figure seated against the wall to her right. She couldn't see his features, but he didn't look at all menacing. She began to feel a little foolish for that piercing scream that had escaped her.

As though he read her thoughts, he said, "You have a first-rate scream. Do you practice a lot, or is it a natural talent?"

"Funny you'd mention it. I'd always wondered if I had one, and apparently it was an undiscovered gift."

The storm was continuing outside, so she lowered herself to the floor opposite her fellow mine inhabitant and prepared to wait it out.

"Would you like that water now?" her mine mate asked.

"Yes, thank you."

In one of the lightning flashes she saw a water bottle extended to her. She felt almost an electrical charge herself when her fingers touched Tom's, and she blurted into conversation.

"Do you hike much?"

"Actually, I do. I have a rather sedentary job, and I find hiking relieves lots of stress, besides allowing me to see some of God's greatest work. When you get up high on a mountain, it puts things into perspective by making you aware of how truly unimportant so many things in life are. I've set a goal for myself to climb all the 14,000 footers in Colorado."

"Are you starting with this one?"

"No. I've climbed all but three. I'm here today because I didn't really have enough time to make it to the northwest part of the state, and I want to keep in shape, so I just thought I'd climb two of my old favorites again but I got a late start."

"You're going to climb *two* today?" she asked incredulously.

"Oh, yes. Grey's and Torry's are close together, and as long as you do one, you might as well do both. Even with a late start, it should be possible."

"Do you think *I* could do both?" she asked hesitantly.

"If you're up this far and not suffering from the altitude, I think you have time yet today, depending on how long the storm lasts. Are you in fairly good shape?"

"I walk a lot at home, ride a bike, and run a bit, but all that is on pretty flat ground in Iowa, comparatively speaking. A friend and I are staying in Georgetown, and I determined to make this climb just to prove to myself I could do it—or that I couldn't do it. Would I have something to brag about at home if I climbed *two* 14,000 foot mountain peaks!"

"In the interest of interstate cooperation, I will volunteer to hike with you, and we'll see if we can't get you started on two 14,000 footers. I may create a monster, and you will be off for the others, but I'm willing to take the chance if you are."

There was a pause before she responded hesitantly, "That's very nice of you, but why would you burden yourself with a greenhorn whom you don't know and haven't even seen? For all you know, I might have two heads or be a robber from New York."

"I knew I liked your scream the minute I heard you. Two heads would allow you to get an all-around view from on top of the mountain, and I don't know if a New York robber would get really excited about a water bottle and some trail mix."

"Speaking of trail mix, is it lunchtime yet?"

"I believe it is. How do you want the special served?"

"Any hand out will do."

She reached out her hand into the darkness and felt the warm fist that emptied the mixture of nuts and dried fruit into her palm. Again there was a charged feeling as though energy was passing between them. She tried to keep her hand steady. This was just a casual encounter; why did she keep imagining more? He might be a sixty year old or have pimples or be married. In fact he probably was married. He sounded mature and confident and happy. He might have six children. Her imagination could lead her into all sorts of scenarios.

"Hello? Are you still here?"

"Yes. I'm sorry. Did you say something?"

"Yes. I just asked if you noticed that it's really dark in here. That means that the lightning has passed on. Maybe we bears can emerge from our cave. I must admit I'm curious to see what the storm blew in."

Nervously she jumped to her feet—and hit her head on the sloped ceiling above her. "Darn it!!"

"Are you alright?" he asked with anxiety.

"Bloodied but unbowed," she answered tremulously.

"Well, I must say that your swearing ability doesn't match your screaming talent. You need to work on that a little."

"You can't see it, but I'm smiling. You're pretty good to bring that about after I've made myself painfully shorter by an inch."

He was on his feet, too, and she felt his fingers on her head.

"Ouch! You found the spot alright."

Now his voice was serious. "I think your head may be bleeding. Let's get outside where I can take a look at it."

As they moved toward the entrance, she was aware of her reluctance to leave this dark womb where imagination reigned. Now real life would begin again.

As they stepped out into the light, both the Smiths tried not to stare too obviously, but surreptitiously each sized up the other.

Sue saw a man about six feet tall with very handsome, regular features. The thing she was most struck by was the impression of strength that he gave. His shoulders were broad as well as his chest that was covered by a blue tee shirt that said, "Be good to your mother," with a view of earth from space. His legs looked a little like tree trunks beneath the khaki shorts he wore.

When he caught her curious gaze, she blurted, "Do you lift weights?"

"Yes, I do. As I mentioned, I have a sedentary job and I want to keep in shape for climbing and a few other athletic activities. Do you do weight lifting?"

"No. Do I look like I do?" she asked nervously.

He laughed. "No. You are much too slender for that. And very pretty, too, I might add."

"I'm glad you did. Thank you. I was about to add a thought of my own about how handsome you are. Is that a pleasure or a problem?"

"No one ever asked me that before. I have found it to be both. People notice me, and girls seem to have been interested, but I find people look at me occasionally as just another pretty face." He laughed self-consciously. "Do you have that problem?"

"I doubt if it's my face or figure, but I do find that men sometimes don't take me very seriously, which can be frustrating.

"Now that we've looked each other over a bit, let me look closer at your scalp and see if you've cut your head." And he did just that, his gentle fingers sifting through her hair and making her knees rather weak. "I think you'll just have a nice goose egg later. Does your head ache?" She quickly denied the pain under the sore spot, so he would take his hand from her head and allow her to regain her composure.

"Let's start walking if you still want to try for the peaks," he suggested as he stepped away.

She looked a bit taken aback, and he quickly added, "We have a good walk ahead of us, and we can talk on the way until it gets steeper. It's not much fun to try to come down in the dark, so let's start and see how it goes. We want to give ourselves plenty of daylight."

Sue looked relieved. "So you're still willing to take a chance on a flatlander?"

"You bet—if the flatlander starts moving," he said with an engaging smile. "Besides, I want to see you from the back."

She looked startled.

"I want to see where you hide your second head," he said, with an easy smile.

Sue led the way at a fair pace, feeling self-conscious because of the man behind her, her thin little tennis shoes, and her difficulty with the altitude. He must have been aware of her breathing because he soon said, "Will you slow down a bit? I can keep up, but I'll be worn out soon. Let's pace ourselves for the long climb. That was on page ten of the Tom Smith School of Mountain Lore manual, but I think I forgot to give you a copy."

"Thank you! I didn't want to slow you down, but breathing isn't as easy up here. Why don't you lead the way for a while, and let me see if I can handle it? And if I'm too slow, you can just give me directions and a copy of the manual and go on your way."

They exchanged places, and Tom settled into a slower, even pace that allowed her to be less self-conscious and to breathe.

It was when they stopped to rest and enjoy a drink of water that she rattled off the questions that had occurred to her on the silent climb.

"What would you do for a living if you could do anything you wanted to do? What do you do now? Do you like it? How long have you worked there? Why did . . ."

He interrupted her with an upheld hand. "Were you sent up here to interrogate me by the CIA? The FBI? The IRS? The SPY?"

"What's the SPY?" she interjected.

"I made it up to see if you were listening. Why all the questions?"

She was now quite pink with embarrassment. "I had lots of time to think on the way up, and I wondered about your life. This is such an unusual opportunity. We live in distant states, we have never seen each other before, I'm quite sure we have no mutual friends, and we'll never see each other again. We can say anything we want, and no one will ever know. I propose—don't look at me with that funny leer—that we each get to ask any question we want, but we have to agree to take turns. Usually when people meet, they're concerned that they say something entertaining or not sound stupid or be careful not to reveal any secrets or to pick their teeth. We don't have to worry about those things."

He thought a minute. "You know, I think it's rather an intriguing idea. I get so tired of feeling my way around in conversations with women, and it would be relaxing to just be right up front. And fun to ask all the nosey questions I wanted. All right, let's do it. Since it's hard to talk walking up hill in tandem, we could make our inquiries when we stop to rest. And that would give us plenty of time to think up *good* ones." He grinned wickedly and held out his hand.

"Agreed!" she said and tried to ignore the tingle she felt from his hand. She was beginning to wonder if the lightning had given him some kind of electrical charge.

"Since you've asked the first questions, I'll answer some of them. I work in a large company in the accounting department. I got my college degree in business, thinking it would be a good general base to get a job. The courses were pretty interesting, and I didn't have a real passion for anything else. I've worked there five years, have moved up to assistant manager in the department, like the people with whom I work, and I'm bored." He looked startled. "I haven't even allowed myself to think that, and here I just blurt it out. But I don't know what else I'd really like to do. I was trying so hard to fit in and do a good job that I never stopped to ask if *I* liked it. I'll need some time to think about what I might like to do. When we get to the top of Grey's, I'll hope to have an answer to your first question.

You really have a knack for asking questions no one ever asked me before. Do you do it for a living? Ah, that's not my next question. I'll come up with another one, and if you're satisfied I've answered well enough, then it will be your turn."

They hiked up a steep stretch on the mountainside, and neither had enough wind to talk, but when they reached a saddle, he flopped down on the ground and she selected a smooth rock to perch upon. When they got their breath, he said, "Now it's my turn. Let's see . . . Are you married or have you ever been married?" In spite of their agreement that any question was acceptable, it seemed to Sue that he looked a little embarrassed.

"Interesting question. No, I am not, and have not been, married. Are you mar—"

"Aha! You were going to ask me a question, and it isn't your turn! Cheaters aren't allowed at high altitudes."

"I noticed I was having more trouble breathing. I guess I'll have to give up cheating if I'm to make it to the top."

She had her question all ready when they reached the next resting place—and he was waiting for it.

"Did you grow up as a happy child in a happy home?"

He had his mouth open to answer but shut it again. "Ah, the unexpected. Yes, I grew up happily with a normal, undivorced family which included my mother, father, and little sister. I also had two cousins who lived nearby and were like siblings to me. It was in Holdrege, Nebraska, on very flat ground. My dad worked for the railroad, so he was gone quite a bit, but when he was home he was truly there, and my mom was always there. I also had relatives around, so I never felt lonely. My uncle and aunt lived on a farm a few miles outside of town with their two children, and I spent lots of my time with them because I loved the outdoors. After I was ten years old, I worked for my uncle every summer as a hired man. He paid me and everything! Since I've grown up, so to speak, I often thank God for my childhood and the freedom and happiness I had. My parents moved to Florida when I was in college, and I've missed the old home place. I still go back to visit my cousins, though.

And now a bonus answer to the questions you didn't ask. I have never been married and am not married now. And these are my own teeth." He flashed her a big grin, rose to his feet, gave her a hand up, and started walking on.

Her watch read 11:00 at the next pause. "I'm glad I started fairly early. Do you think we can still do it?"

"The Lord willin' and the water lasts."

"What's your question, Tom?"

"I'm going to borrow one from you. I want to hear about your job and what you would do if you could chose anything in the world. You may know right off the bat, but if not, I'll give you until the top of Torrey's Mountain. I think you asked a great opening question, and I've been enjoying thinking of my answer. I hope you will have fun thinking of yours. It can be off the wall, but remember, we have to be honest."

"I'll need time to find that answer though. I've taught school for the past few years and have loved it and the children, but I've realized lately that I don't think I want to spend my whole life as a teacher. I have many interests, and I haven't focused on what other things I might want to do. Do you know how you can put that off? When things are fine, it's hard to stop and really examine your life and see if it's truly what you want. I've been putting it off, and perhaps that's why I asked you about your dreams."

"What's a nice fellow like me doing on a mountain with an Iowa school teacher? I thought you were going to say you were a professional belly dancer or a pilot or a cowgirl. No, don't hit me! I'm only teasing you. I liked *all* my schoolteachers, and I'm sure that Iowa is very nice."

She rose to her feet. "Next time it's my turn," she said menacingly.

They were in sight of the top, though not terribly near it when they stopped to get a drink and to let her catch her breath. She was aware that he really didn't need to stop but did it for her.

"Thank you for letting me rest and for helping me do this. I will truly be thrilled if I can climb one of these peaks. I didn't even dream of two."

"You're doing fine, and I'm impressed. Usually a flatlander doesn't even try. What's your question?"

"What have you found is the most important thing in life?"

"Wow! You don't fool around, do you! But I think that's such an important question, one that we have to keep asking ourselves all the time. My answer would have been different at different times in my life, but I think I've found the one that will last for me. I think the most important thing is to know God loves me and to love Him right back.

"What a great answer! And the fact that it was right there and you didn't have to sit and ponder about it. I have to say that I'm impressed, Mr. Smith."

"The one I'm pondering is the answer I have to come up with at the top of the mountain. But I'm having a good time thinking about it."

When at last they stood on top of the world, or at least the world as seen from the top of Grey's Peak, the view was awesome. Mountains rose all around them, divided by long valleys where trees could be seen at the distant bottoms, interrupted by mirrored lakes. Seeking to find a sheltered spot, they started down the trail to Torrey's and soon found an outcropping of rock, which offered them a place to sit as well as shelter from the wind that moved, unobstructed, across the high country.

"I think I'm ready to at least tell you my thoughts, which are still forming. Are you sure you want to hear this?" he asked.

"Absolutely. For one thing it may help me think up my own answer, but more than that, it's so interesting to hear someone's dream."

"One part of my personality is always looking for better ways to do things, and I'm sure that is why this came into my mind."

She looked startled. "I'm that way, too. I always seem to be searching for better ways to do something or more efficient ways. Interesting."

Now it was his turn to look thoughtful. "Here goes. My job is in middle management, and I feel I'm really in the middle. I get directives from upper management that I often have to pass on to the people below me in rank, so it places me in between in some respects. What I see is that the middle men feel pretty helpless. They try to please the guys above them and the workers below them, and they don't feel essential to either group, so their jobs are tenuous. They want to be loyal but have to watch their backs and put in long hours to compete, which leaves them feeling guilty about their families and the stress just grows. When they try to give those families material things to make up for the time they can't give, it puts them in a credit bind, which often means that if they lose their job, they lose their house among other things. And the stress grows greater.

So what can I offer that would make their lives any better? I'm not exactly sure, but there's something I'd like to try. I'd like to combine my love of the mountains with a business philosophy of bonding groups to form communication links as well as emotional links. I find that men have difficulty talking about important things in their lives, and they get into booze and depression but won't allow themselves to say what's constantly worrying them. I want to bring them up here or places like this to test their mettle, to stress them physically, not mentally. I want to find ways to free them to talk to each other safely. I had a psychology minor. I'd have to go back to school to learn more, but I think there is a chance it could help people. I'd want a component of prayer. It would have to be more than an endurance test. I'd want it to change lives. I'd want wives to come up and tell me how much more content and happy their husbands were after their mountain experience. I may be aiming too high, but I'd like to make a difference.

I haven't figured out the particulars, but I have a vision now of what it could be. It'd be a hard sell to busy people, but I'd want a real cross section of a company. I suppose I could just have middle management groups, but I don't think that's enough. I'd like to have men see each other without their corporate hats on, as people like themselves with troubles and dreams and fears and talents. I'd have to find ways of building trust and cooperation and safety within the group. If one person betrayed the rest, my whole program would fail. I'd want to appeal to the best in every man and have him go home feeling stronger and better about himself and his co-workers.

I hope that doesn't sound too odd to you, but that's what I dream of, and I didn't realize it until now."

"It sounds like a fine goal to me and makes me feel easier about telling you my dream. But we have another mountain to climb—tell me it's not far!—and I'll try to have enough wind to talk."

They hiked on across the saddle, and though it took a while, it wasn't as hard as the constant uphill climb that they'd just accomplished. And then they stood on top of Torrey's Peak and marveled afresh at the mountain ranges that lay around them. Impetuously, Sue turned to Tom and hugged him.

"Thank you so much for making this possible for me. It's an ill lightning that doesn't strike some good—or something like that. You must have started on your mission already because you have made me feel better about myself." As she stepped back she added laughingly, "and about my co-climber."

"I guess a fellow has to go to really great heights to impress you."

They looked around for a talking place and found some sheltered rocks to sit on.

"I'll be brief because I know it's getting late. I, too, like to try and make things better. I'd like to get a few talented people together and offer advice to small companies who employ fewer than 150 employees. I'd want someone who was good at figures to go over the books, someone else who would be good at product relevancy and marketing, and I'd like to work with employee relations. I think I'd have to keep my day job (which I really enjoy) for a while because I'd like to charge only for our expenses at first with the understanding that we would get ten percent of the improved profits for the next two years. I'm not sure how this would appeal to a company, but it seems that they'd have very little to lose and only ten percent of any improvement that developed. If there were no improvements, we wouldn't get anything. But if we were good, we might do well. I'm not sure I could find anybody who would work with me on such a scheme, but I find it quite intriguing to look at the ways a system might be made better. And I think the target size would include small companies that had grown but were unprepared to be more than a little business. We could help them grow into a new size, I believe.

I'll give it more thought, but that's the gist of it. What do you think?"

"If I didn't have my own dream and I lived in Iowa, I'd really like to be a part of it. It's just the kind of thing that appeals to me."

The smile that passed between them was deep with shared understanding.

"I guess we'd better start down," she said as she rose reluctantly. "It looks like clouds are starting to come around, and it's almost three o'clock. If it wasn't for me, you'd probably be at home watching TV or getting ready for a big date by now."

He put his hands lightly on both her arms and said, looking straight into her eyes, "I can't think of any place I'd rather be at this moment—or anyone I'd rather be with." And he kissed her on the mouth, on the mountain, in the sunlight.

For one second, she thought she'd been struck by lightning. It seemed that shivers were running through her, and her whole body felt electrified, but instead of her heart stopping, it was hammering in her chest.

Apparently he felt it, too, because when he drew back, he had a startled expression on his face. "You have a high-powered kiss, Ma'am. I just didn't hear any thunder."

He looked undecided, as though he'd like to try it again but shook his head to clear it and reluctantly announced, "It's time we headed down."

The hike back to Grey's summit went quickly but it was downhill from there—and downhill wasn't as easy as she'd expected. She didn't have to lift her weight up, but she had to watch each foot placement more carefully, and her knees were sending her unhappy messages before long. Shadows were lengthening, and though she was getting tired, she felt the urgency of the passing time and didn't want to slow down her guide. He moved like a mountain goat with confidence and grace.

They were going down a particularly steep, rocky part of the trail when a rock slid from under her foot and her ankle twisted as she fell, slithering down through the stones. She cried out, and Tom turned quickly, but he was too far ahead to break her fall.

"I'm so sorry!" she said breathlessly though the pain.

"I should have stopped and let you rest. You have been going along like a trouper, but your muscles aren't used to the downhill jarring. And I forgot you don't have hiking boots on to support and protect your ankles. I'm the one who should be sorry."

"Now that we're both sorry, what will we do?"

"Can you stand on your leg?"

He helped her to her feet, but when she tried to step on her right foot, she fell to the ground with a sharp cry. "It's my ankle."

"Let me take a look at it. I've been trying to look at it all day, and now's my chance," he said, trying to make her smile. She tried.

He felt the ankle, watching her face contort in pain each time he moved it.

"I can't tell if it's broken or not, but I know you can't walk on it and need some medical attention. I could go ahead and get help, but I don't want to leave you here alone. Maybe we'll catch up with someone who can go on ahead and get some help. I don't think there is anyone behind us."

"You can't carry me!"

"Just watch."

He scooped her up in his arms, and though her ankle hurt terribly, she enjoyed the feeling of his arms holding her against his body. That worked for a while, but he couldn't watch his footing with her in front of him, and the evening sun made them both sweaty and slippery. He finally set her down and stood thinking for a moment.

"This won't be easy for you, but I'm going to carry you on my back. I'll try to be very careful of your ankle."

Somehow he managed to stoop down in front of her, so she could put her arms around his neck, and he reached under her legs and stood up. It must have been hard to stand upright with her weight on his back, but he did it.

Her ankle was throbbing, but she managed to say, "I'm impressed. You didn't even grunt!"

"I'm the strong, silent type. Well, at least silent."

The trail seemed endless. They'd progress a little and then rest. He'd try different holds to ease his muscles. One time, she was practically wrapped around his waist.

When they rested, she said the first thing that came to her pain ridden mind. "You've really gotten to know me well with all these different holds to carry me."

He was puffing a bit but managed to say, "I'd like to know you lots better someday."

After she said, "But then I hope I could walk down the aisle on my own two feet," she wanted to crawl in a hole. She turned bright red and stammered, "It must be the altitude that makes me delirious."

He laughed. "I must admit I feel very close to you at the moment. And, who knows? If we marry, you wouldn't have to change your last name, which would be convenient." Then he backed up to her so she could climb on his back again and they proceeded.

When it began to get dark, he reached into his backpack that he'd slung over his arm and pulled out a flashlight. She began to mumble and could hardly see through the pain.

The trail down was a nightmare of slipping and wrenching pain. It had been exhausting to go up what seemed like endless steps, but in the dusk, and then darkness, lit by jerking stabs of the flashlight and punctuated by the jolting descent, it was horrific. She tried not to cry out, but sometimes she was unable to suppress the groans. He must have felt her body stiffen to meet the pain, but there was nothing he could do except hurry.

When they caught up with a young couple who were gingerly making their way down, the woman offered to hurry ahead for help, and the man stayed to assist in carrying Sue. It went faster after that because one could hold the light, and one could carry the wounded. However, transferring her was so painful that they all dreaded each change.

They had started down the last long rocky trail when they saw lights coming across the parking lot ahead. And there was an ambulance and another vehicle in the parking lot with red flashing lights which seemed to shout EMERGENCY in the still, dark mountain air, as well as a few other vehicles.

"Sue, there's help waiting for us. You'll be safe soon." But he couldn't tell if she could hear him over the pain.

The paramedics met them about two hundred yards above the cars and took over immediately, wrapping her ankle and strapping her on a stretcher. Tom tried to stay by her head, and she clutched his hand until the stretcher was swiftly moved ahead to the waiting vehicle. He followed as close as he could but was hustled out of the way and was surprised to see them carry the injured young woman past the ambulance to the next flashing light.

This flashing light was attached to the top of a Clear Creek County sheriff's car where the man in uniform was talking to a tall, dark-haired young woman. He turned and instructed the medics to place the injured girl in the back of a large SUV with her wrapped ankle up on the seat. Tom managed to hold her hand through the transfer before turning to the tall woman to introduce himself and tell her he'd been hiking with Sue when the accident happened, and he would follow them to the hospital. She stuck out her hand and said, "I'm Mary. The sheriff thinks it's okay to take Sue down to Denver to her uncle who is a doctor. See you down there?" she asked as she disappeared into her car and started down the jolting, three-mile rock road to the highway, followed by the sheriff, the paramedics and the young couple (angels?) who had helped them.

Tom was running to his car when a young man stepped in front of him.

"I'm from the 'New Miner,' the local paper. Were you with that young woman? Is she badly hurt? How did it happen? What's her name? Where is she from?"

"I can't talk to you now," Tom shouted as he hurried around him. Dissatisfied, the reporter ran to his own car and followed the disappearing parade.

Wrenching his door open, Tom threw his backpack in the back, and leaping into the driver's seat, he thrust the key into the ignition. As the engine throbbed into life, he slammed the car into gear. Gravel shot from under his tires, but he didn't go far. Swearing vigorously, he opened his door and leaned out to observe his left front tire absolutely flat. By this time there was no one in the dark parking lot, and he knew he had no choice but to change the tire.

"Of all times to get a flat!" he hissed and though not a swearing man by nature, managed to let fly words he'd only heard others use.

It was 10:30 before he got on the highway and raced down to the Sheriff's office in the Clear Creek County Court House in Georgetown in hopes of finding Sue's whereabouts. But it turned out that that gentleman didn't know.

"Her friend said she'd drive her straight down to Denver to get medical aid, and I thought that was better than having her end up in the clinic up here since it would take a while to get the doc out of bed."

"Where was she taking her? She mentioned an uncle who was a doctor."

"She didn't say; probably the closest hospital, maybe Lakewood."

"What was her friend's name?"

"I think it was Mary something. We were in such a hurry to get her out of there that I didn't take down all the information I probably should have. I'm sorry I can't help you more."

"They were staying in a friend's cabin in town. Do you know which one?"

"We were so concerned about the injured girl that we didn't talk about where they were staying. Sorry."

Frustrated, Tom drove down to the Lakewood Hospital. No Sue Smith and no ankle trauma emergency admission. Not defeated, he went home to his condo in Capitol Hill and systematically called every hospital and emergency center in and around Denver. No Sue Smith anywhere. It was as though she'd disappeared. He felt cold fear in his heart, but he tried to stay calm and go over everything she'd told him, in hopes that there'd be some way to reach her.

Sue hung up the phone and leaned back in her high-backed leather office chair with a satisfied smile. Herman Miller had just called to thank her for all she'd done for his company and to inform her of the production figures that had proved her analysis had been correct. That was the meat and potatoes, but the dessert had been sweet indeed. Morale had never been higher, the managers and factory personnel were cooperating as never before, and he'd heard singing as he walked through the plant.

She looked out the picture window beyond her desk into the trees and across the valley that flowed verdantly across the Iowa landscape. When she started the business, she'd had no idea that four years later, her services would be so much in demand that she would be able to pick the projects that interested her. Or that she'd have a lovely home which held her office, overlooking scenery of which she never tired and a staff of four. Or that she'd be given the joy of making others' lives happier and more productive. It had all started on a mountaintop.

Automatically her eyes sought the photo on her desk. It was a picture she'd taken of Tom on the summit of Grey's Peak. He looked so strong and healthy and was smiling his big, warm smile. She knew without a mirror that she was smiling back at him.

For the millionth time she wondered where he was. Now a frown creased her usually smooth brow. She winced as she recalled all the phone calls she'd made to every Thomas Smith in the Denver phone book and in all the surrounding suburbs. Each hopeful beginning ended with disappointment. She was aware now that thirteen of them had climbed Grey's Peak, and eleven had made it to Torrey's top—but not on August 12th, 1988. She tried the accounting offices of some of the large companies in Denver. She ran an ad in the Denver Post. Each summer since then, she'd climbed the peaks and even sat in the parking place and watched the climbers come and go, but it was as though he had never been. If it were not for the picture on her desk, she would have wondered if she had imagined him. Since angels had become so popular, it was tempting to think he had been sent to protect and guide her. He had certainly done both.

With a sigh she returned to the present. Her life was so satisfying! Why couldn't she let him go—a man she'd spent part of a day with? It didn't make sense, and yet in her heart she felt that he was the man God had intended for her. Was she wrong? Where was he? And she was right back where she started every day.

The phone rang, and she heard Reed's deep smooth voice.

"Would Ms. Smith be able to consult with me over dinner this Saturday night at a restaurant of her choice? I'm having trouble relating to a young woman, and I need some advice."

She laughed in spite of herself. "You nut! Where are you?"

"In Paris at the moment. And I wish I could take you to dinner here. Iowa is not famous for its French cuisine. But it is famous for a beautiful consultant with whom I wish very much to consult—and other things."

"I'll be in Dallas this Saturday. Do you want to meet me there?"

"That's as good as any place. Where are you staying?"

"I'll be at the New Britain."

"Want to share a room? It would be cheaper and would save me a phone call."

"You handle phone calls very well, and I know your secretary will do it anyway. Say hi to the poor, long-suffering dear for me."

"You just don't know a good thing when you see it. But I'll keep passing by you, so you can see it more often."

They chatted a bit more and agreed to meet in the Dallas in the new Britain Saturday at 6:00.

Reed was fun and handsome, successful and nice. He'd make someone a fine husband when he settled down from all his empire building. He would be willing to do that if she'd agree to marry him, but she didn't encourage him in the idea. Why couldn't she love him? She liked him a great deal and knew him to be a really fine person. Oh, dear!

One thing her business had done was to bring her into contact with many interesting people—and some interesting men. None of them took her lightly. Though she was apparently physically attractive, she'd had no suggestions for one-night stands. She knew that Reed would have been delighted if she'd taken him up on the hotel room, but he'd also have fainted with surprise. No, the men who'd been interested in her were usually men who'd given their lives to the businesses that she was there to improve and had found it wasn't enough. They wanted a smart, beautiful, charming woman to share their lives with, and she'd had some wistful proposals, but they seemed to suspect that her heart was already occupied.

Wednesday morning, she flew from Cedar Rapids to Chicago on her way to the Thursday meeting in Dallas. She liked to arrive a day early, so she could look over the actual situation and fine-tune her suggestions and assessments to the management.

Not having much time between planes, she hurried between the two concourses but took time to enjoy the colors of the lights on the ceiling as they moved rhythmically across the long space. She idly looked over at the opposite moving walkway and was stunned to see Tom looking down lovingly into the upturned face of a striking-looking brunette who hung on his arm. She saw the top of a little head in the stroller he was pushing. Unconsciously she reached out to touch him, but their moving sidewalks had carried them away from each other. She started to swim upstream to reach him, but looking again at the engrossed couple, let the walkway carry her away from him.

Of course, he must be married, maybe living in Chicago. He was probably off on a business trip and his wife and baby were seeing him off. Sue built an instant life for him with a family and home and job that required some travel.

She felt sick to her stomach and hoped she wouldn't make a scene by leaning over the handrail and losing her breakfast. Ah, she'd reached solid ground at the end of conveyor belt. Stepping aside, she took a deep breath and realized she was crying silently. People tried not to look, but she was aware of their sideways glances.

Then she decided. She *would* try to find him, at least to tell him how he'd changed her life and thank him for that and for getting her safely off a mountain. And if he hadn't told his wife the story, that was his problem. Goodness, she'd looked for him for four years! Why would she let him just walk by?

Darting to the opposite walkway she ran as much as possible on the left side, apologizing and wiping her eyes and nose with the tissue she'd managed to retrieve from her purse. She knew she must be a sight, but she hurried on, driven to find him.

The steps up to the concourse seemed endless, and she frantically looked both ways at the top, wondering which way he'd gone. Then she thought she saw his wife's red blouse far off to the left. She began to run. Dear Lord, let it be him! She prayed all sorts of panic prayers as she hurtled through the other travelers.

"Gate 65 Denver"

There was the brunette stepping out of his arms and trying to get the baby to wave bye-bye. Sue saw him give his boarding pass to the attendant and start through the door to the plane. She couldn't get there in time! And cool, professional Sue Smith yelled "Tom!"

with all the strength she had in her. He turned with a puzzled look and saw a frantic, tear-stained, disheveled woman charging at him.

And he did the oddest thing. He dropped his briefcase and ran to meet her, yelling "Suc!" in a triumphant voice. When they met, he swung her round and round and kissed her at the same time.

When he finally set her down, there was a burst of applause from the bystanders and the young woman in red pushed the stroller up to them and hugged Sue, too.

"At last he found you! I'm so excited! We'd given up."

Sue looked at her in confusion. Tom then hugged the girl in red and turning to Sue, said, "I want you to meet my sister, Nancy, and her daughter, Kerry. She's helped me look for you and began to doubt my sanity when I kept saying, 'I believe God wants this woman for me, and I'll find her someday.' Today's the day!" and he shouted "Yippee" at the top of his lungs before he kissed her again.

It was at this moment that an airline employee tapped him firmly on the shoulder, handed him the forgotten briefcase, and told him the plane was leaving. He started toward the door, saying to Sue, "I'll call you." And then realized he still didn't know where to call her. "I *won't* lose you again!" he said and ran back to hand her his business card as she scrambled through her purse to find hers. They exchanged cards, and he glanced at her card as he again ran toward the door and yelled, "You did it!" He was out of sight when she heard down the corridor, "I can't wait to get to know you!"

She and Nancy were left standing there as the interested bystanders drifted away. Sue looked at his card then and saw:

> Peak Performance
> Motivational hikes led to 14,000-foot mountain tops.
> Have a mountaintop experience with experienced guides.
> Lawrence Thomas Smith 1–303–453–4369
> 734 Vine St. Denver, Colorado

"He did it, too. How long has he had his business, Nancy?"

"He started it four years ago, after he met you. When is your plane? Do you have time for a cup of coffee? I'd love to get to know you better. I can hardly believe that that was my brother who boarded that plane. My quiet, conservative brother shouting and kissing in the middle of an airline terminal! He's also the sibling who sells his mountain idea to big industry, and they love it. I think you've brought out things in him that we didn't know existed."

"I've already missed my plane to Dallas. I'll just use one of the airline phones and ask them to get me on the next flight, which leaves in a few hours, I think. I want to get to know you, too, and more about Tom. I tried so hard to find him, and yet he was in Denver all the time. I had no idea his first name wasn't Tom," she said, looking at his card. "I called every Tom Smith in the Denver area," she said ruefully. "And quite a few of them had climbed Greys and Torreys."

Nancy looked relieved. "I was so worried for my brother that lightning had struck him (pun intended), but perhaps it had missed you.

"I keep his picture on my desk. I've almost given up finding him at times, but no other man has even begun to interest me. I hope we both don't have false expectations but I, too, feel somehow that God brought us together. Why we lost each other I don't know. Or really, how we found each other again—especially in a city in which neither of us live. I hope I don't sound like a fool."

Nancy laughed. "No, you sound just like my brother!"

When Sue got home on Tuesday, there was a message on her answering machine from Tom telling her that he had tried to reach her and that he'd realized that he had a trip during the week that he'd forgotten in the excitement of seeing her. He asked if she would call and leave a message with his secretary to let her know when they could finally get together. She called immediately and talked to his secretary, who introduced herself as Roxanne, to tell her that she could see him the following week. The woman was quite business-like and said she'd give Mr. Smith that message. Sue had the distinct impression that Roxanne had no idea who she was nor had she been expecting the call.

Friday came, and there was no call from Tom, so she called back. Roxanne informed her that Mr. Smith had not returned, but she would give him the message. She was a little curt this time.

Sue called again on Monday, and this time she could almost feel the frost. Then she heard Tom's voice in the background, asking for some letter he needed. Before Roxanne could hang up, Sue said, "I can hear that Tom is there, and I want to speak to him right now." The woman hung up, and Sue was left with a disconnected buzz and a very puzzled mind.

Uncertain about what to do next, she waited until Wednesday, her hand trembling every time she answered the phone. But it was never Tom, and her work began to suffer. She gave up and called him. When Roxanne answered, Sue spoke with more confidence than she felt.

"This is Sue Smith, and I'd like to speak with Mr. Tom Smith, please." There was silence for a moment.

"Miss Smith, I don't quite know how to say this without hurting you." The secretary paused and then said very gently, "Tom and I have had a very close relationship for three years. He didn't want to hurt you because he knew how excited you were to see him, and he seems to have left it up to me to tell you that he isn't interested in hearing from you again. I'm so very sorry."

Sue was determined to hold onto her pride. "Thank you for telling me. I won't bother him again." And she didn't cry until she'd hung up the phone.

How could she lose him again? But this time, it was worse because this was his choice. And he didn't even have the nerve to tell her. Maybe he wasn't the man she'd thought he was. But she looked at his smiling face in the picture on her desk and tried to picture him forcing someone else to speak for him, and she just couldn't.

Sunday night, after a very long weekend, she was trying to focus on some silly television sitcom, which kept eluding her when the phone rang. Listlessly, she answered, "Hello."

Tom said quickly, "Don't hang up! I know you don't want to hear from me, but I just can't let you go without finding if there is some way I can see you and talk about it. I feel we are so right for each other, and I want you to see that, too."

"Tom!" was all she could say before she started to cry.

"Honey, what's wrong? I wish I were right there with you. I'll come if you let me. I'll go to the airport right now and sit and wait until I can get on a flight to Cedar Rapids. I'll call you first thing when I get there unless it's in the middle of the night. Oh, do you want me to come?"

"Yes, more than I can tell you! Just call whenever you arrive, and I'll be down to pick you up. I can't wait to see you!"

"I think I love you, Sue, and I want you to love me right back. I'm coming to plead my case."

"Oh, Tom! I don't think you'll need to plead anything. Just come."

The sky was just beginning to lighten in the east on Monday morning when Sue pulled up to the terminal in her little blue pickup. She saw Tom lounging against a pillar with a small duffel bag at his feet, and her heart leaped in her chest. When she stopped, he threw his bag in the back and gave her a grin as he ducked his head to get into the passenger seat. She knew she was grinning foolishly right back at him.

"Nice of you to pick me up so early. One question we didn't ask each other was if we were early birds or night owls. I'm guessing early birds."

"I'm usually up by six and walking or jogging by 6:15. What about you?"

"I'm up about the same time, depending on whether I have to get an earlier start than that. I'm eager to see Iowa as soon as it gets light. I'm expecting lots of corn."

"Then you came to the right place. But there are trees and rivers and cities and pigs and . . ."

"Don't tell me everything. I want to *discover* Iowa. And some other things, too." He was looking at her so intently that she almost ran off the road.

"I don't think I want to discover the ditches, so why don't we stop for a bite of breakfast and some conversation?"

Sue blushed with embarrassment and managed to keep her eyes on the road all the way to Smithson's Diner. When they got out, he casually put his arm around her shoulders as they walked in. She was in a total state of confusion at his touch.

They had placed their orders when Tom said, "I want to talk to you about Roxanne and me." Sue's heart sank.

"She has worked for me for about two years and is an excellent secretary. She has had to work some late hours at times when a big proposal was due, and one night it was nine thirty when we finished. I felt it only fair to take her to dinner, which she agreed to. We had a pleasant meal, and I drove her home. She seemed reluctant to leave the car, but it was late so I went around and opened the door for her. I noticed she stood very close to me when we said good night but thought she might be uneasy about being out at night, so I walked her to her door and then went home. And that is the only time I've ever seen her outside the office. You can hardly imagine my amazement when I inadvertently heard her tell a friend how she had intercepted your messages and what she'd told you. I could have strangled her! When I confronted her, she blurted out her romantic dream of my interest in her. I couldn't believe it. I'd given her no encouragement!

"She was so embarrassed and a little angry at being found out that she quit. I was relieved because I'd have fired her. How could I ever trust her again? I feel badly about the whole thing, but not *nearly* as badly as if I'd believed her and lost you. I'm sure I can find another secretary, but I don't want to lose you. I've been there, done that. So I apologize for the deception and hope you'll forgive me."

"Of course, I will! I should have realized that it wasn't like you, but I'd known you for such a short time that I wasn't sure. She sounded so thoughtful and sympathetic that I believed the whole sorry tale. So I apologize for my lack of faith in you."

"Gosh, I guess it's my turn next to apologize, but I think I'll have to wait until I do something bad. Can I take a rain check?"

She giggled. "I'm glad it's your turn." And then more seriously, "And I'm so relieved to get this straightened out."

Their food had arrived unnoticed, and now they began to eat their omelets in companionable silence.

"How long will you be able to stay, Tom, and what would you like to do while you're here?"

"Will five days be too long? Without a secretary, things will be a mess at the office, but sometimes you just have to set your priorities. I want to spend some time with you now that you've reappeared."

"Five days would be grand. I'll follow your good lead and take a holiday. Do you have anything you'd like to look at or will you trust me to show you around?"

"The man next to me on the plane said I should see your art museum for sure, but I want to see the things you want to show me. Could you take me to a hotel, so I can register and then we can get started?"

"Would you object to staying at my house? It would save you some money and give us more time to get to know each other." He gave her an exaggerated leer and raised his eyebrows.

She blushed. "Not in the biblical sense!" Then she said, "You can't imagine how many questions I've thought up in four years."

"And, as I recall, you were *always* good at that," he responded with a grin.

Well, I didn't think I'd ever see you again, but some of my questions have been answered already. Like, what is your real name? After chasing down all the Thomas Smith's in Denver I found out you didn't exist. And now I can hardly believe I'm sitting across the table from you in Cedar Rapids, Iowa. Praise the Lord!"

He reached out to take her hand, saying earnestly, "I do!" Her eyes widened as she felt the well-remembered voltage.

He was pleased with her uniquely designed, beautifully sited house on the hillside. While they drank cups of tea by the floor-to-ceiling windows in the living room, he kept exclaiming about the wonderful view down the wooded valley, bisected by a winding stream. Birds darted to and from among the feeders, and the breeze through the open windows was balmy.

"What a heavenly place!"

"It's been a real blessing. This isn't a big house but it's versatile and seems to fit my needs. I do have a guest bedroom on the lower level, but I want you to have my room with the view and the deck. I have a fine daybed that I often use in my office above the garage, and I'll stay there."

"I don't want to put you out," he said.

"I will give you the house," she grinned, "and that includes the kitchen, so you can make some exotic mountain breakfast for me."

231

"Just give me a few minutes in a grocery store, and you've got a deal, lady. A house for a breakfast! I haven't had an offer like that in a long time."

And so it was settled. She showed him to his room, took a few things out of the closet, and soon she was ready to show him the town.

It was eleven o'clock when they arrived at the Museum of Art. She was pleased with his knowledgeable comments about the paintings and glad to add to his information with comments of her own, having been a former docent there. Their minds seemed to meet and spring off each other in an exciting way.

After a light lunch, they walked for a few hours on the local nature trail, so deep in conversation that they were amazed to find the afternoon gone.

Sue drove him back to her house where each changed into less-casual clothing. As they met in the living room, he asked if she would mind if he drove the truck and took her out to dinner. She felt like they were having a real date as he held the door open for her. After a brief stop at the nearby grocery store, they drove to a local Greek restaurant. Sue hardly noticed what they ate, and they continued to talk across the candle-lit table until they became aware that the room was empty of everyone but themselves and a tired looking waiter.

The drive home was quiet and companionable without awkwardness until they were in the hallway, each ready to go to their rooms.

"It's been a grand visit, Sue, from the moment you picked me up at the airport. Thank you so much!"

"Thank *you* for dinner. I've had a wonderful time, and I'm already looking forward to tomorrow. Sleep as late as you want. You do remember where the kitchen is, don't you? I can hardly wait to see what you're serving in the morning," she said with a smile as she turned to go to her room.

She felt his hand on her shoulder as he gently turned her around and gathered her into his arms. The familiar tingle ran all over her body as he bent to kiss her willing lips. Reluctant to move away, he was the one who had to step back, gently releasing her. His eyes looked startled as he said quietly, "Our first day began with lightning and our second day ends with it. Good night, dear Sue."

As usual, Sue was out in her jogging clothes at 6:15 and was surprised to see Tom coming back from a run.

"Great morning, Sue. I'll shower and have that breakfast waiting for you," and giving her a quick, sweaty kiss he headed into the house.

She stared after him before starting off. It *was* a great morning, but her mind kept wandering back to Tom, and she found that her feet wanted to carry her back to him, so she wasn't gone as long as usual. After showering, feeling fresh and clean, she knocked on the kitchen counter to announce her presence. Tom appeared from the dining room, a towel draped over his arm, and a set smile on his lips.

"Madam is ready for ze breakfast?" he enquired in a phony French accent. "Please to follow me to your tabell."

And there on the dining room "tabell" were two places set with placemats, napkins, silverware, and large plates with a small pile of trail mix in the very center.

"It is known to me that Madam likes the trail mix, so is the first course,"

She giggled as he formally seated her at one of the places. Removing the towel from his arm, he sat down opposite her and said in his normal voice, "Do you want to say grace before we eat?"

"Will you, Tom?"

He reached for her hand, bowed his head and prayed, "Heavenly Father, thank You for this new day and a loved one with whom to share it. Please bless us and all we meet, direct us, and help us to see You in this wonderful time. Amen." Then he took his spoon and began to eat the trail "mix."

"This is really delicious," Sue volunteered.

"I make it myself because the food seems to be an important element of my clients' high-country experience. I've played with lots of recipes—not all successful but I won't describe those while we're eating—and it's been part of my learning curve."

He rose, picked up the towel, and asked, "Is Madam done with ze first course?"

Sue nodded, and he whisked the plates into the kitchen. Shortly, he returned with a loaded tray from which he served her orange juice in a goblet, steaming coffee, a lightly browned omelet, and a slice of delicate coffee cake. He then served himself, removed the towel and sat down.

"I'm impressed!" Sue exclaimed.

"You'd better eat it before you say anything," he answered modestly.

She ate and ate and then repeated, "I'm impressed! Everything is especially delicious. You really are talented."

"Thank you. And now may I have the deed to the house?"

"If you'll keep cooking like this, yes!" Then she realized how permanent that sounded and turned quite pink.

He didn't appear to notice as he rose and once more placed the towel over his arm.

"Madam is satisfied? Would she like more coffee?" And the plates disappeared again to be replaced by small bowls of fresh fruit, swimming in delicately flavored juice. When the coffee was poured he returned to his seat.

"Had you thought of going into the restaurant business?" she asked.

"No, but occasionally I think of writing a cookbook. There are so many interesting things to do with food."

"Is there anything in particular you'd like to do today, Tom?"

"I guided you up a mountain, and I'm counting on you to guide me around the cornfields."

"How would you like to go kayaking? Ever done it?"

"I've watched the whitewater kind—on TV—and made a vow never to do it."

"I promise you no white water unless the wind kicks up. I'm suggesting recreational kayaking. I have one, and we can rent one for you at the local lake. Are you game?"

"Lead on, oh Guide."

After creating a picnic lunch together, he helped her load her sleek red boat in the back of the pickup.

The day was sunny and bright with little wind—ideal for their adventure. They stopped at Keegan's boat rental shop and selected a blue kayak like hers, an appropriate length paddle and a PFD (personal flotation device).

She demonstrated how to get in the boat without tipping over by sitting on the back of the cockpit and swinging in one leg at a time before lowering herself onto the seat. When he attempted it, he was perilously close to going over and had to clamber into the water and start again. She laughed.

"A friend once told me that getting in and out of a kayak is a lesson in humility. And I've had plenty of those lessons. Once a young man tried to help me out of the boat, and I almost pulled him in the lake. You're off to a good start!"

Since he was an athletic person, he picked up the rhythm of paddling with no difficulty and his muscular arms made it look effortless. She struggled to keep up.

"Slow down a little, please. You aren't supposed to be that much better at this than me so quickly," she said laughingly.

They settled into a mutually comfortable pace and began to explore Lake McKenna. It had been created by building a dam at the lower end of a valley, and the creek running into it had filled it over a period of a few years. Now it was well seasoned, and the surrounding shore looked as though it had always been there. It seemed like a special day of grace since there were only a couple of fishermen on the far side, and they had the rest of the lake to themselves.

They were able to go near the shore and into little coves with their shallow boats. Wildlife was all around them. Ducks fluttered away as they drew near, and a great blue heron flew ahead of them nervously. They quietly drifted near two does with their fawns who had come down to the water's edge, and around another corner, they startled a red fox who darted away at the sight of them. There was almost a holy quiet, and the kayakers found themselves whispering to each other.

They'd been out almost two hours when Tom said plaintively, "I'm hungry."

"Table for two, please," she said to the sky.

"This way, Madam," Tom said.

He led the way to the middle of the lake where the sun shone warm and the breeze was soft. They held the two boats together, facing each other. She retrieved their lunch from the hatch on his kayak, and they divided it between them.

"May I say grace?" he asked.

She nodded.

"Heavenly Father, we thank You for the blessings You have given us, and for the love that we feel from You. We thank You for this beautiful world with all its blessed surprises and creatures. We thank You for this special day, almost too wonderful to bear. May we in some way give thanks to You with our lives." He paused. "How can we ever thank You enough? Amen."

She had tears in her eyes as she felt the sheer happiness of the day. She must remember this perfect time always.

"Do you think this is what heaven will be like?"

"At least the Iowa part of heaven," she said with a smile.

They savored the day as they ate and then packed up the remains and stowed them away.

"I'm sleepy," she announced. "Let's find a smooth spot on shore and take a nap."

"Sounds good to me."

She led the way to a grassy space where they beached their kayaks, and she produced a picnic blanket from the hatch of her boat. Spreading it on the ground, she lay down with a contented sigh. He lowered himself next to her, and they played the game of naming what the clouds looked like.

"Will you tell me about Peak Performance? How you run it and what some of the results have been? How did you start it?"

"Just how much do you want to hear? It can be a very long story."

"I have the next couple of days. See if you can fit it in."

"You asked for it! When I couldn't find you, I started to concentrate on my dream, just to keep my mind occupied. A friend of mine, Don, had a small company that produced a specialized piece of labor-saving machinery for truck farmers and employed about fifty people. I knew he was thinking of expanding but not sure he could handle a larger operation. I went to him and asked if he'd be my guinea pig. I told him it would be free except for the time involved, which speeded his commitment.

First, I interviewed Don, asking him about his concerns, his dream of expansion, the problems that existed in his current operations, and a little about his financial picture. Then I went to one of the supervisors who oversaw the workers on the production floor. I asked him about his satisfaction, if the workers were good, and how he thought the production might be improved. Each person I interviewed was assured that what they said would be kept confidential. Next, I went to one of the workmen and asked about his job satisfaction, what the atmosphere in the workplace was like, and if he saw ways of improving the operation. I also asked what he thought of a possible expansion. He was surprised at that question."

"You must be a good questioner and a good listener."

"You zeroed in on one of the most important things. If I tried to do this without knowing the current situation, I would be useless.

I went to friends who camped and borrowed their best camping recipes and practiced cooking in my backyard over a campfire. I had lots of company during that phase, so I wouldn't eat everything myself. I didn't want to become too fat to climb the mountains. I also lay awake nights, thinking about what I'd heard and wondering if I would be wasting the company's time. And I prayed that I was on the right track in a way that the Lord could use me.

I ended up asking the owner and four men from the production floor for a week of their time. One man refused because his wife was ill, so I took my fifth choice. On Monday morning, with begged and borrowed equipment, we went camping back in the Arapahoe National Forest where there were no trails or roads. We drew straws for various responsibilities. Don, the owner, drew cleanup duty for the first two days. It was interesting to see how different skills made different people more important. Joe, the last one I'd asked, was a good climber and could efficiently set up camp in no time at all. They all began to ask him for advice and direction, and he became the leader. Don was the most out-of-shape, and they ended up helping him with his pack and slowed down to his speed. Carlos was a terrific cook and a model of efficiency as he produced and served an amazing variety of dishes with the simple ingredients available.

The second night as we sat around the fire, I asked them to talk about themselves. At first, they were reticent, but as we roasted marshmallows and basked in the heat, they began to speak out. We heard their hopes and worries and histories. Everyone was equal. It was as though we had stepped out of time, and that circle of flickering light was all there was of the world. We all made a camper's vow of confidentiality, so what was said would not be shared with others.

The next day I could see that they were beginning to be a team, knowing each other's strengths and weaknesses, and working within that knowledge. Don was such a good sport about his aches and pains and tried so hard to keep pace with the others that he won our respect. So that night, I asked him about his dreams of expansion. The others listened thoughtfully. When he was done, I asked each of them what they could foresee of success and problems in the idea. Some looked at it from the workers' view, but Joe and a short man named Bill saw the larger picture, asking Don about market needs, competition, suppliers, and such. A few times he said he'd check into things they mentioned because he hadn't thought of it. We ended that evening singing old camp songs and teaching each other the ones they didn't know. Not all of them were for ladies' ears, but we had a pleasant surprise. Eddy, the fourth man had a beautiful voice, and finally we just sat around and listened to him sing Irish songs from his childhood."

"I doubt if there were many ladies' ears around back in the mountains."

He smiled. "The fourth day we actually climbed a 14,000-footer. I wanted them to have something to brag about when they got back. That night they were tired but proud, Don most of all. As we toasted our feet and our marshmallows, Bill brought up the subject of expansion again. He'd been thinking about it, but he thought there were some weaknesses in the current operation that should be corrected before enlarging could be considered. He saw the problems as only being magnified by expansion. That set off a spirited conversation. At first, Don was defensive, but he overcame that and really listened. The others felt the supervisor looked down on them and never asked them their opinions or considered them to have any ideas of their own. The consensus was that they just did their jobs but not their best because the supervisor wouldn't recognize it. This conversation made me very glad I hadn't invited the man to join us.

"The next two days were easier because we were settling into a routine. I led them out by a different route, and they were quite surprised when we arrived at the car on Friday evening, the fifth day. It was a weary but happy group who arrived back at the plant. We kidded each other and talked about the highlights (and lowlights) of the trip until we reached the outskirts of Denver where they realized they were back in their own worlds again. There was a good deal of handshaking and backslapping before each went off in his car. And it was over.

"The weekend gave them time to share their trip with their families and relax. You can imagine how eager I was to find out what Don thought of the retreat. I managed to wait until Sunday evening before I appeared at his door. I asked if he thought it had been a valuable experience for him and/or the company and if he had some suggestions to improve it. He did have a few ideas about how different physical abilities might be considered and some changes in the equipment but seemed rather subdued and quiet. I had expected some kind of enthusiasm, and there was none. I went home deflated and questioning myself and the whole idea.

"I spent the next week in a funk, lying around my apartment and looking at help wanted ads in the Denver Post. I had not quite burned my bridges with my old employer, but I was ready for something new. I so wished I could talk to you about it! It seemed real when we were on the mountaintop. The week was very long.

"Don came knocking on my door the following Saturday night. He started talking, and it was as though a dam had burst. It had taken a week for him to process the five days in the mountains. He poured out his whole new philosophy. He had seen that he'd been looking at his business from his point of view—from the top down and had divorced himself from the real production. When he'd had the opportunity to see it through the eyes of the men on the retreat, he became aware of what his workers might be feeling. He realized that his leadership was important, but the product was the thing that mattered and how well it served the customers. He was going to let the supervisor go, and he was going to do the job himself for a while, so he'd really see what production involved firsthand. He'd decided to have an advisory board, and he wanted Joe and Bill on it.

Only after he was sure the plant was running well would he think of expansion. 'I want to have a good model to copy, not a shaky one to worry about. And I think Joe and Bill might be the men to head up branch offices. And I'm thinking of starting a lunch service for the workers, with Carlos to manage it. How did you do such a good job of selecting the men for the trip?' he asked. I told him that there'd been some serious prayer involved."

Suddenly Tom sat up. Shadows were growing long, and he realized he was very hungry.

"You blessed girl! You listened to me all that time and didn't interrupt me. You should have stopped me long ago. I've talked your ears off!"

"I was really interested in what you were saying. Some of the things you talked about are much related to my work, and I wanted to hear how you approached things. We probably *should* head back to the car. It should only take us about twenty minutes if we paddle steadily. But when we get something to eat, I want to hear more."

"You *are* a good sport! I'm eager to hear your stories, too. If you keep being such a good listener, I may have to change my reservation home for later in the week."

She smiled. "I guess I could put up with that."

He smiled into her eyes as he said, "Can you put up with a kiss?" Before she could answer, he pulled her into his arms and gently kissed her—at first. Then his kiss deepened, and she hugged him tightly.

"I think I was a lot hungrier for that kiss than I was for dinner."

They paddled hard under darkening skies and were glad to see her bright pickup as they rounded a headland. By the time they had the kayaks loaded, it was raining hard, and they were soaking wet. She turned on the heater on the way home, so at least they weren't cold.

After showers, they concocted a dinner from the contents of the refrigerator, which they ate in front of a crackling fire. It was so peaceful. When they finished their meal, they pulled the cushions from the couch that faced the fireplace and sat with their backs against its checked cover.

"Tell me what happened to Don's business. By now he must have made some major decisions since that was four years ago."

"There was a bit more conversation that night when he came over to my apartment, but I finally asked him if he thought what I wanted to do was worthwhile and workable. His response was very enthusiastic. 'I have a whole new point of view and I'm excited to see what will come of it!' Then he handed me an envelope and thanked me and left. I thought he probably just wanted to say thanks. Well, he said it ten thousand times! It was a check! I went to my desk and threw all the want ads I'd been saving into the wastebasket. I was on my way. And I did some heavy thank you's of my own to the Lord who had blessed me so much."

Her eyes shone as she reached over to squeeze his hand. "How wonderful!"

"Don did expand his business. He opened a second factory in the valley in California where he could be close to farms that needed his equipment. This also gave him the opportunity to see firsthand what his customers' needs were and the ability to make repairs immediately, so his customer service was excellent. Joe took over the first plant and led some innovations that brought up production as well as worker satisfaction. They made a few mistakes, but when I talked to Don a few months ago, he was delighted with their success, not only financial but product and worker improvement as well. In fact, he tried to give me another check, which was generous of him. I told him. 'I should be paying you for taking a chance on my crazy idea and for so generously starting me out on what has been a most satisfying career—but I won't.' We laughed, and each kept our money.

My next move was to map out a list of firms, which I could approach. I started with the one where I had worked, and since I left with a good reputation, they heard me out and doubtfully agreed to give me a chance to try my ideas. I knew their set-up fairly well and had seen some of the worker dissatisfaction and the lassitude that caused. I wanted to empower the lower ranks since it all seemed pretty top-heavy. The company was an old one, accustomed to control from the top down. I felt there was a more productive way since the workers are so much better educated than when the company started. And I knew who I wanted to take to the mountains.

It worked really well. In fact, they gave me two more contracts and not only gave me a bonus but spread the word. Now I can pick and choose who I think will benefit most from this idea."

"What a great success story! Can you do it all yourself (plus a secretary) or how do you manage?"

"I had a hiking buddy who climbed most of the 14,000 footers with me. We think a lot alike, and I have complete confidence in his mountaineering skills as well as his cool head in times of emergencies. He's literally seen me through some real cliff hangers. We've tried to work it so that one of us stays at the office while the other one is out, but occasionally we're both in the mountains at the same time."

"That was really great of you to take time off to come and see me. I doubt if you expected to be gone now, and with no secretary, it might be a problem."

"I told Ted I'd be gone, following my heart," he smiled and touched her hand, "and he took over a trip for me. I left a message on the answering machine, saying when I'd be back and that I'd return their call. I think that should cover it."

He reached over and gave her a hug as he said, "You listened so patiently to the story of Peak Performance this afternoon and evening. Now I want to hear about your dream come true."

"I think that will have to be for another time because it's ten o'clock right now, and we have a date with some corn and hogs for tomorrow."

Sue had called her cousin who lived on a farm near West Branch, and when she explained that she had a city boy who wanted to see a real farm, Keith immediately invited them out, so Wednesday was the day that was set. They were to come for lunch, so the couple had time to go to the Herbert Hoover Presidential Library in the morning. They looked through the memorabilia and learned much, not only about President Hoover, but about the times he lived in, including the Great Depression. Their faces were sober as they walked out into the park surrounding the building.

"He was blamed for things that he wasn't responsible for. How hard that must have been to have people look at you as though you had caused the Depression," Tom said thoughtfully.

"It reminds me a bit of Abraham Lincoln who suffered such 'slings and arrows' during the Civil War. Politicians would like to solve those problems, but they are only humans, and sometimes the tide of history is beyond their control."

She took a deep breath and with a twinkle in her eyes, asked, "How would you like to go oink at some pigs and whisper into the ears of corn?"

"If I can only have some lunch first, I'll be ready to oink and whisper with the best of them."

She put her arm through his, and they went on their way.

As they drove down the gravel road, she looked at him questioningly. "Since you worked on your uncle's farm, this probably won't be much different than when you were growing up. Do you really want to do this?"

"Yes! It's been a long time since I've been on the farm, and I know there are all sorts of new equipment and ideas."

At this point they pulled into a farmyard, anchored by a large, two-storied white house and a looming red barn with various outbuildings clustered around them. As they exited the truck, they could hear pig noises coming from a pen beside the barn.

"I'll oink with them later," he said in response to her questioning look.

As they started up the path to the house, the door opened and Keith and his wife, Jolene, came out to welcome them. They were both tall and slender, and his browned skin was the only thing that gave him away as an outdoors person—hardly the stereotypical Farmer Jones and his little plump wife.

Sue hugged them both and introduced Tom before they were swept inside. A veritable feast was set out on the table, and after a solemn prayer, with gratitude expressed for the plenty before them and asking for the Lord's blessing, they passed the steaming bowls around. Conversation was limited by consumption.

As they sat with their coffee and apple pie, Keith asked Tom where he and Sue had met. "In a mine in a lightning storm," was the answer. "We were climbing a mountain in Colorado," Sue added. Tom took over with a short version of the rest of the story and finished it with, "I thought I'd lost the love of my life, and you can't imagine my gratitude at finding her again."

Sue looked at him, wide eyed, while a smile passed between Keith and Jolene.

Their host offered to show Tom around, and Sue offered to help with the dishes. When the men had gone out, Jolene grabbed her guest by the shoulders and demanded, "Is this the *one*? The man whose photo is on your desk? The one that you tried so hard to find?"

Sue looked a bit pink but answered gamely, "He is that one. I was startled at what he said to you though, because we really haven't talked about the future. I think we both felt the connection then, and I feel it now. Apparently he does, too. The scary part is that we've not had time to really know each other. He could be a bank robber, and I could have three husbands. And yet I'd trust him with my life—and I have."

The women visited about other things as they cleaned up after the delicious meal before going outside to catch up with the men. They found Tom driving an enormous tractor with a smile that almost went from wheel to wheel. Keith had shown him how to pull the wagon alongside the combine, so he could unload in the field. The women went back into the house after admiring the new farmhand.

"I'm really glad you brought him, Sue. I was doing all that driving, and it's lovely to have the afternoon off. Now tell me what you've been doing in your business."

"Only if you'll tell me where you've been giving your motivational speeches."

"That won't take long because I keep them to a minimum during harvest season, so I'm here to help Keith. The last three were in Wyoming, Japan, and Pennsylvania."

I can't imagine the places you've gone and the people you've met. It makes me feel like a country girl."

Jolene laughed. "Life doesn't always turn out as you imagine. You just have to work hard and grab the opportunities that come your way. You never know where your path will lead, but if you trust in the Lord and seek His will, it's amazing what may happen."

They chatted through the afternoon until Sue happened to look at her watch. "Oh, my, it's 5:30 already. I'm afraid I'll have to leave very soon, and I need to take Farmer Smith with me. He leaves early in the morning, and he'll need to get packed and ready to go. I'm sorry to call a halt to your afternoon off."

Jolene looked at her guest with a twinkle in her eye. "And you'll probably need time to say goodbye, also." Sue had the grace to blush as she shook her head affirmatively.

Keith and Jolene were smiling as they waved the couple off on their return trip to Cedar Rapids. Tom was driving, and when Sue turned to wave goodbye, she saw Keith give her a thumbs-up sign.

They talked briefly about farming and about how farmers were not all like the stereotypical image that urban dwellers often had of them. Tom had to laugh at himself a little during the conversation. "And I never thought of myself as a city slicker. Obviously Jolene and Keith wouldn't fit *any* stereotype."

There were a few idle comments about the countryside before silence settled like a blanket over the occupants of the car. Sue felt as though she were drowning in a sea of unspoken words. When they were almost home, she suddenly thought of dinner and broke the silence. "Shall we eat at home tonight? Then you'll have time to pack and get some sleep before you have to get up in the wee hours. We can make a quick stop at the grocery store and pick up some salad makings and meat if you don't mind starting the grill."

He seemed relieved to be conversing again. "Let's do that, and I want to hear about your business and how you made your dream come true. You were kind enough to listen to me the other day, and I don't want to miss hearing about your adventures. This is my last chance to catch up, and I don't want to miss it."

Her heart sank at the "last chance" phrase. Was this to be the end of their relationship?

She tried to keep things light after that, but her heart felt heavy even though they chatted easily as he cooked out on the deck, and she put together a really interesting salad. After the dishes were done (she washed and he wiped them), they lit a fire in the fireplace and sat on the couch. She tried to relax, but she felt the tension of the future, untalked about, but filling her thoughts.

Sue was feeling very nervous as they walked into the airport at 6 a.m. on Saturday morning. As they walked up to the counter, she realized that her nervousness wasn't related to his catching the plane but to the things that seemed to be unsaid—or that she wished had been said. When he'd called five days before, he'd said something about pleading his case and loving her. Their time together had been so happy, and he'd been affectionate, but he'd never mentioned the future except to invite her to visit him "sometime." Would he say something before he left? Or was he not looking for a permanent relationship? She really didn't know him that well. Maybe he was a nice guy who didn't want to get involved. After all, they lived a long way apart, and how could they manage to live together? She felt a deep sadness.

When he finished checking in, he still had forty-five minutes until departure time. Her anxiety increased.

"Do you want to have a cup of tea in the restaurant?" he asked.

"That would be nice. You still have a half an hour before you have to board. Your corn flakes this morning may not last, so maybe you'll want some breakfast."

They were walking toward the restaurant when a booming voice shouted, "*Tom Smith!*" Sue turned in astonishment to see a heavy-set man barreling toward Tom with his arms outstretched. He grabbed the startled-looking Tom in a bear hug, lifting him off his feet.

"George?" Tom said in astonishment. "What are you doing here?"

"I was negotiating a contact with a local electronic company and thought it would be better to do it face to face. What are *you* doing here?"

"I'm visiting my friend, Sue Smith." He turned to introduce her, but George was already pumping her hand energetically.

"I'm glad to meet you, Sue. You two must be related, with the same last name." He laughed and went right on. "Isn't he an amazing guy! He took me to the top of a 14,000 footer in Colorado, and I'll never forget it. It didn't occur to me that I could do it, but with Tom and help from the team, I made it. It was a proud moment for me, I'll tell you."

Sue managed to retrieve her hand as she said, "He did the same thing for me. It is something you never forget." She glanced at the subject of their conversation, who looked slightly dazed.

"By the way, my name is George Hadley. That experience rejuvenated my company, and Tom knows I'm really grateful to him." He clapped the object of his gratitude on the back as he said, "Let's go get some coffee. I hope you're on your way back to Denver, Tom. I have lots of things I want to talk to you about." By this time he had propelled them to the entrance of the restaurant.

George was still talking when the boarding announcement was made, and they stood to leave. She looked at Tom helplessly and saw him struggle to get a word in edgewise.

"You go ahead, George, while I thank Sue for the great time I had here."

"That's okay, Tom; I'm not in a hurry. I'll wait. I can't get over my luck in seeing you here."

The younger man took her hand and led her to a nearby pillar with his back to George. "This is not what I expected. George is a great guy but not too sensitive to the situation. I'll call you tonight and thank you for the wonderful time. I'll never forget it." She thought he was going to say something more, but George boomed, "We'd better get a move on, Tom, if we're going to be able to get to sit together."

"I'll call you tonight," he repeated. He kissed her on the mouth, sweetly. Then George grabbed his arm and proceeded to march him toward the concourse, calling over his shoulder, "Nice to meet you, Sue."

She watched them walk away. As they reached the top of the stairs, Tom managed to turn around and wave at her. She waved back, hoping her smile didn't betray her tears. And then they were out of sight. She had a sudden premonition that she would never see him again. It was so strong that she wanted to run after him and beg him not to go. Then she reasoned with herself and grinned ruefully as the thought of chasing him through another airport crossed her mind. But her heart was breaking.

The day seemed to drag even though she worked hard on some of the things she'd ignored while Tom was visiting. She thought he might call when he got home, but the phone didn't ring all day. Finally, evening arrived, and she decided to read in bed by the phone. She finally turned the light off at 2 a.m., but sleep is hard to find when you're waiting anxiously. As the sky began to lighten, she finally slept.

The phone rang at 1:00 on Sunday, and she answered it with, "You're home!" Ralph, her partner, answered, "Yes. And since you answered the phone you must be, too. How was your holiday? Any big news?"

"No. He was as wonderful as I'd imagined, but when he left he said he'd call me last night, and he didn't." She started to cry.

"Sue, he's only been gone a day! Give the guy some time."

"You haven't heard of any plane crashes, have you? I had the feeling when he left that I'd never see him again. I can't seem to shake it. But you're right; all sorts of things could have come up. Thanks for reasoning with me. Ralph. And I did finish writing up the Dawson report, so that's ready to go."

They talked on for a few minutes, and when she hung up, Sue decided to go on a run. It helped, but she kept thinking of him running on the same path just a few days ago. She wished desperately that he were beside her now.

By Wednesday, she was beside herself with worry and fear. She'd called his home and his office, and there was no answer. It had been almost five days. She wondered if this was one of those famous men's lines—"I'll call you"—with no intention of doing so but as a safe exit line to an unwanted relationship. Would he have said something if it hadn't been for George? She'd never know apparently.

Sue tried to analyze the situation. She'd only known the man for less than a week, all together. How could she feel so devastated? Was he her dream man or a figment of her imagination that she'd convinced herself was perfect? If she'd had a chance to see him in other situations, would he have looked so wonderful? Was he the reason she'd never had a lasting relationship with any other man? Was it easier to imagine a relationship than to have a real one? She asked herself all those questions and then thought of the man she'd just spent five days with and burst into tears again.

After crying herself into exhaustion, she finally fell into a deep sleep. When the phone ran at 3:30 in the morning, it took her a minute to figure out what the noise was. She picked up the receiver and heard Tom pleading, "Answer it, Sue!"

"Tom! Are you all right? I've been so worried."

"If you'd known where I was, you would have been more so. I'm on a pay phone in a police station and haven't much money, but I'll call you as soon as I get home. Trust me! I love you, Sue."

"This is the operator, and you will have to put in another fifty cents."

"I don't"—click.

Now her mind was filled with other questions. Why was he in a police station? What had he been doing that would have worried her and apparently was the reason he hadn't called? Had he been arrested and unable to get to a phone? Why didn't he have any money? Her mind made up all sorts of answers, and she finally drifted off to sleep, wondering if she dared love a criminal.

Sue stayed as close to the telephone on Thursday as her work would allow, picking it up eagerly each time it rang, only to be disappointed when she didn't hear Tom's deep voice. About one o'clock, she decided to take a walk to try to relieve the tension she felt. She imagined that the phone rang as soon as she walked out the door, so she was only gone about ten minutes. Running to her desk, she saw the answering machine light blinking. Pressing the button, she heard Tom say, "I didn't get home until this morning, and I just fell into bed. I need another ten hours of shut-eye, but I must talk to you. Please call me back as soon as you can. I'll sit right here by the phone."

Her fingers shook as she dialed the number. He sounded groggy, but at last she could talk to him. "Tom, are you all right? When you didn't call on Saturday, I imagined all sorts of terrible things. Just tell me you're okay, please."

"Yes, I'm fine, now. I won't tell you the whole long tale right now, but if you have time I'll explain part of it."

"If you're not too tired, I'd really like to know what happened. Why were you arrested?"

"Arrested? I wasn't arrested. What made you think that?"

"You called me from the police station and I assumed that was the one call you were allowed."

He laughed. "I never thought of that. The police picked us up when the helicopter dropped us off and stopped at the station before driving us back to Denver. I just had time to make that call before we left for the city."

"Helicopter? Police? Are you going to tell me some wild story?"

"I guess it is sort of wild. When I got back to Denver on Saturday, I went straight to the office to see if there was anything I needed to do. I found Larry, the young man who fills in for us occasionally and sometimes goes on the climbs with us, pacing the floor. He was frantic. Ted had taken the trip I'd been scheduled for and gotten caught in a surprise early fall snowstorm. No one had heard from him, and they didn't know where to look because he'd taken the maps with him and apparently your phone number as well because Larry had no way of getting in touch with me. He had the van all loaded, called the Mountain Rescue Team, and was hustling me out the door almost as I walked in."

"Did you find Ted and the group? Are they safe?"

"Do you always go to the end of the story when you start the book? I'm teasing you, Sue. Yes, they're safe, and you can relax through the rest of the story. Do you have about fifteen minutes to hear it?"

"I have the rest of the day, if you can afford to pay for the call."

"That might be a problem since I'm out of work now, but I think I can manage."

"Out of work? Out of work? You're gone six days and you call me from a police station, go off on a mountain rescue, *and* you've lost your job? You've been a busy man."

"Absolutely—and I'll tell you how it all happened.

The Rescue Team had a helicopter waiting near the Georgetown Lake, ready to take off as soon as we loaded our gear on board. They flew us up to the top of Guanella Pass since the road had not been plowed yet. Ted and his group had started from the pass on their way to climb Mt. Berstedt, which was the place I had planned for the trip. They landed the helicopter as close to the mountain as they dared, so we wouldn't have to wade through any more snow than necessary. It had been a dumper up that high. The snow was about three feet deep on the level and higher in places where it had blown. We put on our packs and had just stepped away from the copter when it took off in a whirl of snow. They'd warned us that the wind was coming up, and they had to get out while they could.

Are you still there, Sue?"

"Hanging on every word!"

"We started up the mountain, but it was slow going because of the depth of the snow, and we had to feel our way where we thought the trail was. Fortunately, it was a climb I had done fairly often, so I knew it well, though not with three feet of snow on it. We were aware that the wind was picking up, but it kept getting stronger until the snow was blowing around us in a whiteout. To make a long story short, we pitched our tent and stayed in it for two days and three nights. We couldn't get in an area sheltered by the mountain, for fear the snow would bury us, and we'd not have enough air, so we were out where we listened to that howling wind until we thought we'd go crazy. We finally kept talking until we were hoarse just to keep our minds off the incessant roar.

We talked about our childhoods, our philosophies, our families, our educations, girls we'd dated, friends, and what we were glad we'd done and what we regretted. I don't think I ever knew as much about anyone as I know about Larry. We prayed for Ted and his group, for ourselves, and those we love. And we began to wonder if we'd come off that mountain feet first. We were getting cold, and the food was running low.

Then on early Tuesday morning we were wakened by the sound of silence. It really did seem like a sound after all that noise. We looked out of our tent at an absolutely pristine world, unmarked by man or beast. It was awesome—and cold. Have you gone shopping or anything?"

"You must be kidding. This is fascinating. I'm almost shivering as I sit here listening. What in the world did you do next?"

"We knew we couldn't leave Ted and the clients on the mountain, so we packed up our gear and fought our way up. There were times that I just wanted to lie down and give up, but I knew that I'd never get up if I did that, so I just plodded on. It was about five hours later that I knew I was in real trouble or at least *more* trouble. I heard singing. I've read that you see a beautiful light and hear wonderful music but I never imagined that the angel choir would be singing "Take Me out to the Ball Park." I turned to look at Larry, and I saw the same astonishment on his face that I must have had on mine."

"Weird!"

"I was afraid to ask him but I finally blurted, "Do you hear singing?" He looked relieved as he answered with a positive shake of his head. I shouted, 'Ted,' and a face appeared from the bottom of a huge mound of snow. 'You called?' he asked with a grin."

"I must admit this is a strange story. Are you sure you didn't just go on a binge, and you're making this up as you go along? And to think that I thought you were a normal person."

"Where did you get that idea? To go back to the story, it turned out that when Ted saw the beginnings of the storm, he stopped where they were, set up camp, and waited it out. They had plenty of food and a combination of quite a bit of body heat, so they played cards and sang songs and waited. I don't know when he planned to go down but probably when the food ran low.

"We had a short-wave radio with us and let the Rescue Team know that the lost had been found. By this time I wasn't quite sure who was lost and who was found. They said they'd meet us with the helicopter on the pass the next afternoon so we got the group packed up and started down. They even fed us since we'd brought so little food on our 'rescue' mission.

"It was slow going on the way down because people were sliding, and one guy fell and twisted his ankle badly. It turned out that he'd really broken it. We made a sort of sled from one of the tents and pulled him on it. We hadn't reached our first camping site by dark, so we set up the tents where we were and spent the night.

"We reached Guanella Pass by noon of the next day, about an hour before the copter. That 'thunk, thunk, thunk' was a mighty welcome sound. They took the injured man and five others and flew them down to Denver, so he could get to the hospital. That left Ted, Larry, and me and the other three clients to wait for the whirly bird's return.

"We were packing up everything to transport it out while the others were talking over the trip and what it could possibly mean to their business. That's when Larry asked me if I'd be willing to sell my part of Peak Performance. I looked questioningly at Ted who said, 'It's okay with me. I'd miss you, but I have a feeling you're ready to move on. Larry's done a good job helping us, understands our philosophy, and is a heck of a mountaineer. You started it, but if you're willing to pass it on to us, I think we'd do a good job. If you want to continue the way we are, that would be fine, too.' I was pretty stunned. And then I realized it was actually an answer to prayer.

"When Larry and I had been caught in the wind and snow, we talked about what we regretted, and I told him that I regretted not telling you I believed that I loved you and figuring out a way we could be together and really get to know each other. I was afraid I'd not have a third chance with you. And I thought of looking out over your green valley while I was sitting on a bare mountain on an adventure that I might not be able to survive."

He heard her take a deep breath.

"We set a price, there on the pass, and Larry agreed to pay me half and the rest over the next ten years. The three of us shook hands on it. I had lived my dream, and now it was time to pass it on. I felt a little sad and a lot excited.

"And that brings me to you. I hope you won't be frightened if I move to Iowa. I just want the time to know you better, to meet your parents and have you get to know mine, to know what you're like when you're mad and when you're sad, and what makes you smile. And to see if we fit together well enough to make it last a lifetime. And if it turns out that it's not what you want, I can quietly get out of your life and move on. Are you willing to give it a try, Sue Smith?"

"When you didn't call, one of the things I imagined was that you didn't want to see me again. 'I'll call you' is a great exit line. I sat by the phone and waited, hoping each time it rang that it would be you. I cried myself to sleep more than once.

To answer your question, yes, Tom Smith, I want to get to know you, and if you can't come here, I'll meet you any place. I think there may be a job for you here. I can hardly wait to feel your arms around me. When you get off the plane, you'll recognize me. I'll be the one carrying a big sign that says WELCOME TO IOWA!

UP ON THE ROOF

Mark 2: 1-12

When after some days he returned to Capernaum, the news went round that he was at home; and such a crowd collected that the space in front of the door was not big enough to hold them. And while he was proclaiming the message to them, a man was brought who was paralysed. Four men were carrying him, but because of the crowd they could not get him near. So they opened up the roof over the place where Jesus was, and when they had broken through they lowered the stretcher on which the paralysed man was lying. When Jesus saw their faith, he said to the paraslysed man, "My son, your sins are forgiven". Now there were some lawyers sitting there and they thought to themselves, "Why does the fellow talk like that? This is blasphemy! Who but God alone can forgive sins?" Jesus knew in his own mind that this was what they were thinking and said to them: Why do you harbour thoughts like these? Is it easier to say to this paralysed man, "Your sins are forgiven" or to say, "Stand up, take your bed and walk"? But to convince you that the Son of Man has the right on earth to forgive sins"—he turned to the paralysed man—"I say to you, stand up, take your bed, and go home". And he got up, and at once took his stretcher and went out in full view of them all, so that they were astounded and praised God.

Simon was late! We didn't know what to do. Baruch, David, Simon, and I had everything planned—we thought. The four of us would carry Philip to Ben Ibram's house, but we figured we had to get there early in the morning. We didn't know when the rabbi would be healing and speaking. It was only by chance that we heard he'd be there. Simon's (where was he?) cousin knew one of the healer's disciples and had heard from him that there would be a meeting at Ben Ibram's house on Tuesday. The local scribes were always protective of the faith, and they wanted to hear what this man was preaching, so he had agreed to come and talk to them and anyone who wanted to hear him. The trouble was that since word had gotten around about his healings, though they might not be true at all, everyone wanted to see him. Stories about healings had gone around our culture for years, but these seemed more persistent, and a few local people claimed to know someone who had physically been changed. Naomi swore her father knew a man who had been blind from birth and suddenly could see after being with the rabbi. But we all knew Naomi liked to be the center of attention, and she'd say anything if she thought we'd really listen to her. However, what did we have to lose? Except now that Simon was so late, we were going to lose whatever chance might have been!

Philip had always been the leader of our group of boys, all of us growing up together in Capernaum.

He was always eager and quick, ready for any adventure, but he was also kind, loyal—, and funny! I remember some of the really amusing tricks he pulled off. In fact, I smile just thinking of them. They were never mean, so people always smiled and said, "That Philip!" when they saw they'd been fooled. Everyone loved him.

And the girls—why any girl in town (or outside of it) would have given her dowry if he'd just shown a little interest in her. But his smile was for all, and his heart was with us—mostly. However, occasionally, when we'd gather in the evening we'd find him at Sarah's house, talking with her family. We teased him unmercifully, but he never got angry when he well might have. He'd just say he liked Sarah *and* her family.

Really, we couldn't blame him. They were a wonderful, God-fearing family. We knew that Ben Isaac had studied at the temple in Jerusalem and had planned to be a rabbi, but his family had needed him at home, so he did the proper thing and come home and now was taking care of the small family vineyard. It was a far cry from his dreams, but he knew the Fifth Commandment of Moses and honored it. And Sarah was special! I think we all felt it without understanding it. She had a quiet dignity that set her apart and the beauty (and she was *beautiful*) was not only outward but inward, as well. Most of the time she was quiet and thoughtful, But just when you thought you understood her, she'd burst into peals of laughter over some funny thing that happened in the village, and you just had to laugh with her. And could she dance! Sometimes we'd all just stop and watch her. It made my heart beat faster just to see her grace. We all knew that Sarah was special.

Where could Simon be? I don't know whether to be angry or worried.

We boys had been growing up at the happiest time of our lives. We worked hard with our families but had few responsibilities. We had each other and all sorts of dreams about what lay ahead.

And then Philip fell, and his dreams ended. It was almost a year ago when he decided to repair the roof of the crazy Egyptian widow who lives down in the valley in that decaying building. All she ever did was babble about her childlessness. Of course, that is a problem because who's to take care of her since her husband died. They were never accepted when he was alive. He shouldn't have married a foreigner. We're warned against that all the time at the synagogue. They must have come here because no one knew them, and he had no family to embarrass. And then he died. His widow still lives on the edge of the village, and no one has anything to do with her except some of the pious folks who leave food at her door from time to time. I guess it does say somewhere in the sacred writings to be kind to foreigners because when our ancestors wandered in the desert, they were considered foreigners ourselves. But that was a long time ago.

Come on, Simon! We're all waiting for you! We can't go without you because we need someone to carry the fourth corner of the litter.

Anyway, the rotten roof gave way, and Phillip fell. The crazy widow came shrieking into the village, and we knew something was really wrong because she'd never dare forget her place. When we got to her hovel, we found Philip lying on the ground with his head twisted to one side and a frightened expression on his face as he said, "I can't move my arms or legs." And it was true. He never moved his limbs again.

We carried him carefully to his house where his mother started shrieking. It was awful, and then quiet Sarah stepped up, bathed his face with water, held his hand, and calmly said, "Let's get him inside."

In the year he has been unable to move, he has shrunk before our eyes. Every time I go to see him, his eyes look deeper in his head and his bones seem more prominent. As we've matured, he has to be taken care of in every way, like a baby. I wonder how much that must bother him to see us looking like men and growing the way we all assumed we would while he cannot. We boys all visit him often, and he hasn't lost his sense of humor, but there's despair in his eyes. Sarah is often quietly there, and they seem to communicate without words. I realize now that they would have married if the accident hadn't happened.

Thank Yahweh, Simon is running up the road!

We'd all asked our fathers for permission to have this day to go hear the rabbi and had done extra duties, so we would be allowed to do it. Our parents seemed surprised by our sudden religious interest, but everyone was talking about the man Jesus and wondering who he really was, so it didn't seem too unusual.

Philip's parents were the only ones who knew of our real reason. They worried that he might fall or be trampled by crowds (we'd heard that sometimes there were thousands of people pushing to see the Rabbi), but we pledged that we would take care of him. He just listened and then said, "Thank you for wanting to try, but what can this man do? He isn't Yahweh. You will be wasting your time. I'm grateful that you'd do this for me but . . ." His voice trailed off. We ignored him. Having come this far, we weren't going to give up now.

"What happened, Simon? It may be too late to go now."

He was panting and his face, so manly, was streaked with tears. "I'm so sorry. The cow wandered off during the night, and my father said we had to find her. Tomorrow it will be the Sabbath, and we couldn't do it then. I was frantic, knowing that you all were waiting for me, but there was nothing I could do except run faster, looking everywhere I could think of for that stupid cow. We found her at last, almost a mile away, and my father kindly said he would drive her home. I ran all the way here!"

He was so upset that we couldn't be angry. We quickly gathered our corners of the litter and carried Phillip out of the house. It must have been the first time in a long time that he'd been outside because he shut his eyes immediately and opened them only gradually to the sunshine. How strange it must have seemed to him to see the world from such a lowly position. It made me aware of how fortunate I was to be able to run, to carry, and to cover our eyes against the sun's bright light. He never had complained, and he didn't now, as he was jostled and jarred. It took us a while to coordinate our efforts, and we almost tumbled him off the mat on which he lay, but that made him laugh. Oh, he is dear to us!

It was about three miles, and we were wet with sweat as the sun rose higher in the sky. We could recognize Ben Ibram's house because a big crowd of people were gathered at the front of it. We set Phillip down in despair. There must have been five hundred of our countrymen there, straining to see and hear what was happening inside. Phillip looked up sadly and said, "You came all this way for nothing."

"We haven't given up yet!" Baruch said boldly. We each grasped our corner of the carrying poles and marched right to the edge of the crowd.

"Excuse us, but our friend is sick, and we want to bring him to the rabbi. We've come a long way. Will you let us through, please?" No one seemed to even hear us. Instead they were straining to hear any sound from inside the house. Next, we tried pushing. We are four strong young men, but the size of the litter, the press of the crowd, and our natural aversion to rudeness didn't allow us to move far.

Sadly we backed out of the tiny progress we made and sat on the ground beside Phillip. It was quiet as people strained their ears, and we could hear a bee buzzing as he landed on our friend's nose in the sunshine.

We watched listlessly before David realized that Phillip couldn't brush it away. The sheer horror of what his life must be like gripped us. I knew I'd want to die if I were in that position, and then I realized that he probably wanted to, too. I stared at him and saw my thought echoed in his sad eyes. In addition, he couldn't even do that for himself!

"Oh, Yahweh, in the Psalms of David he talks about Your constant love. In the name of that love, will you show us what to do?" I never prayed so earnestly in my life. In fact, I wonder if I've ever prayed because I always thought the religious leaders would do that for us.

My answer came in the form of a big hawk who swooped above us, casting a moving line of shadow as he flew over our heads—and landed on the roof! Why couldn't we make a hole in the roof and lower Phillip into the house? It was such a crazy idea that I hesitated to mention it, but this was *not* a normal day or situation.

First, I walked around to the back of the house to see if there were crowds there, too. It was empty because there were no windows in the wall. And there was no building on top as was often done, so families could sit out in the evening and catch the higher breezes. I had no idea how we would get through that thick roof or how we'd explain to Ben Ibram or our parents why we tore apart the house, but we were desperate!

When I proposed my great idea, it was not met with enthusiasm. "My father would kill me," said Simon. "Think of the mess," was David's thought. Baruch just sat there with his mouth hanging open and a look of disbelief on his face. I was beginning to doubt when

I noticed Phillip's face. The look of hope on it was unmistakable. It was a look I hadn't seen since before he fell. That settled it.

"You think I'm not afraid? I'll probably grow old in my room at home and never be let outside. But Phillip will do exactly that for sure, *if* he lives very long. I take full responsibility. You can tell everyone that I went crazy, and you tried to stop me. But help me now. I beg you! It's our last hope.

Disbelief was clear on three of the four faces. "Oh, Yahweh," I prayed. "If this is the answer for Phillip, please open our hearts to do this."

David was the first to rise to his feet. "I think this sounds crazy, and we may be in trouble forever, but . . . I don't have any alternative plan, and at least, it's different."

The others looked around as if for rescue. No one appeared. They slowly got to their feet and asked me, "How do we go about this weird plan?"

I threw my arms around them and answered, "There is none. We make it up as we go along."

Carrying Phillip around to the back of the house was the easy part. Getting him up on the roof was not.

A very red-faced Baruch was boosted up, and we heard, "I don't like this!" as he tumbled over the edge of the building onto the roof. After a minute, he peered down at us and announced, "There are ropes stored up here." Praise Yahweh!

After several failed attempts, we sort-of rolled our friend up in his mat, tied ropes around him, and pulled him up. I have no idea what he suffered in that, but we were aware that the rabbi might leave soon, and then we'd be left with a lot of trouble and no help for Phillip.

Then we all scrambled up on the roof, hoping it would hold us. There were other things stored up there, and among them were three harvesting knives. I carefully poked a hole through the heavy matted roof and could see Jesus for the first time. I just marked his location and the scribes seated across from him. I did notice that they sat on stools while he sat on what looked like an old camel saddle. It was the space between them that I studied carefully, just about the size of the litter that we planned to lower. I marked the place in my mind, and we frantically set to work. The sun was burning down on us, and I wondered if we'd soak through the covering with our sweat.

Ben Ibram needed a new roof, we decided. The one we stood on was brittle, old, and dark. We could only hope he'd see it that way as we began to cut the current one apart. We couldn't avoid the dust and straw that fell into the room below, but we caught each piece of roofing material, so it wouldn't fall on anyone. Oddly enough, no one seemed to look up as we went about our work. Every eye was on the teacher, and every ear and mind was focused on what he was saying. Why they didn't notice the growing light in the room, I never will understand.

When we had an opening big enough for the litter, we tied ropes to each corner carrying pole, stopped breathing (but I didn't stop praying), and lowered our friend into Ben Ibram's house. For one horrifying moment, I thought Phillip was going to roll off onto the scribes, but David lengthened his rope just in time and righted the "flying carpet."

There was an indignant outcry from the occupants of the house, and we looked down into angry faces and raised fists. Simon was so frightened that he almost fell through the hole, but I grabbed him in time. We knew we were in trouble, *big* trouble. My friends tried to move away from me. I couldn't blame them. I had lead them into disaster.

But it was too late now. I called down to the rabbi, "Our friend is sick, and we want you to heal him." Then I saw Ben Ibram's red, important face and stammered, "Sorry about your roof."

Suddenly it was silent. I thought perhaps I had gone deaf. However, as I looked down into the face of Jesus and his eyes met mine, I knew he could see right into my heart. All my sins lay bare before him. Then I knew somehow that they didn't matter now because he only saw my love for my friend, and I felt his love for me like a physical force. May I never forget that look! Baruch, David, and Simon felt the same way, as I found out later. His look blessed us for loving our friend enough to do anything we could to help him. Then he turned those wonderful eyes toward Phillip and said, "Your sins are forgiven." I didn't know what that meant. We hadn't brought Phillip here because he was a sinner. He was always a good person, or at least a lot better than the rest of us. In addition, how could this man, who had grown up near here, forgive sins? I realized we'd made a big mistake. But I was grateful for the love in the look that he gave me, even though he was a charlatan.

Now the silence was shock! I think everyone was wondering who he thought he was that he could forgive sins. Only Yahweh could do that, and it seemed that he rarely did. But Jesus looked at them, aware of what their thoughts were apparently because he said, "Why do you raise such questions in your hearts? Which is easier to say to the paralytic, "Your sins are forgiven" or to say, "Stand up and take your mat and walk?" But so that you may know that the Son of Man has authority on earth to forgive sins"—he said to Phillip—"I say to you, stand up, take your mat and go to your home. Your friends' faith has made you well."

And Phillip did! I had been watching Jesus so breathlessly that I hadn't looked at my friend. I forced my eyes to leave the teacher and saw Phillip move his arms and legs and push himself off the floor, and he looked healthy and whole! And then I wept and didn't see him walk through the parted crowd and outside.

Sound suddenly exploded into that vacuum of silence. I wanted to leap down and protect Jesus! But he didn't need it. He just looked at them calmly, with great authority and confidence, got to his feet, and walked out of the room. I felt a hand on my arm. "Come, Joshua, we must go find Phillip." David said softly. I don't remember getting down to the ground or skirting the murmuring crowds.

We found our friend in a tight knot of people, all arguing about whether he'd really have been paralyzed or was it some kind of hoax. Simon almost got into a fight when they questioned his word. However, it was Naomi who made them believe. She and he parents came rushing up to Phillip, and she stared at him through tears, completely overwhelmed. Her parents were stammering, and her father kept squeezing one of Phillip's newly vibrant arms. No one could doubt their sincerity. They told anyone who would listen about the fall and his atrophy. Meanwhile the object of their attention said not a word. He looked in shock, but there was a light about him, almost as though he was surrounded by some kind of—glory? It was Baruch who began to move us homeward. I found my feet reluctantly joining them, but my heart wanted desperately to go sit at the feet of the Master. I wondered where he'd gone, where he could find rest when everyone wanted something from him, when did he eat, who were his friends—and who were his enemies.

We talked of normal things on the way home, too close to tears and emotions to put into words our feelings and impressions. We knew we'd spend a great deal of the summer putting a new roof on Ben Ibram's house, but until that got done, we hoped he'd enjoy the sunshine and fresh air. Fortunately, there wouldn't be any rain for the next few months. Our hearts were so light that I think we could have flown to the top of his house.

Sarah was waiting for us on the edge of the village. She must have somehow known because she didn't look shocked when she saw Phillip walking toward her, just radiant. We boys——no, men—walked on to our homes, still living in the day that changed our lives forever.

CPSIA information can be obtained
at www.ICGtesting.com
Printed in the USA
LVHW081919130519
R14788200001B/R147882PG616982LVX4B/1/P

32/1